PERFECT LIKENESS

J.M. PHILLIPPE

Blue Zephyr Press
2661 N. Pearl, #360
Tacoma WA 98407

Cover art by **LILT**.

ISBN-10: 0692513159
ISBN-13: 978-0692513156

To

Jeneane & Jason

DReam a little DReam

"You don't want to do that."

Ally's low voice echoed off the high ceilings of the marble room. The glass cabinets along the walls surrounded the center display, where Ally'd just used a fancy-ass tool to cut a perfect circle out of the top pane. She slipped one sleek, black-gloved hand inside and seized the biggest, most expensive necklace that ever existed, ever. Ally slowly moved the large glittering necklace closer to the pouch at her side while maintaining perfect eye contact with the blue-collared security guard nervously pointing a Taser her way.

"Really, I'm telling you, you don't want to do that." She breathed the words out, calm, serene. "You want to turn around and pretend you never saw me."

The guard, the buttons of his shirt straining against his trembling belly, thrust the Taser further out, a desperate attempt at regaining control.

"You're under arrest!" he squeaked. "By the authority of the state of California…and, um, my citizenry…"

"How much do you make?" Ally interrupted. "Ten, maybe

eleven bucks an hour? Is that really worth risking your life over?"

"My life?" he repeated. She could see his sweat beading, the low light of the room sparkling against his forehead. The necklace was almost safe in the silk bag, and as soon as it was secure…

"Allyson Smart."

Ally closed her eyes. The voice had all the authority the security guard's voice didn't have: deep rich tones that she knew vibrated in a wide muscular chest. At any other time, she would have been more than pleased to greet its owner in the warmest, most sensual embrace.

But she didn't want to see Jared while she was stealing a priceless heirloom from him. She opened her eyes and turned to face her lover.

"This isn't what it looks like," she said with a flippant smile. The necklace was secure now. All she had to do was get past the two men and she was home free. Well, as free as any woman wanted for over thirty career-making heists can be. Which is still pretty damn free.

"Hands up, Ally," he said. She looked at his empty hands and grinned a hundred-watt grin.

"Or what? You'll lecture me to death?"

"The police have been called—you'll never make it out of here."

Ally's grin dimmed to sixty watts and she made her move, rushing toward the guard. As though anticipating her, Jared went toward him too, sweeping up something along the way that Ally didn't quite see. Ally kicked the guard in the stomach, and while he was bent forward, grabbed the back of his head and used her body weight to force him face-down on the marble floor. Ally found herself on the wrong end of a long, antique and very sharp-looking sword.

"You don't want to do this," she said, more desperation in her voice than she would have liked.

His eyes floated over her body, and she was proud to see that he was still haunted by the hunger she knew only she could satisfy—if only he didn't impale her.

"I can make it worth your while," she offered.

His gaze intensified and then he frowned. The point of the blade pressed against the hollow of her throat. She could feel the slightest prick of her skin, and a warm drop of blood trickle down.

"You're not giving me much of a choice," he said. "That necklace is worth more than your life."

Ally attempted to shrug despite the sword point pressed against her flesh.

"That's kinda why I'm stealing it."

"And that's why I'm going to have to kill you." Ally was beginning to worry.

She slid her hand down her side, her fingers finding the edge of the knife she kept strapped to her hip. Almost...just a little more. She'd have to keep him talking.

"Listen," she began.

"Ally," he interrupted, but his voice was not his own. It was higher, and yet familiar in an entirely different way. "Ally," she heard again. His voice seemed to be coming from his lips and from beside her as well.

"Ally?"

She whirled away from the sword tip at her throat. The marble walls gave way to lukewarm pastels, the glass cases to black filing cabinets and the low light to annoyingly bright fluorescent. Ally blinked away the fantasy she had been building around herself and peered into brown eyes she knew as well as her own blue. Better even; she looked at Michael tons more than she looked at her own reflection.

"Where were you just now?" he asked, leaning against the table pushed up against the wall of the filing room. Ally sat at that table, a stack of too-thick patient charts next to her, and the green billing sheets she was supposed to be reconciling in front of her. She blinked rapidly, trying to reorient herself.

"I was just…"

"Day dreaming," Michael said with a smile. "Anything good? Or better yet, anything naughty?"

Ally's face reddened; she hated it when Michael caught her daydreaming. "Did you need something?"

"Your sister is waiting out front. It's lunch time."

Ally glanced up at the clock and tried not to frown. "Already?"

Michael grinned.

"Time flies when you're avoiding work."

"I'm not avoiding, I'm multi-tasking," Ally said, and flipped her brown hair over her shoulder as she followed Michael from the room. Her corduroys rubbed together as she walked, a sound she was overly aware of.

"You guys are going costume shopping, right?" Michael asked, his own cords zipping along. He didn't seem to notice the sound. *No one cares that your thighs rub*, Ally told herself. But she also vowed not to wear those pants again.

Shorter than Ally, Michael still managed to give the impression of being taller. He always seemed comfortable in every space. He hadn't always been like that – before he came out as gay in high school, he seemed to constantly be editing his movements and shrinking into himself. *What a difference a few years makes.*

"Yeah," she said. "We're going to try that place near Pavilions."

"They have a great selection," he told her. "And in all sizes too."

Ally felt her chest constrict. *All sizes.*

"Yeah," she said, and tried to walk quickly past him. He took her hand. It was warm and hers felt cold in comparison. He forced her to look at him.

"You'll find a great costume," he said in a warm voice, his brown eyes staring steadily into her hazel ones. It was the tone of voice some of the doctors used when talking to their irate patients, designed to be soothing, non-threatening and yet authoritative all at the same time. Michael was studying to be a therapist and had that intonation down. "You shouldn't even care what the size is, just how you feel in it. I'm excited to see what you get."

"Sure...how I feel in it," she said, breaking his hold and forcing her face into a mask of pleasantness. "I just think I'd feel more fabulous if I were a different size."

"Fabulous doesn't have a size."

"Tell that to Victoria's Secret," Ally said. "I sized out of their fabulousness a while ago."

"Victoria's secret is that she's a sizist bitch," Michael countered, and Ally laughed. He followed her out to the front office where their boss, Ella, was talking to a patient through the slide-open office window.

"And how are we today, Bobby?" Ella asked, brushing a silver-chunk of hair behind her clip-on-earring-bejeweled ear.

Bobby, a chubby boy with dark hair spiked up on top of his round head and who dressed in an over-sized tank top with Gir from Invader Zim on it, gripped his backpack strap tighter. In Bobby's other hand was a sketchbook, its cover stained and bent, pages poking out the sides. Ally wanted to compliment his shirt but felt unsure about it. Two months into her job as an administrative assistant at the Child and Family Center and she still wasn't sure what all the protocols were yet.

"I'm doing okay," he said. His eyes flitted across the glass, and for a moment, met Ally's. She smiled at him and decided to go for it.

"Great shirt," she said. "He's one of my favorite characters, too."

Bobby smiled slightly, and then looked away quickly, pulling his bag up higher on his shoulder.

Ella turned back to Michael and Ally.

"Bobby was just sharing some of his drawings with your sister, Ally," she said. "He's a very talented artist."

Ally looked past Bobby at a short blonde sitting in the small waiting area, scrolling through something on her phone.

"Here she is, Misha," Michael called out from behind Ally, and Misha looked up, tossing a section of her golden hair over her shoulder with an ease of movement Ally had never managed to mimic.

Misha's heart-shaped face was a perfect mask of annoyance. "About time," she said. "What took you?"

As Misha stood and walked toward the front window of the reception area, Ally could see her jeans riding just below her jutted-out hip bones, a stretch of tight, flat stomach—complete with sparkling belly-button ring—and a form-fitting, lace-topped pink shirt under an open light-weight sweater. Ally couldn't see her sister's feet. She knew they would be in an expensive pair of stylish boots, just as she knew Misha's nails would be manicured, her hair perfect, and her jewelry flashy.

Ally's button-up brown shirt, somewhat baggy black corduroy pants she was never wearing again, and scuffed black boots felt frumpy in comparison. She turned away from her sister and walked back out of the front office, around the corner, and through the security door that separated the staff of the Child and Family Center from its potentially-psychotic patients.

The Child and Family Center was a two-story complex with a ground floor reception area and secondary upstairs patient check-in area. It housed a foundation that raised money for the center, an education center, and a section that provided a variety of services focused on children and their families. Michael was currently working as a part-time case manager while going to school to become a marriage and family therapist. He was the one that got Ally the administrator job after her post-graduation employment search kept coming up empty.

Ally smiled at Bobby again as she walked out of the security door, but he was staring down the side hallway. Dr. Beverly Barclay, a regal woman with short reddish-blonde hair giving way to gray and a youthful stride not giving way to anything, walked toward them.

"Hi Bobby," Dr. Barclay said, and the boy shrugged recognition.

Ally watched Bobby's eyes dart back at her and away, as though he was afraid of getting caught staring.

"So you showed my sister your drawings?" she asked. He nodded, and Dr. Barclay smiled.

"That's great Bobby!" Dr. Barclay said.

"He's super talented," Misha said. "Reminds of the kind of

stuff a friend of mine draws, and he's a professional comic book artist."

"I wish I could draw like that," Ally offered. Bobby shrugged again and turned slightly away. Dr. Barclay glanced meaningfully at Ally, and Ally nodded back. It was too much attention for Bobby.

✳

"We should go," she told Misha, glancing down at her watch. "We don't have a lot of time. Later, Bobby!"

Ally led Misha down the stairs to the first floor and through the front doors, and stepped out into the overwhelming orange outside. The sky was overcast, yet still reflected the mid-day sun through the clouds of smoke, concentrating it, giving everything a vague yellow-gold glow. Ally looked up at the sound of a helicopter buzzing above like a giant dragonfly, most likely on its way to one of the two fires that were currently burning in the Santa Clarita Valley, one of five fires in the greater Lost Angeles area. Ally watched the helicopter float across the sky and tried not to choke on the smoky air. Ash floated around her as though she were in a snow storm. Flakes fell against her sleeve, and she blew them off again. They swirled on an invisible eddy and, watching them, she was distracted.

"Are you coming or what?" Misha asked over her shoulder, now several feet in front of Ally. Her voice broke the spell the ash had cast, and Ally hurried past the large round planter, surrounded by the signature cement-and-brick design found in all California suburbs, to catch up to her little sister.

"So what's wrong with him?" she asked Ally.

"Who, Bobby? I'm not allowed to talk about that. Confidentiality."

"But like, is he sick sick, or just like, a little depressed? Some of his drawings were super dark."

"Dark how?"

"Like, there was this one comic that kinda looked like him, but it kept saying really mean things. The lettering was really good though. So, is he like crazy crazy?"

"I told you, I can't talk about it. Anyway, I only know what I read in the charts."

"What does his chart say?"

"Imagine if you were the patient. How'd you feel if people talked about your diagnosis?"

"Whatever," Misha said. Their conversation took them to Misha's bright blue Honda Civic, a bribe from their parents to get Misha to enroll in school again.

"Anyway, like I said, I already have that one costume for you," Misha said. And I don't know why you can't go as a fairy-god-mother for both parties."

"Did you bring the other costume?" Ally asked.

"I told you—Julie has it. She'll bring it to the party."

"Then I don't know it will fit," Ally said. "So I should have a backup."

Misha rolled her eyes and Ally wondered if they might roll out of her head. She pictured them bouncing off of Misha's bony shoulders, landing with a soft squish on the cement, and rolling down the ash-covered pavement until the blue eyes turned gray. *Heh.*

"I think we should take separate cars," Misha announced, bringing Ally's attention back to her. "I don't want to have to drive back up here with all the fires going on and stuff. I only drove out here now because it was on the way from Jeff's."

"Fine," Ally said, having no clue who Jeff was. "I'll meet you there then."

"Don't drive slow!" Misha commanded through the open window of her car.

Ally exhaled hard, and it came out as a snort. She got into her white Camry, a car she bought herself with her own money. She ran her windshield wipers to remove the worst of the ash from her windshield, and put her car in gear. She turned the rearview mirror until she stared at herself. Her eyes said it all. *You don't want to do this.* She checked her mascara and wiped a few tiny black flakes off her cheek.

Ally knew she'd never get out of it though. Both Michael and Misha had invited her to Halloween parties, one on Friday and Halloween proper and the other on the day after, and she needed a costume. However much she wanted to be by herself lately, she couldn't ditch both parties. Misha was sort of doing her a favor to go costume shopping with her, even if she seemed annoyed with Ally about it. Then again, Ally felt like she was annoying everyone lately. With a sigh, she put the mirror back in position and pulled out of the lot and headed toward the costume shop...at a perfectly respectable speed that Misha would not look kindly on.

WHICH WITCH

There was the Sexy Witch and the Feathered Witch. Ally compared the two costumes. Sexy Witch, with a shorter, low-cut dress and fishnet stockings, was the kind of witch who would sashay into a party and have demons and pirates and vampires all over her. Oh, my. Feather Witch, with feathers along her hat brim and dripping from her sleeves, was the kind of witch who would follow around a pack of kids door-to-door, dipping into their bags to eat all the "unsafe" candy. Big sigh.

This was the problem with plus-sized clothes—they looked like they belonged to the type of people who try very desperately to believe that big is beautiful. *If big was beautiful, the clothes would match.* She stared at the costumes with a discerning and disappointed eye.

Sexy Witch claimed to fit all women sizes 7 to fourteen. Feathered Witch was for all women sizes fourteen to twenty-two.

Sexy Witch had sexy makeup and sexy hair. Feathered Witch had a bright shiny purple belt cinching her non-existent waist.

"Have you picked one yet?" Misha asked, coming around the corner with a basket full of decorations.

"Aren't you getting one?" Ally asked.

"Already have mine." She took the Sexy Witch costume from Ally and looked it over. "They call that sexy?"

Ally snatched it back and put it back on the shelf.

"I'll just get this one," she said, trying to shield the Feather Witch costume from Misha's wandering blue eyes. Misha grabbed the edge of it.

"Lemme see," she said. It was either play tug of war with her sister, or give up the package. Ally relented, feeling bitter. She could see Misha's eyes flicker up to the size label in the corner, and Ally wanted to dissolve into a little pile of goo. Clean up, aisle sixteen, emphasis on the sixteen.

"Make sure not to let the feathers get wet," Misha said, handing the costume back to Ally. "They're just dyed and they give off color. Happened to me last year with my feather boa."

Ally nodded, and felt her face redden. Why was she always thinking the worst of her sister these days? That was actually a pretty good tip. She walked quickly toward the counter, her sister a slow, meandering shadow behind her. Ally checked her watch—her lunch hour was fading fast and she hadn't even eaten yet.

"What's your return policy?" Ally asked the woman behind the counter, and the clerk frowned.

"We don't allow costume returns," the girl told her. "But there's a bathroom in the back where you can try them on if you want." She smiled encouragingly.

"She's fine," Misha said from behind Ally. "It's a fine costume—sides, if you don't like it, you still have that other one."

"That I still don't know will fit me," Ally said, trying not to grit her teeth.

"So, are you going to try it on?" the clerk asked. Ally pictured herself in a tiny stall, bumping into the walls, dropping her clothes in the toilet, sweating, breathing hard from trying to change fast. She shook her head.

"I'll just take this one," she said.

"It's a pretty costume," the clerk said. "I think you'll look great in it."

Ally looked back at the bag. That was a very hideous purple

belt. Did the clerk not see how horrible that belt was? Probably, the clerk was trained to say something nice about every costume that people bought. It was the only explanation.

"It's nice you guys carry the larger sizes," Misha piped up from behind Ally.

The clerk nodded. "And a pretty good selection, too." She smiled at Misha, who leaned forward, her elbows on the counter.

"I even saw some of the smaller sizes—zero to seven—that's just great. It's so hard to find clothes in my size."

"I bet," the clerk said. Ally looked up and caught the clerk's eye. "Being a different size than average can be difficult," she said, that same understanding look aimed at Ally.

"I'd settle for being mode-sized," Ally said.

Misha dumped her basket on the counter.

"Was that a math joke? No one ever gets your math jokes."

"Well, that was just mean," Ally countered, and the clerk chuckled.

"I don't get it," Misha said.

"Average – mode, mean, median. Get it now?"

"Ug." Misha rolled her eyes. Again.

Plop plop. Ally stifled her own giggle, watching the imaginary trajectory of Misha's eyeballs bouncing off the counter and rolling to the floor. She wondered if the clerk would say something polite if Misha's eyes actually fell out. "Those eyes look great on the floor! They really bring out the tile." Ally turned away so she wouldn't be caught grinning.

As the clerk focused on Misha as a customer, Ally tuned out. For the next few moments she concentrated on her reflection, just visible in the glass opposite her. If only she could change it by sheer will—shrink it down, firm it up, become beautiful. Successful. Better than she was. Happy.

The clerk's declaration of "have a nice Halloween" returned her back to her reality, and she smiled politely before being tugged away by Misha. On the way out the door, Ally bumped into a display hard enough to knock a few candy bowls off the shelf. She bent down to pick them up. Misha bent with her, her oversized purse slamming into Ally's and knocking both to the floor, scattering contents everywhere.

"Damnit!" Misha declared. Ally rushed to grab what she could and shove things back into both purses without paying much attention to what went where.

"I didn't mean…you were rushing me, and…"

"It's fine. Let's just go." Misha stood up and looked away from Ally. Ally imagined that Misha must feel embarrassed to have a sister like her. She felt embarrassed for herself at any rate.

"I'm sorry," she said, hiking her own purse up on her shoulder.

"It happens," Misha said. Ally was extra careful not to bump anything on the way out of the store.

"So then, I'll see you Friday," Misha said to Ally as they walked out to their cars. Ally stopped and stared at her.

"We're not having lunch?" she asked.

"Already ate," Misha responded. "So, see you later then?"

Ally nodded her head, biting back her annoyance.

"And you're welcome, by the way," Misha added.

Ally stared at her, confused.

"For shopping with you." Misha had one hand on her hip, her head cocked to one side.

"Gee, thanks," Ally said, sarcasm coloring her voice. Misha gave her another patented "whatever" look and got into her Honda. She sped out of the lot before Ally even finished walking to her Camry.

Ally took out her cell and pressed the photo of Michael until the phone automatically dialed. Two short rings later and Michael's voice was on the line.

"So, did you get one?" He was cheery, as usual, and Ally felt better just hearing his voice.

"Yeah," she said. She took the plastic-encased costume out of the shopping bag and eyed it warily, tilting it to avoid the glare from the sun.

"So, what are you going to be?"

"A witch," she said. "I just got one of those bag costumes."

"Didn't I tell you they had a great selection?" Michael asked. "So what does it look like?"

She stared at the purple belt and the model's matronly face.

"Like an old woman's costume," she decided.

"Oh, so like a scary hag-like witch."

"No, like this is the costume some mother would wear to hand out candy, eating every third piece herself."

"And why do you think it looks like that?"

Ally sighed. He had that therapist tone again, and it was starting to grate on her nerves.

"The model is like in her late thirties, and there is this horrible purple belt—it's just not the costume I wanted to get."

"What kind of costume did you want to get?"

"One I won't feel fat in." Ally shoved the costume to the side in disgust, more with herself than with the costume. She didn't know how to be big and proud when everyone and everything told her she should be small and sexy instead. She rubbed the shoulder that slammed into the display and wondered if it would bruise.

"Ally," Michael began, and Ally could feel another one of his

boats of peppy platitudes about to embark. She decided to ward
it off.

"Oh, I know," she told him. "It's never as bad as I think it is."

"You've been thinking things are pretty bad lately."

"Yeah," Ally agreed. "I don't really know why. It's probably
my diet or something."

"Have you eaten yet? Low blood sugar never helps anyone."

"No." Ally looked at her watch. "I'm not even sure I have
time."

"You have to eat."

"Maybe I'll swing by the school and find some nice juicy children. Or do you think feathered witches eat, like, birds?"

"Ooooh, feathers. I love feathers."

"Your boa collection is proof of that."

"I'm just a sweet transvestite..."

"Damnit, Janet, I'm gonna be late getting back."

"I'll cover. Get food. Self-care and all that."

"Sure thing. Say hi to Rocky for me."

"I wish. See ya."

Ally tossed the phone down on the passenger seat, and pulled
out of the space. A quick and ill-advised trip through a fast-food
drive-thru, an agonizing debate with herself over grilled chicken
or a burger, and a last-minute decision to get a meal, with fries,
which Ally almost instantly regretted, and her mood continued to
drop. It's not like she had a lot of choices when going through the
drive thru of foods she could eat while driving. Salads and steering
didn't mix. Still she'd have to make up for the extra calories later,
do a double session on the treadmill, eat an extra-light dinner. It
was depressing.

Why did she have to live in a world that made French fries

and then told you not to eat them? How fair was that?

As she ate, she watched the ash fly against her windshield and felt a little stirring of rebellion. *Damn the diet! Damn the skinny! Up with the supersized!* She grabbed a handful of salty fried potato bits in an act of rebellion and let her mind wander. The television had reported on the million fat-woman march on Washington. On Jezebel, they talked about all the plus-sized models being fired for being too thin. There were infomercials selling products that would help people pack on that oh-so-desired extra poundage...

As Ally realized she'd eaten the entire container of fries, her images of rebellion faded. She crumpled up the take-out bag in horror and suddenly felt very guilty. Then angry for feeling guilty. Then guilty for feeling angry. And then just generally confused. She didn't know if she was more mad at being fat or at wanting to be thin. She hated dieting. She also hated feeling like a failure for being fat.

Ally got to Golden Oak and was ready to turn right when the train-crossing bell jangled and the post came down, so she had to wait for a freight train to go by. Her eyes wandered over to the witch costume—she didn't like it. She just spent forty bucks on something she didn't like and didn't want to wear. She stared at it with new hatred, blaming it for making her so late, blaming herself for taking so long to admit that she was in fact "plus-sized," and blaming the world for making her feel so useless because of that. The train chugged on by, seeming to go on forever. Ally's thoughts followed it down the track, destination depression.

"For sizes fourteen thru twenty-two."

Halloween was three days away. Ally idly wondered how much weight she could lose before the party.

More ash fell from the sky.

COPY Jams

"Am I in trouble?" Ally asked, rushing into the upstairs reception area. "I lost track of time, didn't know I would be so late."

"No one's here," Michael said, running his hand through his hair in a casual movement he seemed to do every ten minutes. "Ella went to lunch shortly after you did. She won't be back for a while." Ally handed Michael a drink, which he took with a surprised "thank you."

"It's diet," she told him. He smiled gratefully and followed her as she walked into the file room.

"Anything happen while I was gone?" Ally asked.

"The copier jammed again." They both looked toward the mammoth gray machine on the other side of the filing room. Ally sighed.

"Dr. Delkey?" she asked.

"She thought it was best to wait for you—she thinks you have the magic touch."

Ally stared at Michael. "How bad is it?"

"I don't know—I was too afraid to look. You're better at those things than the rest of us. It's like your superpower—you speak machine."

"Is it too late to get a better superpower? What's the return policy on those things?"

"You can't get unbitten by a radioactive spider."

"Or a radioactive copy machine." She sighed dramatically. She walked to the offending machine, its red light blinking out its distress. "How did I end up here again?"

"The Economy." Michael said, following her. He steepled his fingers together in a mock prayer pose, eyes down.

"The Economy," Ally agreed, duplicating his pose. After a moment they both crossed themselves and feigned spitting to the side. "May it rest in peace."

Michael laughed.

"With your computer skills and my people skills, one day we'll be running this place." He waggled his neatly trimmed and shaped eyebrows at her. Ally just smiled briefly.

She had no intention of one day running the Child and Family Center—her aspirations were higher. Not that she had a plan, per se. But she had lots and lots of dreams, and those seemed just as good.

Michael was more practical. "I'm already a case manager part time, and when I finish school I'll be a doctor here too. You could easily work your way up. Ella started in the front office too, you know."

Ally kept her eyes on the copier screen which blinked out the path to the jam. "Yeah, well Ella is happy with what she does. I'm just not sure I'm assistant material."

"Okay," Michael said gamely, taking another long pull on his straw. "What do you want to do then?"

"Something else," Ally said, stalling.

"What something else?"

Ally went through the options, all the things she was in her fantasies: spy, dancer, vampire-slayer, witch, singer, empath, jewel-thief, model, astronaut, time traveler, Amazon, Bionic woman, actress, spiritual leader, mercenary, and princess of a small exotic country.

"I don't know," she said at last. "Something that doesn't require filing."

"You should take one of those personality tests that tells you what job you would be best at," Michael said. "I think Buzzfeed has one. Why don't we do that tonight, after we eat dinner? Sandra's making us something special. You're still coming over, right?"

Ally nodded absently. She couldn't imagine what Michael's new-age new roommate would think was special, and she really didn't want to think about how she was going to meet her calories for the day after her overly fattening lunch. *Air, maybe I can just have air for dinner.* She went back to opening doors and pulling out bits of the copy machine to dislodge a paper. She put all the right parts back in the right places, and closed the final door with a thwack. The machine buzzed to life, fully functioning once again.

"Delkey's probably going to want me to bring her these copies, isn't she?"

"She's totally your favorite."

"She keeps me in the lifestyle to which I've grown accustomed. If I work really hard I may get a promotion to the sixth level of hell!"

Michael laughed. Ally smiled at him as she started pulling packets from the printer tray. When she turned her back to him to sort the stacks out, she couldn't hold the smile in place. She was not meant for this—making copies, fixing the problems of the Delkey's of the world. She didn't know what she was meant for, but was sure there had to be something more to life than fixing copy jams—she just had to find it.

✳

After taking the copies to Delkey, Ally went to file. Anyone with a basic understanding of the alphabet could do most of the duties of her job, and Ally felt only slightly more intelligent than an orangutan as she sorted client charts into neat stacks on top of the filing cabinets they would eventually go into. Once all the stacks were arranged alphabetically, she started with the A's and shoved overly-thick folders into increasingly-smaller spaces in the drawers, doing her best to avoid a massive folder shift. The center had recently transitioned to electronic files, but kept physical files as backup, which many of the therapists still preferred to use. With her hands busy, Ally's mind wandered, walking familiar paths.

She followed it down a favorite trail—Fantasy Man and his brilliant biceps.

Fantasy Man was working his legs at her gym the first time Ally saw him two weeks ago. He held hand weights by his side, his chest heaving with each muscle contraction, his face tight with concentration, sweat dripping off his strong chin. He was dark haired, pale for a Californian after a hot summer, and looked like a Greek god. No, Roman god. No, Spartan Warrior…oh, yes, she could just see him in Gerard Butler's leather skirt. He was Gerard Butler, or as close as she would ever get to someone like that in real life. He was a total T'DAH: tall, dark and handsome.

Ally had never heard him speak. She imagined his voice like a mocha brown. If it was an ice-cream flavor it would be triple chocolate fudge—thick, rich, and delicious. She didn't know him, so, of course, he was perfect, and the perfect star of all her most recent fantasies. Jared the rich art collector, Mark the fellow secret agent—whatever man she created, she created in his image.

Ally let her mind wander as she shoved musty charts into crowded drawers and counted down the minutes until her day would be over.

❋

A shout echoed down the hall and into the filing room. Suddenly Doctor Delkey ran in, her stilettos sticking to the carpet, shortening her strides. She ran right up to Ally and grabbed her arm, bosom heaving.

"He's out of control!" Her perfectly lipsticked lips trembled.

"Who?" Ally asked, "What's going on?"

"Please, now!" Delkey said, and her voice went from Betty Boop to Minnie Mouse—squeaking and squealing. "I don't know what to do!"

Ally let herself be dragged out of the room, down the hall and through the door to the front lobby of the Center. The scene was straight out of a network TV drama. A teenager was standing in front of the elevator and waved a gun around the room. Ella stood behind the front-desk counter, the bullet-proof window open. Doctor Delkey was next to Ally, her hands on the sides of her head. And a strange man with gray hair was standing on the wrong side of the protective doors, glaring at the teen. *The teen's father?*

Michael was on the wrong side of the safety glass too.

"You don't understand!" the boy shouted, waving the gun around the room, pointing it at each person in turn. "None of you can possibly understand! You don't know what it's like. You read books, act like you care, pretend to know. But you don't know!"

"John, don't do this. I'm your father!" The gray-haired man mustered up the last of his courage, and his authority, and stepped forward. He got a face full of gun for his troubles and he stepped back, his mouth falling open and his mighty speech lost in the drool pooling on his lips.

"Oh God, oh God, oh God…" Dr. Delkey chanted to herself, her hands up by her mouth, manicured fingers bent in, bright red nails between her teeth.

"Doctor Delkey, control your patient!" Ella demanded. The gun oscillated between the scared, but stoic office manager and the hyperventilating, hussy therapist, and Delkey fell back against the glass window of the reception area and slid to the floor in a dead faint. Only she wasn't dead, Ally noted wistfully. Delkey's large breasts continued to rise and fall with each shallow breath the shallow woman took.

"She doesn't know shit," John said. "And her breath smells."

He was right. Dr. Delkey did have a breath issue.

"Listen, John, if you could just calm down," Michael said. It was the wrong thing to say, and the gun was pointed squarely at Michael, the best friend Ally had ever had, and the only person in the world she could truly say really loved her.

Ally's moment had come. She wiped her hands against her corduroys, took a deep breath, and stepped boldly forward between the gun and Michael.

"John, listen to me," she said, her voice calm, steady. "You're right. None of the people here can possibly know what you're going through."

"What the hell are you doing, Smart?" Ella stage-whispered at her. John waved the gun in Ella's direction and she whimpered. Ally took another step forward.

"And you have every right to be angry," she continued.

"What the hell do you know?" John asked.

"Nothing," she said. "But I can guess. I'm not that far out of school, I remember what it's like. The whole world is against you. And there's pain, so much pain, and loneliness, and yet all this stupidity coming at you from all angles, all these people who have dibs on your time, your life, your future."

John's pimpled chin trembled. Tears rolled down his cheeks

and he brushed them angrily away with his shirtsleeve. It was a SpongeBob SquarePants shirt.

"I just want to make them understand," he said, his voice breaking on the last syllable of the word. "Is that so wrong?"

"No," Ally said, and inched closer and closer with each word, "but this is. Give me the gun, John. This isn't the way."

John shoved the gun more solidly in Ally's face. She could see the little posts that you were supposed to line up in order to aim. They were all pointing at her. She swallowed hard, her mouth suddenly dry.

"Be careful!" Michael whispered from behind her.

"You won't be a kid forever, John," Ally said carefully, staring into the teen's eyes, keeping them focused on her. She slowly moved her hand up. "And when you turn eighteen, there's not a damn thing they can do to you. Your life will be your own. You only have to hold on till then."

"Too long," John said, a crackling in his voice. "I can't wait that long."

"Just a little while," Ally said. "One day at a time. You can do it."

"Don't feed the boy lies." Ella said. "The boy is going to be locked up when he's eighteen, locked up for the rest of his life!"

"No!" John whirled the gun in Ally's boss's direction, his finger on the trigger, ready to pull. Ally grabbed the gun, shoving her finger in the space behind the trigger and blocking any effort John made to squeeze it. She twisted his wrist, made him let go, and then, in the same movement, grabbed him in a controlled fall to the floor. They landed on their knees and Ally held John to her.

"They can't do that, John," she said. "You be strong and they won't be able to do that."

He sobbed into her shoulder and she held him, letting him cry himself out.

"Miss?" said an unknown voice, a voice like mocha almond fudge. Ally looked up and into the piercing eyes of Fantasy Man; he stood, perplexed, at the top of the stairs and wore a tight Sheriff's uniform. He took a careful step forward. "I think I may need to take that from you." He motioned to the gun. Ally smiled at him, her teeth glittering white, and held the gun up, dangling it off her manicured finger. He took the gun, his fingers brushing hers and sending chills down her spine, and to other places.

Ally let the police take the boy away, and stood with Fantasy Man as he took the report.

"She saved all of us," Dr. Delkey told him, magically revived. Fantasy Man looked at Ally, admiration in his generous brown eyes as they met her sparkling blue ones. She looked down, shy, and noticed her flat stomach, her slim thighs. Her perfectly comfortable four-inch heels. Then she smiled at Fantasy Man. He moved closer to her, almost touching her, and spoke in a low, husky voice:

"I get off soon," he purred. "Maybe you would like to…"

✳

But Ally never found out what he would like to do. Michael burst into the file room then with his brisk efficiency and started asking her a question about a chart she had reconciled.

"The notes don't match the billing sheet," he said, and it took a moment for Ally to focus her real-life hazel eyes on his face, and on the reality of the file room around her with its glaring fluorescent lights, black filing cabinets and wide flat desks next to the humming copier, and a multi-colored carpet that wouldn't show stains.

"Which one?" she asked, shaking her head to break the spell of her daydream.

"On October twenty-fourth," he said, and showed her the sheet. She bent over the folder, looking for the discrepancy, and silently mourned her interrupted fantasy.

A shout echoed from down the hall. Ally and Michael looked at each other, startled. A second shout made its way to them, and Michael dropped the chart and hurried down the hall. Ally followed close behind.

A very upset young man stood in front of the elevator, waving something in the air.

Ally felt her heart constrict. She held her breath and blinked hard as though that would change the scene in front of her. Her fantasy was coming true.

TOUCHED

Two stories up, the sun glared through layers of smoke-clouds and tinted glass to light up the scene that greeted Ally as she entered the lobby. Everything was touched by its hazy intensity. Sunlight glinted off the dark brown, gelled, angry spikes of Bobby's hair, infused his pale skin with an unearthly glow, illuminated his large, soft bare arms, round face, and gray, terrified eyes.

"He's taking my life!" he shouted, struggling as Dr. Barclay tried to hold him. "Robert is taking my life!"

"You are Robert!" a woman with a long dark braid wailed, circling the two bodies like a tether ball, coming ever closer to the center. "Bobby, please! You are Robert. My own sweet Bobby."

"Michael!" Dr. Barclay shouted, her voice straining to stay calm as she tried to wrestle something from Bobby's hand. He waved it beyond her grip. Ally still couldn't see what it was. "Michael, get Mrs. Dominguez out of here!"

Michael nodded, and rushed forward to take the woman's arm. Small though she was, she shrugged him off forcefully.

"Bobby, oh Bobby, please!" She reached out to touch her son. He flinched violently away from his mother.

"He will infect you," he said. "You're too weak; he'll take you over. I have to fight. I have to fight. He's taking my life!" And he doubled his efforts to hold onto whatever it was the doctor was trying to get from him.

"Bobby, we just need to take this from you, for your own safety." Dr. Barclay reached for the object in Bobby's hand.

Bobby wriggled it away.

Michael stepped forward, tried again. "Mrs. Dominguez, please, I think you're upsetting him more."

Whatever was in Bobby's hands glinted in the light and Ally found herself rushing forward, reaching out to the object, trying to snatch it away. She was surprised by her own movement, by her own nerve.

"You!" Bobby shouted then. "He wants you!" He lunged toward her, thrust his pudgy hand out and onto her arm, gripping it tightly. His eyes met hers. "I can't take it anymore. I'm sorry," he whispered. His eyes were filled with tears. "He'll let me go, he'll go to you." And then his eyes were filled with…something else. A silvery-blue sheen shone out from them as Bobby stared intently into Ally's eyes.

Ally fought the urge to scream and tear away. It wasn't as though she could—Bobby's grip was too strong. She felt a shudder go through her and closed her eyes. When she opened them, the silvery-blue glow in Bobby's gray eyes was gone.

"You!" he said again. "Not me anymore."

Dr. Barclay grabbed Bobby's wrist, gently pried it off of Ally.

"It's okay," the doctor said. "We're okay now, Bobby. It's okay."

Now freed, Ally backed away shakily, back into the eerie glow of the sun.

Bobby stopped struggling then, looked at whatever he had in his hand, and then let out a squeal of joy.

"He's gone," he said. "It's just me. He's gone!"

Dr. Barclay stopped trying to force Bobby's hand, and instead reached out her own. "Can I have it now Bobby?"

He looked at her, smiled, and showed it to her. The sun glinted off it again, almost blinding Ally. She shielded her eyes, looked again to see what Bobby fought so hard for: a small square mirror.

"Look," he said, and angled it so that he was reflected in it. "Just me." Dr. Barclay smiled, nodded.

"Just you. Can I have it?"

Complacent now, he gave the mirror to Dr. Barclay and she handed it to Ally. Ally couldn't figure out why they had wanted to take it from Bobby so badly.

Mrs. Dominguez rushed forward to her son, wrapping her arms around him. He returned the hug and smiled all the while as Dr. Barclay led him and his mother away.

Ally stared down the hall, her heart still pounding, and then looked down at the flat shiny surface of the mirror. Her brown hair, her dull hazel eyes, her unibrow growing back in from the last pluck session. Her, just her. She looked up at Michael.

"You okay?" he asked.

She shrugged. "I think so. Do you have any idea what that was about? Why they wanted this?" She held up the small square mirror. He took it from her, his brown eyes dark.

"Sharp edges," he said.

She looked at him blankly—the mirror's edges didn't seem particularly sharp to her. He seemed to understand her confusion.

"Break it and you can slit your wrists or cut someone else."

Ally looked at the mirror, startled.

"You think he would have…?" She couldn't finish the idea of what Bobby might have done. Bobby, who'd shown his beautiful drawings to Misha earlier that day…how could he be this disturbed?

"Bobby has a thing for mirrors," Michael said with a shrug. "We've been trying to get him away from them. But especially when throwing a fit like that." He shrugged again, and Ally knew that whatever he was thinking, it was deep. And dark. And the kind of thoughts she didn't want to have.

Michael knew dark. After his step-father kicked him out, after his mother disowned him for being gay, Michael had gone so dark Ally hadn't known how to reach him. All she could offer was a couch to crash on and a shy suggestion that maybe he talk to someone, a professional someone. He told her, years later, that going to a therapist saved his life. It's why he wanted to be one. It's why he could look at patients like Bobby and see something of himself. But it also wasn't something she knew how to talk to him about.

Her eyes followed Michael as he made his way back into the office, and Ally felt the sudden backlash of adrenaline as a shaky weak feeling overcame her. She glanced back down the hall, as though waiting for Bobby to come back, for answers to come her way.

She hurried to the door, waved her security card over the gray box next to it, and when the light blinked green, turned the handle.

Security doors and glass windows separated the staff from the clients and she looked at them with new appreciation for their purpose, their significance. Mostly the clients were people she announced, names on charts and cards and schedules—just kids who happened to see therapists now and again. She had never really thought of them as troubled, or as different from any other kids. She rubbed her arm where Bobby had grabbed her. She remembered, in her training, how they had talked about the possibility of one of the kids becoming violent, possibly bringing in a gun. The glass between the lobby and the office was supposed to be bulletproof. The security badges were supposed to prevent unauthorized access into the back offices—people got in trouble if they propped the doors open. There were measures in place to protect the staff from the clients, if need be.

And yet Ally had been touched.

HARDER TO BREATHE

Hours later, and Ally caught herself holding her own arm where Bobby had grabbed her. For the rest of the work day she'd thought about, or tried not to think about what happened. She hoped a good work out would help shake the unease from her.

Once upon a time, Ally had a dream. Actually, she'd been dreaming from the time she was a very small child, and in almost all of them she was stronger, faster, and fitter than she was in real life. She was the savior, the leader. She was important. She mattered.

Lately she'd been dreaming more than usual. The part of her that still secretly believed she had it in her to be a Charlie's Angel became obsessed with the idea that if she was just stronger, fitter, and thinner, things would fall into place. She'd get what she wanted —whatever that was—and be who she always was meant to be. Life would be exciting.

And maybe she could dream a little less, and live a little more.

It was in that mindset that Ally joined the Santa Clarita Valley Athletic Club. And while it was a big step, and certainly the first of the thousand miles Ally knew on some level she would have to travel to get to her fitness fantasy, she still daydreamed about something more instantaneous. She hadn't anticipated it being so hard, or taking so much effort. Patience was never a trait she expressed through her daydreams.

"You sure you okay?" Michael asked as they stood just outside the locker room areas. "That was pretty intense this afternoon."

Ally nodded.

"I kinda don't want to think about it. He's okay, I'm okay. Everything is okay."

"Well, a hard-core sweat session will help get your mind off it all." He winked at her.

Ally smiled at him. Yes, project Charlie's Angel would definitely help make her stop thinking about Bobby and mirrors with sharp edges and that weird light that left his eyes.

"Ready to kick some butt?" he asked.

"Ready to shape some butt, at least," she said.

"You going to work out with me today?" he asked. It was a hesitant question and a sore spot between them.

The SCVAC had a woman's only section, smaller, set off in its own little space, right near the women's locker room. Ally looked into the greater gym, and there he was: Fantasy Man. She found herself staring, then blushing. If he caught her blush, he didn't mention it. He was good about things like that.

"I think I just want to blast music. There are always more treadmills in there, and..."

Michael nodded.

"One of these days though, you should come do weights with me. Or a class. Or, something. I feel like we don't get to talk much anymore."

"We see each other all day, every day! We talk all the time."

"That's work talk. I mean, real talk. Talk talk."

"Talk talk," Ally repeated, raising an eyebrow.

Michael sighed.

"You know what I mean."

Ally did. But she turned away from him anyway.

"I just want to blast my music," she said again. "It helps me focus."

Michael smiled at her and nodded. The smile seemed a little forced, but Ally accepted it for the gesture it was.

"Okay, we'll talk talk later then."

Ally stuck her tongue out at him, and he laughed, a real laugh, as he walked away. Then she entered the sanctuary of the smaller gym-within-a-gym dedicated to women.

Ally claimed her traditional treadmill closest to the door and furthest from the wall of mirrors on the other side of the room, and put her headphones in, pressing play on her workout playlist. She stepped onto the dull black belt, pushed some buttons, and set the treadmill for thirty minutes, the max allowed on any of the aerobic machines. The engine whirred to life beneath her. She sped the treadmill up to two miles per hour, finding her stride, warming her muscles up. Slowly she moved the speed up, peaking at three point five miles per hour—a good base walking pace.

She pumped her arms at her side, looking down briefly at the spot where Bobby had grabbed her earlier that day. *It was the weirdest thing, being grabbed like that.* More than that, she had felt something when Bobby touched her, something she couldn't describe. *An energy maybe?* She shook her head, tried not to think about it. *It's just my imagination,* she told herself. She looked around the room, scouring for a distraction.

The older woman next to Ally—gray-haired, spandex-wearing, magazine-reading—sped her machine up, matching Ally's stride. Ally felt like she was in a race then, or a synchronized walking contest. She looked at her reflection to see how she and Spandex Lady looked.

She never even saw Spandex Lady in the mirror, Ally was so awestruck by her own reflection.

Look at you. The thought whirled around her head, taking each body part in. Her breasts bounced merrily up and down, the right one, slightly bigger, flopping higher and more energetically than the left. *Disgusting!* Below her breasts her stomach also bounced, shaking like the bowl full of jelly that jolly red guy sported. But did she feel jolly? Her arms jiggled, her thighs quivered and her chin trembled—Ally suddenly wanted to cry.

She turned away, pulling at her shirt as though she could magically stretch it into some sort of shape that would hide the bouncing beneath it, then looked back at the treadmill console. She told herself to concentrate on her breathing, to think of the good she was doing by working out, to realize that everyone started somewhere and someday when she ran she would look more like a Baywatch babe and less like an excited walrus. Breath in, step, step, breath out. You can do this. This is easy. This is good. No one's looking anyway.

Or are they?

Ally snuck a peak around the gym, just to make sure. Two thin blonde women, obviously friends, were chatting while working their inner and outer thighs respectively. Spandex Lady's attention was fully on the star-studded magazine in front of her. *See,* Ally told herself. *You're just being paranoid. And you're doing fine, keeping up with Spandex Lady and everything.*

It had been several minutes now and it was getting harder for Ally to control her breathing. She took a deep breath, tried to will her heartbeat to a steadier pace. *Me and Spandex Lady are one. I can do this as long as she does.* Ally focused on the TV screens, on a rock video, on her music, on Raymond being yelled at by his TV wife on reruns. The sound of the Spandex Lady's machine changed, and Ally looked over at it hopefully, thinking that the older woman was going back to a walk now. Instead, she had increased the speed.

Not to be outdone, Ally did too, trying to match her stride with Spandex Lady's without making it look obvious.

It was getting harder and harder to breath.

Then Spandex Lady increased her incline, idly flipping a page of the magazine. Ally ignored this and concentrated harder on breathing. *I can do this, I can do this,* she chanted to herself.

No, you can't. It's too hard.

Her face was flushed, sweat dripped down her forehead, and she flexed her fingers to make sure her arm wasn't going numb. She held out for another thirty seconds until the pain in her chest made her push the button to slow down the machine. She took it all the way down to two point eight, gasping and holding onto the handles of the treadmill. She was afraid to look around, afraid to see who had witnessed her failure.

As her breath settled back into a rhythm, she closed her eyes and forced her mind away.

✳

Bullets were whizzing by her head as she leaned over the handlebars of her sleek black motorcycle, her boots and form-fitting jacket the same midnight shade. In the next turn, she leaned so far over her knee grazed a pebble in the road, and then she was back upright, revving the engine so that the front wheel came up off the pavement. Wheel back down, she dodged around the car in front of her and risked a glance back over her shoulder.

He was gaining on her. He was on his own motorcycle, flanked by two black SUVs. The bullets were coming from them. She had to take them out.

Ally veered wildly to the right, her back tire skidding, and barreled down a narrow alley. It was wide enough for a car, if just, and she could see one of the SUVs had made the turn and followed her down. Ahead was a large green dumpster, and as she roared past it, she slowed just enough to aim a kick at it hard enough to set it rolling. She heard the crash behind her but couldn't take her eyes off the path in front of her. One down. Another corner, another skidding turn back onto the road.

He caught up to her at the next intersection, the second SUV still with him. Up ahead was a park, a steep set of stone steps leading down to a grassy area. A quick hop of the curb and Ally was skidding down them. He followed her. The car didn't.

Only one to go.

She was thankful for the cover of darkness, the lack of people on the path. She aimed for a clump of trees, her street wheels slipping on the wet grass and making her back tire fishtail. A glance back showed that he was doing better. And gaining.

A small embankment led down to a lower path circling an artificial lake. She launched her bike down it and let go of the handle, flinging her body to the side in a controlled roll that separated her from the bike. The hill wasn't that high, and she hoped it was enough to give her cover as she rolled forward, freeing her gun from the holster on her hip at the same time and whirling around to aim at him as he came over the hill.

But only his bike came over.

Ally whirled again. He was already behind her, had anticipated her move. He should have. He was the one who trained her.

He charged her, knocking the gun from her hand and slamming her onto her back, holding down her arms above her head. The breath had been knocked out of her, and as she stared up into his eyes, she began to rethink her life as a double agent.

Fantasy Man leaned down toward her and....

But again, Ally missed the next moment with Fantasy Man. The treadmill beeped at her, telling her that it was time to cool down. She'd made it through the first thirty moments of her work out. After glancing around to make sure no one was waiting for a treadmill, Ally programmed in a second thirty-minute countdown. She had fries to work off.

Ally peeked at her reflection in the mirror. At first she thought she saw a glimmer of something around her, a blurriness to her reflection. The glimmer faded quickly and her overstretched t-shirt and baggy pants bounced back at her. Things quieted down to a small jiggle the slower she walked.

That jiggle is why you're still single.

Ally was jarred by the thought. She also knew it wasn't true. She'd been smaller when she was younger, and just as single then. *But you have even less chance now.*

Ally watched the minutes of her time on the treadmill count down and felt heavy. Her arms hung at her sides, her shoulders slumped forward, and her chest felt tight in a way that had nothing to do with exercise.

Just once she would like to know what it felt like to feel proud of her body, to feel comfortable in it.

She wiped sweat away from her face and imagined that she was wiping fat away with it.

Someday, she told herself.

No, she reprimanded herself. *Someday soon.*

A new sort of bounce kept her company, her determination lightening her step. Head up, shoulders back, and chest hitched to a star, as her mother used to say, although she was never really sure what that meant. Whatever it meant, she was going to do it. She was going to succeed. She had to. She just needed something to go right, something to change.

She didn't want her life to be the same anymore.

After the gym, Ally followed Michael's Jetta back to his house, her window open to let the cool night air dry the sweat off her face.

Michael had just moved in to his place over the summer, and Ally still wasn't comfortable going there. Michael lived in a three-bedroom set up in one of the older neighborhoods in Saugus. It was, in fact, the same neighborhood both he and Ally had grown up in, although both their parents had long moved away, Michael's to Santa Monica and Ally's to Ventura.

Ally had to admit it was a nice house. It not only boasted a decent-sized backyard, but a partial view of the valley as well. It was a one story ranch with a large living area. Michael had three roommates. Billy was ruggedly handsome, a dirt-bike rider and surfer and general extreme sports enthusiast with an aura of cool permanently tattooed on him; his hair always spiked, and his clothes the right kind of careless style that made him look good without making him look like he was trying. And he had the longest eye lashes Ally had ever seen—every time she talked to him she had to stop herself from staring at his eyelashes, or at him period. He was the kind of good looking that made her palms sweat. Until Fantasy Man, Billy had been featured pretty heavily in Ally's fantasies. Well, up until she found out he had a girlfriend.

Ally had met Billy's girlfriend, Lisa, twice before, and each time she was impressed not only with how pretty Lisa was, but how nice. It was hard to hate someone who complimented you in a genuine way. Ally couldn't daydream about kissing Billy without feeling like she was betraying Lisa in some way, so she stopped.

Michael's second roommate was a short workaholic who they

almost never saw. The few times Ally had met Tina she'd been on her way out of the house, and Ally's general impression of the woman was that of a red-haired pixie flying past her in the night. Michael said that Tina worked in the Industry and that's why she was always gone. Ally could never understand why anyone wanted to work in the film and television industry. As far as she could tell, the hours sucked, the work was hard, and unless you were the talent, your work went mostly unrecognized. Still, she was impressed with Tina. She couldn't even really say why.

While Billy and Tina each had their own rooms—the ones located at the front of the house—Michael and Sandra shared the master bedroom. Ally had once asked how they managed dates while sharing a room, and they both had stared at her.

"We don't bring our dates home," Sandra had said. "We go to their houses."

Michael had nodded matter-of-factly, and they both exchanged amused looks at Ally's expense.

It was moments like that which made it hard for Ally to warm up to Sandra. Ally was supposed to be the one exchanging looks with Michael. In fact, he had asked her to move in before Sandra did, and Ally often thought about what it might have been like to live in that house. She also knew she could never do it—she would never feel like she belonged.

Ally parked at the curb in front of the house. Michael was already out of his car and waved at her as he headed toward the door. Ally unhooked her seatbelt and went to open the door. But she couldn't do it. Her breath caught in her chest, and her heart started pounding. Billy, Tina, Sandra. People she didn't know, not well, not really. She closed her eyes. It was happening again. This was the third time in as many months, and the idea that this would keep happening made her heart rate increase.

"I'm okay," she said out loud. Michael's roommates weren't going to judge her. They weren't mean people. It wasn't rational to fear spending time with people she didn't know well.

Her breath was becoming more ragged and she fought to control it. The idea of not being able to get catch her breath – *what if I pass out?* – made it even harder to breathe and she gripped the steering wheel hard, tried to center herself.

"I'm okay. I can breathe. My fears are irrational. I'm okay."

That wasn't working. She was trembling now, nauseated. She opened her eyes and grabbed at her purse, digging into it for her bottle of water. Her hand closed around a small pill bottle, and she was confused enough by it that she forgot to panic about not being able to breathe for a moment.

The bottle rattled with little yellow pills. She turned it in her hand and read the name: Michelle Smart. Klonopin (clonazepam) 1 mg prn. Only doctors and teachers ever called Misha Michelle— her unique nickname started when she was born and Ally couldn't quite say her name. Misha had been Misha ever since.

Ally stayed focused on the bottle, and on what it meant. She wasn't exactly sure what Klonopin was, or why Misha was prescribed them, but she knew Michael would know. And he was just inside the house. Just up the sidewalk and through the door. She put the bottle back in her purse and closed her eyes again, taking more deep breaths.

I'm okay, I'm okay, I'm okay.

She looked up in time to see Michael come down the walkway toward her, a concerned look on his face.

"You okay?" he asked. Ally forced herself to smile and then nodded. She picked up her phone and waved it at him.

"My mom," she said. She hoped the sound traveling through the car would hide the shake in her voice.

This time she was able to open the door, grab her bag, and walk with Michael toward the house, taking as many slow breaths as she could.

"You want to take a shower first?" he asked her. She nodded at him. He called out "hello" as he walked in. Ally could smell something spicy wafting through the house. Sandra emerged from the kitchen, a frilly pink apron standing out against her black pants and dark-green shirt, large hoop earrings dangling from her ears. A bandana kept her dirty-blonde hair out of her face, and Ally wished she was cool enough to wear bandanas like that.

"Good workout?" Sandra asked.

Michael nodded. "Smells fantastic—what'cha making?"

"Okra," she said. "Rice. Some chicken for you meat eaters, some tofu for me. Hey Ally," Sandra said, and gave Ally a little wave. Ally waved back.

"Hi."

"Ally's going to shower before dinner," Michael said. "She got time?"

Sandra nodded.

"If she hurries." She turned to Ally. "Wash your hair with the stuff in the purple bottle. You'll love it!"

Ally followed Michael into his bedroom—his and Sandra's. When they'd moved in together, Sandra and Michael decided to make the most of the space they had by having platform beds hanging over their desks on opposite sides of the room. This was the arrangement they needed to pay for school on part-time salaries. Ally found the entire arrangement very dorm-room like—the decorations around the room just added to the feel. On Michael's side hung a large "The Lost Boys" poster next to an equally large poster from "Pirates of the Caribbean." His other contributions to the room had been a large arm-chair and his painted-so-many-times-it-was-several-inches-larger-than-when-he-bought-it-at-a-garage-sale desk.

Sandra's stuff was equally dorm-like—Goth candle holders, a large poster of fairies, and everything covered in scarves. Sandra said she was a practicing Wiccan. Ally was never sure what that exactly meant, except that Sandra always seemed to be wearing some sort of stone jewelry, didn't eat meat, and believed in the great energy force of life, or something like that. Michael said he found a crystal hanging over his bed one day, and when he asked Sandra about it, she said it was to promote good dreams. He left it there and when Ally asked if his dreams improved he said that they had, but that it could be a placebo effect as much as magic. Either way, Ally wouldn't have minded a magic stone or placebo effect. She was regularly plagued by nightmares, and didn't sleep well as a rule, particularly lately.

Once she was alone in the bathroom, she put her hands on the sink edge and bent over it, waiting to see if she might throw up. Several gulps of air later, she knew she wouldn't, and the panic feeling she had in the car began to fully subside.

Ally tried to hurry to get done with her shower, but the water felt good running over her fatigued muscles, and the stuff in the purple bottle did smell wonderful—clean, with a hint of some sweet spice. Worried she had taken too much time and still feeling shaky, Ally dressed hurriedly back into her work clothes, the only other clothes she had with her.

Her hair was still wet as she made her way back toward the kitchen. She heard voices floating out of it on another spicy-scented draft and slowed down to hear what they were saying before she stepped inside.

"Have you talked to her about it?" Sandra was saying.

"I keep trying to," Michael's voice responded. "Every time I bring it up, she gets defensive. If she was anyone else, I'd have no problem. But she's not just anyone – she's Ally. She's always been a little sensitive. I mean, I get it, with her parents, I would be too. I just don't want to make her feel worse, you know?"

"But you said that you've seen signs for a while. Like, with this diet…"

Ally paused just outside the doorway. She wasn't sure if she wanted to hear more. Was this the talk talk Michael had been wanting to have with her?

"She's become sort of obsessed. I think she thinks if she can control her weight, she won't feel so disconnected from her life. But that's how it can start, you know? That need for control…"

Ally definitely didn't want to hear more. She inhaled slowly, and stepped forward.

"Hey," she said as she entered the kitchen. Sandra and Michael were sitting at the kitchen table in the corner, Sandra's feet folded up under her. She looked small in the high-backed padded chair.

"Ready to eat?" Michael asked, and jumped up, grabbing a plate from the table in front of him. He couldn't look directly at her. Ally didn't blame him and didn't want to look directly at him either.

"I was just telling Michael about this guy at my work," Sandra said. "Seth. He's a real crack up."

"Oh?" Ally said, sitting at the table. She thought briefly about calling Sandra out on her obvious lie, but what would that accomplish? Michael took Ally's plate from her and handed her one laden with strange looking glops. He smiled brightly, and, Ally thought, more than a little guiltily. She forced a smile back and sat down with her meal.

The yellowish blob on the plate turned out to be rice and the greenish-brown one okra. The chicken was skinless and covered in a light sauce that had a spicy-lemon edge to it. After timid bites to make sure she could handle the spice, Ally did her best to dig in. She didn't have much appetite.

Sandra continued to talk about work and Ally nodded along, pretending to listen while secretly scrutinizing the smaller woman. Sandra moved with physical confidence, like someone who never had to be extra careful not to knock things down when moving through tight spaces. She'd spent a lot of years practicing ballet, Ally knew, and she had the dancer's body to go with it. Her arms looked strong, her stomach flat, and her thighs thick with muscle. High brows arched down to a long, thin nose and pointy chin. Her sharp face was softened by a wide smile that created crinkles around her green-ish eyes, giving her an impish look. Ally wondered if Sandra appreciated her body, appreciated being pretty and thin and strong, or if she was one of those women constantly searching her near-perfect body for any tiny flaw, like Misha did. Like Ally and Misha's mother did. Ally wondered what it would feel like to be in a body that never doubted its movement, its place in the world. A body that could leap and jump and spin with grace. Ally had never felt graceful a day in her life.

Why would Michael worry about her trying to lose weight so that she finally could?

Ally shook off the depressing thought and tried to concentrate on the conversation.

"You're really lucky you managed to get all your classes on two days," Sandra was telling Michael.

"I'm not taking a full load this semester," he said. "It'll take me longer to get through it all, but I really think the experience I'm gaining at work will help me in the end."

"Definitely," Sandra said, sliding a piece of tofu onto her fork. "What about you?" she asked Ally. "You ever going back to school? You could become even more of a master website design-er."

Ally shrugged. "They aren't really teaching the right programs in a lot of schools. So I don't think going back would really help." She had helped Sandra with her website, dedicated, of course, to the art of Wicca, and Sandra was convinced that Ally was some sort of computer goddess because of it. Ally had been surprised that Sandra had needed help with it. Wordpress sites practically built themselves these days.

Michael slapped the table and made both of them jump.

"We were going to take that career test!" he said. "Ally needs to know what to do with her life."

"Ooh," Sandra said. "I want to play too!"

The dishes were cleared away quickly and the three of them gathered around Michael's computer. It felt dark and cave-like under his bed. They made Ally sit in Michael's desk chair, while Michael sat on the work out ball and Sandra moved her own chair near. Ally could feel herself shrinking in, trying to take up as little space as possible so as to make room for the others. She was over-ly aware of her thighs pressed against the armrests of Michael's chair.

"And this will tell me what to do with my life?" Ally said, turning her attention back to the screen.

"Well, you could just decide for yourself," Michael teased.

"What would be the fun in that?" Sandra said, smiling. "Let's let the computer decide."

"Computers always know what's best," Ally said. "Ask Skynet."

"Hal," Michael offered.

"Jarvis," Sandra said with authority, and Ally laughed, startled.

"Good one," she told Sandra. "Let's see what vision The Vision has for me."

The test ended up being a comparison thing. "Would you rather be an FBI agent, a plastic surgeon, or a tax accountant," she read.

"Be honest," Michael said. "It works better that way."

Ally picked FBI agent. The rest of the test followed the same "what would you rather be" pattern. Most choices were pretty easy. Some took careful consideration. "An Undercover Agent for a Drug Enforcement Agency, a psychiatrist, or an art gallery owner."

Ally easily dismissed psychiatrist, but had to weigh and measures the pros and cons of art gallery owner or undercover agent. Both sounded glamorous, although drug enforcement wasn't as much fun as say, the CIA. She didn't think there would be much opportunity for really cool clothes as a drug enforcement agent. She pictured dirty street corners and men with long greasy hair and the shakes, wiping their noses and telling her about some big deal going down. And she liked the idea of being surrounded by fine art and the kind of rich people who could afford it. So art gallery owner won out that time.

Some of the choices made her pick the best of the worst, like a billing clerk, a landscaper, or a substitute teacher. A substitute teacher had a temporary feel to it, like it wasn't something you would do for the rest of your life, so she picked that one.

As she went down the list, she mentally explored the most extravagant lives for each profession. As a high school drama teacher she could directly change the lives of the troubled kids she worked with, and give one of those rousing speeches that made them suddenly care about their futures. She would probably be fired, or threatened to be fired, because of her high ideals…and probably end up having an affair with the very handsome father of one her students.

No boring job stayed boring for Ally—in her head, at any rate.

Finally, she answered the last question and clicked the submit button.

"So, what do you think it's going to be?" Michael asked.

"Based on some her answers, something with a lot of adventure," Sandra said, laughing.

Ally sat silently waiting for the website to reveal her future to her. She had a sudden feeling that this was going to be the answer she had been looking for, that this site was going to give her the solution to the formula she'd been struggling with – what added up to "Allyson Smart." As she waited she took a better look at the site, the advertisement banners, the color scheme, and the menu options. She wondered who kept up the site, how the test answers were read, what program compiled the information and chose one of the pre-set profession ideas, and wondered if she could hack into it, fix the program to always give her the best results.

"Based on your responses, the career area best suited to you is math and science," Michael read over Ally's shoulder. She felt disappointed, though she wasn't sure why or what she had been hoping for.

"Careers in this field often demand that you enjoy thinking analytically, have strong reasoning skills and the ability to approach a problem from a variety of angles. You're not content to just question. You're motivated to test your ideas to see if they are right. Even if it's not a common perception, people who enjoy math and science are highly imaginative and intuitive."

"Math and science," Ally said, trying the title on for size. "What does that even mean?"

"Stephen Hawking?" Michael offered.

"That's physics."

"Spy," Sandra suggested. "Like, a code-breaker."

Ally grinned again.

"Now we're talking. But I really was hoping for something more concrete, something like 'you should go get this kind of job at this kind of company, and oh, by the way, here is where you submit your resume.' I feel let down by the algorithm."

"That's because you're trusting the wrong source. If you really want to know what you're going to be, you should let me do a tarot card reading for you," Sandra said. Ally glanced at Michael, who shrugged.

"It could work. I mean, why not?"

"Will it come with a link to a job listing?" Ally kept her tone light.

"Not so much," Sandra said.

"Yeah, well, that's okay," Ally said. "I suppose if I knew what I was supposed to be, I would have to actually try to be that." She smiled to try to play off the joke.

"Sure. Well, if you ever change your mind." Sandra walked

over to a small wooden box on top of what Ally assumed by the number of scarves and candles was Sandra's dresser. From inside, she pulled out a deck of tarot cards and showed them to Ally. "Your future is right here," she said, brandishing the cards with a smile. Ally smiled back. She still felt oddly disappointed. The future looked too big and gray and unknown for a deck of picture cards to figure out for her, when even a computer couldn't.

You can't really tell the future anyway.

"Anyway, enough future talk—who wants dessert?" Michael asked.

Ally stared at him. "What about my diet?"

"This is the kind of dessert you can eat," he said, and impishly flicked her nose as he got up. "Follow me."

Dessert turned out to be fresh fruit and whipped cream—which was good, and diet friendly, but also, like the online test, oddly disappointing. It also, Ally noted, put her over her calorie totals for the day. Stupid French fries.

"So, guess what Ally is going to be for Halloween?" Michael said to Sandra.

"Uh, a pirate?" she asked.

"Nope." He grinned at Ally conspiratorially.

"An Eskimo?" Sandra tried. "Or Wonder Woman?"

"A witch," Ally volunteered. "I hope that doesn't offend you."

"That depends," Sandra said. "I hope you're not giving into the patriarchal mythos of hags and witchcraft. You're not going to be an evil witch, are you?"

"Depends on if I get to eat any chocolate on Saturday," Ally said.

Michael and Sandra both laughed.

"You're doing great on trying to take better care of yourself," Michael said. "Although I am still not sure about the calorie counting." Ally glanced at Sandra to try and read her face. Was Michael really going to have the talk talk in front of her?

"I know that it's hard to change habits," Sandra added, her face carefully neutral.

What have you ever had to change? The thought felt harsh, even to Ally.

"The secret to changing is positive thinking."

Sure, you just think your positive thoughts. Ally suddenly felt very tired.

"You know, I forgot I have laundry to do," she said, getting up from the chair and awkwardly moving out from under Michael's desk. "I should get home to get it in before the laundry room closes."

"Oh, okay," Michael said, following her. "Thanks for coming for dinner."

"Thanks for inviting me." Ally turned to Sandra. "And thank you so much for cooking. It was really good."

Sandra smiled.

"No problem," she said. "Anytime."

Michael walked Ally to the door.

"Everything cool with you?" he asked. Ally nodded at him.

"I just seriously don't have anything to wear tomorrow," she said. "You know how I put things off till the last minute."

"Sandra really likes you, you know," Michael said.

Ally smiled at him.

"And I like her. She's really nice."

"I know the Wicca stuff is weird."

"No, it's cool."

Michael nodded.

"We ever gonna have time for a real talk?" He pulled at a lock of her hair. "I have been missing quality Ally time."

"So you said earlier," Ally said, turning away to look down the street as though there was something interesting out there catching her eye.

"I know I've been busy with school, and you've been working on your own thing."

"We'll make time," Ally said, turning back to him with a smile she hoped he wouldn't notice was forced. "Soon. Maybe at the party?"

Michael nodded.

"Okay." He gave her a hug. "Drive safe."

"Safely," she corrected automatically. It was a habit she picked up from her mother, and one she used to drive her little sister crazy with.

"That too," Michael said with a wink.

As Ally walked to her car she tried to shake off the bitter feeling crawling up her skin. She got into her car and stared at the house. She hadn't asked Michael about Misha and the pills. She hadn't told him about her own panic attacks, or the weird feeling she'd had all day since Bobby touched her. And he hadn't told her about his worries about her diet. What else wasn't he telling her?

She turned on her car and pulled away from the curb. She focused on the road, on the music on her radio, on anything other than the thoughts that made her chest tight. She couldn't wait to get home where she could escape into a world where she never had to worry about losing her best friend.

ASH WEDNESDAY

The phone rang "Life Would be a Dream" and Ally picked it up, seeing Michael's name on the caller ID.

"Work's closed because of the fires!" he said, incredibly chipper for six thirty in the morning. "All the schools are closed and people are being told to stay indoors because of all the smoke. And the sky looks positively bizarre. I mean it, you have to get up and look!"

Ally glanced at her clock radio, then after a moment of staring at the red neon, thought enough to reach over and turn off the alarm. She peeked at her window. The blinds were closed.

"Very bizarre," she agreed anyway. "So, no work today?"

"No nothing today by the looks of it. It's all the news is showing."

"All fires, all the time," Ally said, nodding.

"God, it feels like the end of the world," Michael said, sighing. "Do you think this is what the end will look like?"

"If it's the end, it won't look like anything," Ally said. "The world will be ending so there won't be anything to look at. Cuz, probably, we'd be dead already."

"But I bet this is what it's like to be in a war-torn country."

"I have to pee," Ally announced. She wasn't in the mood to feel sorry for people half a planet away this early in the morning of a day she didn't have to get up for.

"Call me later?" Michael asked.

"Sure." Ally hung up the phone, stumbled to the bathroom, stumbled back to bed and fell into it. She knew she should get up.

Or you could just sleep some more.

She hadn't slept well the night before. Again. She probably could use more sleep. Falling back to sleep wasn't easy, not after being awake enough to talk on the phone and walk to the bathroom.

Close your eyes. Dream. Fantasy Man. A grand adventure. You, looking stunning, the most perfect version of yourself.

Ally thought about it, and then closed her eyes, picturing what the most perfect version of herself might look like, going from head to toe—hair, neck, shoulders, breasts, stomach, ass, thighs. She imagined more detail than she ever had before. Instead of keeping her awake, it seemed like the effort to create that image made her sleepy. Soon, she'd drifted off.

Juxtaposition. Ally had never liked the word, but it was the first to come to mind as she stared into the swirling surface of what seemed to be a lake. At least, her dream-self labeled it a lake; it was really just a mess of blue-grays and silvers whirling together, liquid, and yet very unlike water. Floating on top were two images, juxtaposed: Ally as she was, and Ally as she dreamed herself to be. They circled each other, overlapping at times, morphed into different poses and angles. The distinction was clear.

Plain Ally. Beautiful Ally.

Fat Ally. Thin Ally.

Round, soft Ally. Hard, athletic Ally.

Smart Ally. Sexy Ally.

Round and round they spun, until, finally, the images merged into one, perfect vision of Allyson Smart. The vision reached out her hand and took hold of dream-Ally's arm, where Bobby had grabbed her, and then pulled Ally into the liquid silver of the lake. Ally swam through it, feeling both chilled and warmed, encumbered and free, safe and scared.

She burst through the other side of the lake, and fell hard onto a grassy field. Her eyes were closed, but she could feel the little blades of grass poking her through her clothes, tickling her bare arms in the breeze. She could smell the wet dirt beneath her and a hay-flavored wind blowing over her. She opened her eyes to bright sunshine, and pushed herself up to a sitting position.

The lake, calm and silvery-blue, was to her right. A line of leafy trees were to her left. In front of her was a white horse, grazing. The sky above was dotted with a few fluffy clouds. The field around her was peppered with purple and yellow flowers. But more than these things, Ally was aware of herself, her body.

She was thin, and strong. She looked down at herself. Firm, supple breasts poked out of a long, flowy sundress, with toned, tan legs folded under her and glass-slipper-perfect feet wiggling cute-as-a-button toes.

And then, from behind her, a voice spoke—chocolate peanut-butter, thick with flavor, dripping with bitter and sweet all at the same time.

"Ally, are you getting cold?"

She turned to look, and there he was, Fantasy Man, his pale, perfect arms almost glowing in the sunlight. He knelt by her in one easy movement and took her hand in both of his.

"It's getting late. Maybe we should start heading back before Beauty gobbles up all this sweet grass." He smiled, nodded to the white horse who suddenly wore a saddle—or perhaps Ally was noticing the saddle for the first time.

"Beauty was a black horse," she managed to say. Her mind felt muddled, her senses sharp, and the contrast was disorientating. Ally looked down. She was sitting on a checkered blanket that again, either just appeared or was there the whole time and she just didn't see it. She felt, though, that it must have just appeared, and looked over to see if there would be a basket to go with the blanket. There was, wicker-handled, the kind Little Red Riding Hood held when she met the Big Bad Wolf. Ally shivered.

"Beauty is a black horse," Fantasy Man said. Ally looked again, and sure enough, the horse was now ebony. "You're cold," Fantasy Man said, and wrapped another blanket around Ally, pulling her close. She no longer cared what color the horse was or where she was or why this dream felt more real than any other she'd ever had. She breathed in his scent—musk, sweat, hay—and leaned into him, feeling his arms tighten around her.

"I don't want to go yet," she whispered. He chuckled, a low rumble in his chest.

"We can stay as long as you want," he said. He pulled back then, running one finger down her cheek and to her lips. "I always want to be here, in this moment, with you."

Ally's breath caught on her pounding heart—she held it there. He leaned toward her. Ally closed her eyes.

And then he rang.

Ally pulled back, and where Fantasy Man's face was supposed to be was a giant phone. She shook her head and felt as though she was falling, back through the lake of sliver, back to her bed.

Ally opened her eyes to the cold sight of her clock radio, the colon separating the hour from the minutes blinking indifferently at her. 10:47. The phone rang again, and, feeling slightly dizzy, Ally reached out for it.

"What?"

"Are you still in bed?" Michael asked her.

"The world is ending. I'm planning on sleeping through it."

"Just checking in on you. You feel like company today? I can come over…"

"No," Ally said quickly, looking around at the mess that was her bedroom. Even with the laundry she'd done the night before, there were still piles of clothes everywhere. "Maybe later. Or I can come over there. I just want to get some things done around here first."

"Sure, okay. Later. And get up already. You're missing Ash Wednesday."

Ally hung up, flung back the covers and swung her legs over the side of the bed. The walls spun around her and she fell back against the pillows. She tried to picture the lake again, the trees, Fantasy Man bending in to kiss her. Her bladder distracted her. She was fully awake now, and however real it had all felt, it had been a dream and there was no way for her to go back to the peaceful surrealness of the lake.

In typical network news fashion, all the major channels were covering the same fires, using the same shots and giving the same information, all at the same time. And they all felt compelled to do so live, interrupting regularly scheduled broadcasting. Brave reporters stood in pressed slacks and yellow fire-jackets and pointed to burning brush or smoke behind them. Eye witnesses agreed that the fire was scary and the ash was everywhere, and back in the studio they continued to warn people of the poor air quality, saying again and again that it would be best to stay indoors.

Ally agreed.

She checked her e-mail, noted that the fires were big enough to make the national news sites, found out which celebrities were sleeping with whom, and then checked out a few of the more esoteric web sites—she briefly considered going back to the personality test and hacking her way to a better career but decided against it. She checked out a few online auctions for some computer parts she wanted to get. She was working on putting together a better computer system for Michael for Christmas and figured she could get what she needed online. She didn't find anything worth bidding on.

So instead, Ally decided to celebrate her very first fire-day by making chocolate-chip cookies.

I won't eat that many, she told herself as she got out the ingredients. She was still optimistic about her diet working, for once. She also felt a strange emptiness that seemed to demand chocolate chips. And a few cookies wouldn't kill her diet. Anyway, the world was ending. Chocolate might be the only thing that could save her.

Ally's was the kind of kitchen that always had the ingredients to make chocolate-chip cookies. They were the only things she regularly baked. Even her baked potatoes were nuked in the microwave. Sometimes she "baked" frozen French fries, but really her oven was rarely used, except for the process of tuning blobs of cookie dough into round, still-slightly-soft cookies.

So after a breakfast of bran cereal and low-fat milk—see? she wasn't cheating on her diet—Ally turned off the never-ending fire coverage and turned on Pandora to a station Michel had made her, blasting a mix of energetic female-empowering songs. She got out bowls, measuring spoons and cups, and her bag of chocolate chips.

And then the phone rang. Ally glanced at it and saw Misha's perfect headshot on the screen. Ally let it ring four times before her compulsion to pick it up got to her.

"Hello?" she said warily.

"Aren't you supposed to be at work?" Misha's voice always

managed to sound bored, even when she was being accusing.

"Work's closed because of the fires."

"Whatever," Misha said, and Ally could picture the flippant hand movement Misha usually did when she said that. Misha was probably wearing something pink—her favorite color—and something tight or low cut. Ally checked the clock. It was still early enough that Misha could be in her customary boxer-shorts and pink tank-top that she always slept in. Ally was still in her pajamas after all.

"What's up Misha?" Ally asked.

"Did mom call you yesterday?"

Ally thought back—she went to work, she bought her costume with Misha, she had that weird moment with Bobby, she went to the gym, she went to Michael's.

"Nope," she said. She pulled her phone away and checked the voicemail indicator. "No new messages. Why?" She wedged the phone between her shoulder and ear so that she could start measuring things for the cookies—talking to her sister made her want chocolate that much more.

"No reason—I just figured she'd call to bitch to you or something."

"Why, what did you do?" Ally asked, measuring out the flour and spilling a large amount of it on her shirt in the process. Misha let out a snort of disgust.

"Nice, just assume she'd bitch about me," Misha said.

"Mom thinks you're perfect. She just worries about your decisions sometimes," Ally said.

"She never bugs you about yours," Misha pouted.

"She bugs me about other things," she said, and felt a new wave of guilt wash over her in the middle of measuring out the baking soda. Her mother would not approve of her making cookies. She had approved of the diet though. She always approved of any effort Ally made to look more like how she thought Ally should look. Ally was newly glad that her parents lived a good hour's drive away.

"Anyway, what are you doing today since you're not working?" Misha asked.

"Nothing much," Ally said, knowing her sister wouldn't care anyway, and not wanting to mention the cookies.

"I'm going out. Santa Clarita sucks today. I'm going to Santa Monica and hang with Scott and his band."

Ally nodded. She had no idea who Scott was, but every other person Misha knew was in a band, so she didn't feel any need to clarify which one Scott was in. Ally didn't know anyone who was in a band. Michael could play the trumpet and that was about it as far as the musical talent Ally associated with.

"Have fun," Ally said, hoping that was going to be the end of the conversation.

"You're just going to stay in?" Misha asked.

"I didn't say that," Ally said. "I said 'nothing much.' I meant, nothing much that would probably be of interest to you."

"Like what?"

"Like making cookies, which is what I'm doing now."

"I like cookies."

"Yep, sure, you bake all the time."

"Whatever," Misha said again. "Look, if mom calls, tell her that tattoos aren't that big a deal, okay?"

Ally stopped mid-measure.

"Of what and where?" she demanded.

"I haven't gotten it yet," Misha said, her bored voice taking on an edge. Ally shook her head. Her sister had a perfect body. She couldn't imagine wanting to mar that perfection with some repulsive design destined to fade, wrinkle, and otherwise detract from her sister's beauty.

"Just tell her, okay?" Misha said. Ally contemplated going over all her own reasons why Misha shouldn't get a tattoo, but really, she just wanted to get back to making her cookies in peace.

"She won't listen to me anyway," she said out loud, meaning Misha.

"Mom listens to you," Misha said.

"Yeah, I'll tell her," she said. "Have fun at Scott's."

"Wait," she added, suddenly remembering. "I have your pills!"

"What?"

"When our purses spilled, I think I accidentally picked them up."

"One sec," Misha said, and after a small pause she came back, and Ally could hear her ruffling through her bag. "Klonopin," Misha said. "They're not everyday ones. Just for when I have anxiety or whatever and need to feel, like, normal. Bring them to the party, okay? Don't forget."

"You won't need them before then?"

"If I did, I'd tell you. Anyway, don't tell mom you have them. She freaks out about shit like that."

"Wait, how long have …"

"It's no big deal, and anyway, I have to go. Have fun with your cookies and stuff." And then she hung up.

For anxiety and stuff. Ally thought about the pills, and about her own anxiety attacks. She wondered if she should, could, talk to Misha about what had been happening to her. Misha might understand.

You really want to do that to yourself?

Ally chewed on her bottom lip. Misha cared. Misha always called her to talk. Misha helped her get a costume. Misha invited her to her party. She cared.

Cares about looking better than you.

Ally took a deep breath and tried to exhale all the negativity out. It was if her thoughts were not her own, darker, even more depressing than usual. She didn't want to think them anymore. *Cookies. Focus on the cookies.*

The most important part of the process was the brown sugar. According to the package it needed to be firmly packed. She did this by putting some sugar in the measuring cup, and then used a smaller measuring cup to press the sugar into a compact mold. In Ally's mind, the brown sugar wasn't properly packed unless it retained the shape of the measuring cup when dumped into the bowl. She smushed it and the white sugar into the butter, added eggs and vanilla, then all her dry ingredients. She stirred while dancing along to the Carole King version of "Natural Woman." Finally she added the chips, working hard now to mix them into the thick dough, hard enough to burn calories, she told herself. She covered the bowl and shoved it into the freezer, leaving a not-as-large-as-normal spoonful out to eat while she waited for the oven to preheat and the dough to chill. *I'll only eat a few and take the rest to work with me tomorrow,* Ally told herself firmly, licking dough from her finger-tips.

Sure you will.

Ally took the spoon with her as she stared out over her deck and to the church parking lot behind her apartment complex. Shania Twain was feeling like a woman on Ally's computer. Ally didn't agree. She couldn't say how she felt, but feminine wasn't on the list of adjectives that floated across her mind as she rubbed her arm. Safe behind the glass, she gazed out at the eerie orange of the day, the falling ash, the smoky air. It gave everything a spooky feel, rather appropriate for Halloween, Ally thought. She decided she wanted to watch a scary movie.

A quick survey of her Netflix options and she narrowed it down to two choices—Carrie, the remake, and World War Z. She went with the latter on the grounds that it had Brad Pitt. She was pressing play when Michael called again.

"It's well past later," he admonished her. "You didn't go back to sleep did you?"

"No, I was just working around the house," she said. Stirring cookie dough was definitely work, she decided.

"Are you done yet? You should come over."

Ally eyed the remaining cookie-dough on her spoon.

"Nah, still have things to do," she said.

"Skip it, come over. We're having a barbecue."

"The valley is burning," Ally said, shaking her head. "The sky is full of smoke."

"Yeah, it really put us in the mood to fire up the grill," Michael said. "It's just chicken, and some of Sandra's tofu-dogs— good healthy fare, if you're worried about that. We're watching the news and rating the reports. It's going to be fun."

Ally pulled at her pajama top—she still hadn't gotten dressed. She remembered her panic attack the day before, her overheard conversation, Michael wanting to talk, and felt an unsettling in her stomach.

"I really think I just want to hang out around here," she told him. "But have a tofu-dog for me. And thanks for thinking about me."

"You've been staying in too much," he said.

"I'm a home-body."

"You're anti-social."

"I'm hanging up."

"Love you too, sweetie. Hey, have you tried on your costume yet?"

Ally stared at the bag still sitting on her entranceway table.

"Nah, haven't had time." She cringed at her own lie. In truth she was trying to forget the costume, and the reason for buying it, even existed.

"Well, I'm sure it will look great. Let me know, huh?"

Ally nodded, still looking guiltily at the bag.

"Ally?"

"Yeah, sure," she said. "I'll let you know. Have fun at the barbecue."

"Bye. Call if you need anything."

She hung up the phone and looked at the plastic-wrapped costume just peeking out at her. Then she picked up the cookie-dough spoon and settled on the couch, pressed play on the remote to her streaming device. She took a large bite from the spoon and crunched a chocolate chip. She'd try the costume on later.

✳

By the time Brad was figuring out that the zombies avoided people with terminal illnesses, all the cookies were baked, and Ally sat with a peanut-butter-and-jelly sandwich, dunking the crusts into milk and eating them soggy. When the credits rolled, Ally flipped back to the menu and started making her way through the Harry Potter series, skipping her least favorite scenes, which pretty much meant any that Hermione wasn't in. After that she made a dinner of a frozen health-conscious version of fettuccine alfredo—health conscious apparently meant flavor-free—and decided to wedge herself into her tiny apartment-sized bathtub and soak while reading about her favorite make-up-saleswoman-turned-secret-spy's latest adventure. She rationed out three cookies and took them with her—that would make a grand total of five cookies, plus two spoons of cookie dough, and Ally felt that she was being very good indeed to not have eaten more. She logged them dutifully into her food journal before getting in the bath.

Eventually, the cookies were devoured, the book dropped to the side of the tub, and Ally's eyes dropped close. Head filled with zombies, magic, and sexy gun-wielding women, Ally's imagination re-created herself as a wise-cracking telepath who talked with dead people, rode a flying broom, and solved crimes in the middle of a zombie apocalypse. Or tried to—something just didn't feel right. She couldn't shake the lake dream from her mind. She rubbed her arm. It didn't feel bruised, but it didn't feel right either.

She opened her eyes and dared a glance down at her body; the bathtub was tiny, and she felt even more huge than normal in it. With the water covering less than two-thirds of her, her breasts and stomach floated above the water line. She ran her hand over her skin, tried to imagine what it would feel like to have smaller breasts, a flat stomach, thin thighs, to fit, once and for all, the tub, and the world. She closed her eyes quickly, tried not to think about her body as it was, and create instead the body she wanted to have, the life she wanted to live. She went back to the image of the perfect self she had created earlier.

She was Ally's same height, but her hair became the fiery red of Amy Adams' hair, with all the bounce of a Pantene commercial. Her hazel eyes became blue, and then Ally pulled from the people she knew. She added Misha's smooth tan, her mother's tiny feet, and Billy's eye-lashes. Guy or girl, they were still the best eye-lashes she'd ever seen. Finally, it was the advertisements she'd seen that completed her picture-perfect self. Crest-white teeth, CoverGirl-perfect lips, Neutrogena-clean skin. Once the Frankenstein-version of Allyson Smart was completed, she spent a few moments admiring it. This is what she wanted to be. This is what she imagined she somehow could be, if she was rich, or better disciplined, or born with better genes, and maybe had color contacts. And that version of Ally would know what she wanted to do with her life, would have a boyfriend, a family she felt understood by, and a life that was exciting to wake up to in the morning.

Ally scratched her stomach—her fingers were all pruney, her skin cold. It was time to get out of the bath, away from the fantasy. She de-wedged herself, stood up, and wrapped herself in a towel that didn't quite go all the way around her body. She stepped from the tub and thought wistfully how nice it would be if she could just close her eyes, make a wish, and step in front of the mirror to see that perfect version of herself starring back at her. Maybe if she just wished hard enough...

Ally laughed at herself. It had been a long time since she believed in magic. It was silly to try and believe in it now. All this wishing, and no doing, had gotten her where she was in the first place. Wishing for a miracle diet or to suddenly have someone come along and save her from herself wasn't getting her anywhere. Ally was living in denial of her problems, of what she had to do to solve them. She needed to face reality, and make some real changes. She took a deep breath and then stepped in front of the mirror, ready to face the real her.

The real her wasn't staring back at Ally. Crest-white teeth.

CoverGirl-perfect eyelashes. Neutrogena-clean skin. Amy Adams' hair, Misha's tan, and blue eyes.

Ally shook her head, tried to clear her eyes.

She looked again.

Her reflection in the mirror stayed as perfect as before—not fat, not pale, not Ally, but the most perfect version of herself that Ally could ever imagine.

She looked down at her body, barely hidden under the too-small towel. She looked back at her reflection—the towel went all the way around, with room to spare. The towel in the mirror was somehow fluffier too, less dingy. Ally touched herself, felt to make sure she was real, and even as her hand ran over her squishy arm, her hand's reflection caressed the tight, toned skin of mirror-Ally's perfect arm.

Ally stared at her reflection in horror and wonder.

And then her reflection winked at her.

MIRROR MIRROR

Ally dropped her towel. If her jaw could unhinge itself and fall to the beige linoleum, it would have. Instead it gaped.

Her reflection had dropped her towel as well, and was smiling at her. Mirror-Ally tilted her head to the side, thrust out a perfect hip, and slid one leg slightly in front of the other. She was posing, Ally realized, flaunting her perfectness. Then Mirror-Ally's eyes scanned down the real Ally's body—and she smiled again.

Ally wasn't sure what her other self was smiling about, but embarrassment penetrated the confused, horrified fog of her brain, and she swiftly re-covered herself with the towel from the floor. Mirror-Ally politely followed suit. Even more disturbed by this connection between herself and her mirror-self, Ally jumped to the side, away from the mirror, holding the towel and shaking slightly. She didn't know what to do. *I must still be asleep.* She looked at the tub, half-expecting to see herself still lying there. The bathtub was empty.

She sat hard on the toilet seat and considered her options: One, that she was dreaming. Two, that she was insane. And three, that she ate some bad chocolate chips and was tripping. While she'd never heard of anyone hallucinating because of chocolate chips, she was more willing to believe in that possibility than that she was insane. She didn't feel insane. She wondered if she would. Ally pinched herself, told herself to wake up. Nothing happened.

Eggs. She'd eaten a lot of raw cookie dough—three spoonfuls if she was really being honest. Maybe that was making her hallucinate. *Yes,* Ally decided, *it was the cookie dough, had to be.* And now that she knew what was causing the hallucination, it obviously wouldn't be there anymore. Several deep breaths later, Ally peeked over the sink and into the mirror.

"Boo!" her reflection said, and Ally screamed, flailed back, and fell off the toilet seat, hitting her knee hard and landing harder on her ass. She could hear the lyrical laugh of her Mirror-Self as she rubbed her knee and looked up at the reflection with new shock.

"You…" she managed. She tried again. "You…." But her mind would not function well enough to get words out.

"Me, Allison, you, Jane," Mirror-Ally quipped.

"I'm Allyson!" Ally said, struggling to stand up and hold on to her towel at the same time. "You're just a hallucination and I would really appreciate it if you would go away now."

Mirror-Ally rolled her eyes merrily and shook her head. "Just a joke, silly."

"You're not real," Ally repeated, although she felt less positive about it than ever. Were hallucinations supposed to talk? And if so, were they supposed to crack jokes?

"I'm not a hallucination," her reflection said. "I'm very real."

"You're me…." Ally stammered, "Allyson."

"No, not quite you. You but different, like, Allison-with-an-'i.' It's prettier that way anyway. You should consider changing it. You could dot the i with a heart."

It was Ally's turn to shake her head.

"You have my same name, but you spell it differently? And you look like me but…"

"I look like you the same way a child's finger painting looks like a Monet. The elements of paint and color are there, but the composition is altogether different. Both are art, I suppose—just by different types of…painters, and therefore entirely different."

"You're in my mirror," Ally said helplessly. "And my towel." She looked down to make sure, then back at the reflection. Both were blue and white striped. "Yes, it's the same towel." But fluffier. "Maybe."

"Yes, the same. But better." The way Allison-with-an-i was looking at Ally made Ally pull her towel tighter. Allison very carefully looked away, as though to save Ally some sort of embarrassment.

Ally was getting fed up. Her knee hurt, she was hallucinating, and her hallucination pitied her. "You're not real," she said more firmly, closing her eyes and rubbing them. "Go away."

"The thing is, if you knew why I was here, you wouldn't want me to go away," Allison said. "You did a fantastic job, by the way. Perhaps you lack a certain originality, but still…" The pose she fell into would have made Vanna White jealous. "Everything to your very special order. Aren't you the least bit proud of what you made?" She tilted her hip to one side, pouted her lips, gave her best bedroom-eyed stare. "Mary Poppins couldn't be more perfect." She smiled, her teeth gleaming.

"I made…?" Ally said, trying to keep up with Allison.

"You. Made," Allison said, talking unbearably slow. "Me." She held her hand out, presented herself as a prize. Ally had the urge to buy a vowel.

As she stared at the mirror-girl, suddenly it clicked. The fantasy version of Allyson now existed in Ally's bathroom mirror. This was real. And this was…terrifying.

"I'm insane," Ally said out loud, calmly and reasonably. "I made you because you're a hallucination. And people who hallucinate are insane. My friend is studying to be a psychologist, so I know about these things." She nodded her head to herself, satisfied with her explanation. She tried not to think about its greater ramifications.

"You're not insane," Allison said, tossing her perfectly curled reddish-brown hair over her shoulder. Ally's hair was only wavy, and she resented the fact that her mirror-self's hair was curlier. And redder. And bouncier. "You just have an over-active imagination."

"Of course!" Ally said, pointing at Allison in her excitement. "I'm just imagining this!"

"Yes," Allison said. "And no. Yes, I come from your imagination, but no, you are not currently imagining this. I am real." She tapped the glass of the mirror to prove it, making it bend out toward Ally. Ally jumped back from the motion, banging her hip into the door handle.

"Ow!" Allison said the same time Ally did, rubbing her much thinner hip in the same spot Ally was rubbing hers.

"You're my reflection," Ally said, still confused.

"Inner-reflection," Allison corrected. "How you see yourself on the inside, in your fantasies. I'm what you believe you could be, should be, and want to be. In that way, I am your reflection—I wear what you wear, am injured when you are injured. But also, I'm separate from you, because, and I'm saying this nicely, you don't really look a thing like me."

Ally cringed under Allison's judging gaze.

"Really, this is a good thing, if you only let it be. Isn't this what you wanted to see when you looked in the mirror?"

Ally pulled further back into herself, confused.

"I wanted to be you, not see you." She shook her head, which suddenly seemed to pound with every beat of her heart.

"Baby steps," Allison said sweetly, and Ally stared at her with new suspicion.

"What are you?" she asked.

"I already said—you, but, not you. But possibly the answer to all of your dreams."

She grinned white teeth and Ally had a sudden vision that those teeth were rather predatory. Her head was pounding even harder now, and it was hurting to stand up. She shook her head again.

"My head," she mumbled, cradling it in one hand.

"Sleep is a wonder-cure," Allison said.

Ally decided that was the sanest thing she'd heard yet, and she stumbled from the bathroom and toward her bedroom.

She tumbled straight into her bed. She didn't bother getting into pajamas and dived under the blankets, pulling them over her head, hiding and shivering beneath them.

This isn't real, she told herself, rocking back and forth. *She isn't real.* But Ally's hip really was bruised, her knee throbbed, and her head pounded. If this was all a hallucination, it was taking a very physical toll on Ally. She curled up under the blankets and sent up a silent prayer that this was in fact, just a dream. *When I get up there will be no one in the mirror but me,* she told herself. *Just good ole fat and pale me. My inner reflection my ass.*

✳

A phone ringing startled Ally awake and she reached blindly for her cell.

"Hello?" she said, shaking off sleep.

"The fires are almost all put out," Michael said as greeting. "We have work today."

"Shit," Ally said.

"Wow, you okay?"

"Yeah, just…don't feel that great," she said, rubbing her head. Truthfully, she felt a little headachy.

"You want to call in sick?"

"No, I'm fine." She looked at her closed bedroom door and wondered what lie beyond it. "Hey, Michael?" she began.

"Yeah, sweetie?" She thought about telling him, thought about what he might say. Then she thought better of it. He was already talking behind her back about being worried about her. This would certainly just make him worry more. And talk more.

"Thanks for calling," she said instead.

"Sure," he said, and sounded surprised. "What are friends for?"

Ally hung up and carefully got out of bed, sitting for a moment on its edge before standing up. She felt slightly dizzy, brushed it off to the tossing and turning she did last night. She walked carefully, quietly, to the bedroom door, listened for sound outside of it, but heard nothing. She opened it slowly, peeked outside. The bathroom door was still shut.

Ally eased herself out of her bedroom and to her walk-in closet in the hallway across from the bathroom, and winced at the sound of the light clicking on. She glanced back at the bathroom door as though expecting it to open. Her bladder tried to get her attention. She ignored it. She dressed quickly and as silently as she could in the closet. She kept the silent routine up as she made her way to her kitchen, and she took her cereal to the corner of the apartment, as far away from the bathroom as she could get.

Finally, she couldn't avoid the pressure in her bladder anymore, let alone the need to brush her teeth.

She stalked her bathroom door, walking to it in stints of quiet movement, standing still and listening for any sound coming from behind it. Finally, she made it to the door knob, turned it quietly while standing to one side, letting the door swing open. She took a deep breath, then dashed inside, not looking at the mirror as she went directly to the toilet. She cursed as she lifted the lid, danced a little as she undid her pants, and sat with sudden relief.

Her bladder happy, she eyed the sink warily, tried to figure out how to reach her toothbrush and toothpaste without actually facing the mirror's surface.

"Oh, just get over it!" Allison's voice shouted from the mirror. Ally jumped, hitting her head on the plastic sliding shower door. "I'm here, and you are just going to have to deal with that."

Ally wiped herself and pulled up her pants. She flushed the toilet and then stood solidly in front of the mirror. Allison smiled sweetly back at her, batting her thick black lashes.

"Not a hallucination," she said. "But you can think you're insane if you want to."

Ally blinked.

Allison blinked. She was wearing a trimmed-down version of Ally's outfit, her shirt fitting tighter and showing more cleavage, her pants hanging lower on her hips. Everything about Allison was better than Ally.

"You know, you have outfits that may be more…flattering on you," Allison said carefully. "A more fitted shirt maybe, and pants without pockets…"

Ally shook her head, refused to talk to a figment of her imagination, and especially refused to take fashion advice from one. She looked down at the sink, willing Allison to go away.

"You don't have to look in the mirror for me to exist here,"

Allison said. "I exist here independently from you."

"But you're my reflection!" Ally exclaimed, looking up in surprise.

"Yes and no," Allison said with a sigh. "I already explained this to you last night. I'm your inner-reflection—I'm with you everywhere you go."

Ally stared at her in horror.

"Everywhere?" she asked.

"In a way," Allison conceded. "The thing is, I'm real. So you really should just get used to me."

Ally shook her head again and reached for her toothbrush. Allison reached for hers too.

"I hope you're going to floss," Allison said. "It's very important—helps your breath, your gums—everything. Gotta keep those pearly whites pearly!" Allison grinned, and her pearly whites were blinding. Ally pulled her lips over her own non-luminescent teeth.

She grabbed the toothpaste. Allison mirrored the movement, so Ally turned on her heel and walked out of the door, slamming it shut behind her.

"Hey!" she heard Allison call. Ally ignored her.

She brushed her teeth over the kitchen sink and managed to get through the rest of her morning routine without going into the bathroom and rushed to her car, anxious to get to work and around all the therapists. If she was insane, surely one of them would be able to pick up on it.

Ally got into her car and closed her eyes.

There will be nothing in my mirrors, there will be nothing in my mirrors, there will be nothing in my mirrors. Nothing except my regular reflection, she added as an afterthought.

She took a few deep breaths, primed herself for the big reveal. If Allison was in her rear-view mirror Ally wasn't sure she would be able to drive. And she felt the desperate need to be around all those doctors.

There will be nothing in my mirrors but my regular reflection, she told herself one more time, concentrating very hard, as though her determination could make it true.

She took a deep breath, held it for a moment.

One.

Two.

"DaDa Dum!"

Ally let out a small surprised scream. It took her a moment to recognize the sudden sound as her cell phone playing "Life is but a Dream, Sweetheart."

She pulled her cell from her purse and glared at her sister's photo on the screen. Sighing, she pressed the talk button.

"What, Misha?" she asked. Her eyes were drawn to her mirror, pulled there by curiosity and fear….she didn't hear what her sister said back.

"Uh huh," she said blindly. Ally couldn't see into the mirror from this angle, and it was bothering her.

"Good. So then come at 5:30 or 6 so we'll have time for it."

Ally pulled her attention back to the conversation she was almost having with her little sister.

"Time for what?" she asked.

"Your make over. You just said you wanted one."

"I never said…"

"Look, it's not that big a deal. Julie just thought we could do your hair and makeup and stuff to match the costume."

"Misha, this really isn't the best time. I'm just leaving for work, and I hate to drive and talk….can we talk later?"

Misha sighed a huge, deliberate sigh, making sure Ally knew how much that would inconvenience her.

"Sure. It would only take a minute though…"

"Later. I'll call you later," Ally said and waited just long enough to hear Misha's, "fine" before hanging up. She scooted herself over and looked into the rear-view mirror, reaching out to tilt it toward her.

Her own hazel eyes glared back at her, the mascara imperfectly applied in the living room without benefit of a mirror, while still shaking from her encounter with Allison, the whites showing red from restless sleep. These were not the perfect eyes of Allison, and Ally's shoulders unhitched themselves from her ears in relief. She flipped open the vanity mirror, and framed between the lights was her own pore-showing skin. She smiled at herself, suddenly very happy to see the small zit on her happily imperfect forehead.

She put the car in reverse and contemplated her conversation with Misha as she backed up. A make-over before the party? Ally was feeling less and less sure about his party.

"We're all going to be fairytale characters," Misha had said when first telling her about it. "You got picked as the fairy godmother; I already have your costume."

At the time, all Ally could think about was how she got stuck with the matronly character, to go with her matronly figure, and how all the princesses and princes would treat her—the pathetic fat sister of wonderful Misha. Ally shook her head, wishing just once she could walk into a room full of people and not feel huge and gross, wishing she could be thin like Misha, and beautiful, and….

She eyed the rearview mirror warily. That's what you got for wishing too hard. Hallucinations in your bathroom mirror.

Now that she knew it was just her in in the reflection, she was able to actually see what she looked like. Her mascara was a bit smudged, and her shirt fit a bit tighter than she was comfortable with. In fact, in her rush to get out of the house as quickly as possible, she had pulled a shirt from the back she'd been avoiding for a while because she thought the color was too bright. Ally sighed.

As she drove down Soledad towards work, she briefly reviewed everything she knew about hallucinations: sounds or images that weren't actually there, proven by the fact that no one else can see/hear them. So she had to first determine if Allison was something only she could see. Which would mean having to tell someone about her, or at least get them to go look in her bathroom mirror with her. This would take some planning. It would probably have to be Michael. If he saw Allison, they could solve the problem together.

Ally was slightly comforted by that thought.

But what if he didn't see Allison? She felt the familiar knot in her stomach that seemed to be keeping her company more and more often. She had been having panic attacks. Maybe it was worse than she thought? Her palms were damp against the steering wheel. *What if I really am crazy?* She pushed the thought away.

FIRE Season

As Ally trudged past the lower reception area and up the stairs to the second floor of the Child and Family Center, she looked out the tinted windows. Smoke still clogged the sky, casting an eerie gray over everything, made darker by the glass. Ash still flew around, but somehow with less intensity than it had earlier in the week. Maybe that was just because Ally knew the end of the fires were in sight. She took one more moment to stare out the window of the upstairs lobby, and then made her way past the small gathering of waiting people and back to the fish-bowl front office.

The Center was offering free therapeutic screening to people dealing with fire-related mental health issues. The lobby was full of people waiting to speak with someone, kids restlessly kicking at their chairs, young worried parents waiting to ask for advice in dealing with their children's as-yet-unseen anxiety. Many of the parents weren't even from the neighborhoods that were evacuated, and just wanted reassurance that their kids weren't going to have psychological scarring from watching the fires on the news.

That wasn't fair, Ally chided herself. You didn't have to turn the TV on to see the hills burning, and that could be a very traumatic experience for young kids. Not as traumatic as seeing the wrong reflection in your mirror, but still, traumatic. Ally laughed a little at herself as she grabbed a new stack of trauma flyers to put out in the lobby. Michael passed her on his way out of the office, and smiled back at her.

"Busy day," he said good-naturedly. With all the extra people to see, Ella had taken Michael off the front desk and let him help people under his title of case manager. Not technically a therapist, he worked to help screen the merely anxious people from the ones actually suffering. That meant that Ally had more work to do. She didn't mind since working kept her mind off her own could-be insanity.

She nodded at Michael. He walked cheerily past, in his element in the center of all the chaos, a calm port in the storm. She knew Michael was going to be an awesome therapist. She also knew she should talk to him about what had been going on, from the anxiety attacks to the appearance of Allison. But obviously he was too busy to talk. Or at least, that is what Ally told herself.

A while later, Ally finally found time to sit down at the computer when no one else was around. She tried to keep her body in front of the screen and looked around to make sure no one watched what she was doing. She went to a popular self-diagnosis website, and typed in hallucinations and then stared at the results: schizophrenia, depression, bipolar disorder, medications. Seeing things was considered a serious problem, and in all the little summaries she read, it was also a sign that you needed some serious help. She went for the least psychotic sounding disorder and read up on depression. Other symptoms included sadness, wanting to avoid social situations, feeling lethargic, not having interest in things you used to like, having trouble sleeping…

All of that sounded just a little too familiar, and Ally stared at the screen for a while. Yeah, she probably was depressed, at least mildly, but she wondered if somehow it was worse than she was aware of. She'd felt like this before, back in high school. It had eventually gone away even if it had taken Michael dragging her out of the house on a consistent basis. When his life imploded when he came out to his family, she was too busy trying to be there for him to worry much about herself.

But seeing a reflection that was not hers in a mirror might suggest things were worse than back then, worse than she was aware of.

"Symptoms of depression," Michael said, reading over her shoulder. Ally quickly closed the Internet window and turned toward him.

"Something wrong?" he asked her, genuine concern in his brown eyes.

"Just checking up on things. I figure if I work for therapists I should know something about what they treat." She smiled brightly at him.

He narrowed his eyes. "Are you sure you're okay? You've been quiet all morning. And when I called you…."

"You know, I didn't get much sleep last night. Stayed up late reading. Bad me." She smiled again, got up. "I'm sure there's filing to do."

"Yeah," he said absentmindedly. "Oh, great outfit by the way—I've been meaning to tell you all morning. Very flattering." Ally tensed, uncertain of how to respond, then smiled quickly and hurried off to the filing room.

She spent the rest of the morning continuing to avoid Michael. As much as she wanted to talk to him about what had happened, she was also scared to. Telling Michael would make it real. And she didn't want it to be real.

Finally, it was time for her morning break, and she fled to the break room, getting a Dr. Pepper from the machine absent mindedly. *Maybe she won't be there when I get home,* she told herself. *I'm not crazy. I can't be crazy.* She flinched as the door opened, and relaxed marginally when she saw it was Dr. Barclay.

Dr. Barclay smiled at Ally as she went to the fridge and took out an apple and some pre-sliced cheese.

"How's it going Ally?" she asked, washing the apple in the sink. "You look pretty today—great outfit."

"Thanks," Ally said. She avoided Barclay's gaze as the woman sat opposite her, and concentrated instead on her Dr. Pepper bottle. Her eyes fell to the calories per serving. *Not too bad.* Then looked up at the servings per bottle part. Two point five. She did a little mental math and looked at the bottle with new horror.

"Shocking, isn't it?" Barclay said. "Exactly why I don't drink those anymore. Well, except for special occasions. Other people break out the good wine or champagne. My husband and I break out a bottle of our favorite full-sugar soda."

"How is he?" Ally asked distractedly, picking at the Dr. Pepper label, wishing she hadn't bought it. She was always glad to talk about Barclay's husband, a character actor that was in one of Ally's favorite TV shows when she was a kid.

"Fine. He's got another job, a small part, but still... He's been all over TV lately. I caught one of his old TV shows and nearly died laughing, he looked so different."

"Does he ever watch any of his old stuff?" Ally asked.

"Nah. But he gets a kick out of people telling him about ones they've seen. He'll start remembering the stories behind the episodes and tell everyone all the behind the scenes stuff."

"Must be fun to be an actor."

"Has its ups and downs like any job. What about you? What do you want to do?"

"You mean besides work here?" Ally asked with a wry smile.

Dr. Barclay grinned at her. "I have a feeling you have bigger ambitions than this place."

"Not sure I'm meant for anything bigger than this place," Ally said, looking wistfully down at her bottle. *Why did I have to buy it anyway? I knew better* ....

"Why do you think that?" Dr. Barclay asked.

"I don't know," Ally said. "Because I don't even know what I want to be, let alone how to begin to get there."

"Maybe you just need time to figure some stuff out?"

"How do you know if you're crazy?" Ally asked.

Dr. Barclay laughed.

"Why, you been hearing voices lately?"

Ally felt her face burn and shook her head.

Dr. Barclay looked at her more closely for a moment, and then went back to her casual smile. "The thing is, there is no normal, and yet that's what everyone wants to be. So everyone at one time or another thinks they are going crazy. But really, most people are normal. Maybe they're having an unusual feeling, or reaction, but that doesn't mean they're crazy. Very few people are actually 'crazy.' Crazy is the kind of problem that can't be fixed, either because we don't know how to fix it, or because the person doesn't want to fix it. Everything else is just being different."

"But like, schizophrenia, or psychosis, those are things that make people crazy, right? Seeing things, hearing voices...."

"All symptoms of an issue that can be addressed. Medication, therapy...most of those symptoms can be treated, managed."

"But what causes them? I mean, can you wake up one day and suddenly see something that isn't there? Don't there have to be triggers or something?"

"There's no blanket cause that covers all cases. People develop things for different reasons. The root is often a chemical imbalance, and we really don't know what causes that imbalance. Sometimes there's a traumatic event. We have theories, correlations, but no actual explanations. Usually it's not a sudden thing. Usually there are other symptoms before that."

"Like depression."

"Like severe depression. The kind of depression most people have isn't severe enough to cause hallucinations. Untreated, it can get to that point, but, it's still rare."

"I think I may be depressed…." Ally offered tentatively. Dr. Barclay tilted her head.

"Why do you think that?"

"I've been having trouble sleeping, been eating a lot lately, feeling sort of sad…"

"For how long?"

"A while. I don't know. Isn't it normal to get a little depressed now and again?"

Now that Dr. Barclay was taking her seriously, Ally wasn't sure she wanted to continue the conversation, tried to back-pedal out of it.

"Yes. But that doesn't mean they don't need help for it. How sad have you been feeling?"

"Just a little down. Nothing major. I still get a kick out of The Daily Show and all that, so I don't think it's severe."

Dr. Barclay laughed. "You've read up on the symptoms I see."

Ally nodded.

"Well, periods of feeling down or stressed out are normal. If the symptoms increase or last longer than two weeks, it could be a sign that maybe you need a little help dealing with them."

"But if you're working on them, doing things that you think

will help, that probably means it's not that bad, right?"

Dr. Barclay paused as though she was considering her next words carefully.

"I think 'not that bad' may be relative. How have you been dealing with feeling down?"

"I've been going to the gym," Ally offered. Dr. Barclay nodded.

"Exercise is a great mood booster, once you get over wearing the clothes."

Ally laughed.

Dr. Barclay glanced at the clock and sighed. "I've got to get ready for my next appointment." She stood up. "If you ever want to talk, my door is always open," she said, smiling down at Ally.

Ally nodded and smiled back, but she was pretty sure she'd never be able to talk to Dr. Barclay about Allison.

As the morning gave way to afternoon, activity giving time the wings it needed to fly, Ally found it more and more difficult to take her own problem seriously. The extra clients meant extra work, and taking on Michael's tasks was even more work. All that work made the day feel mundane and made Ally feel further and further from crazy. By the time Ella sent Ally to lunch, she wondered if she had imagined the entire thing. And of course Allison wasn't going to be in her mirror when she got home. She probably never existed in the first place.

Ally rubbed the bruise on her hip.

✳

Ally drove down to the local sandwich shop for lunch, determined to stick to her calorie goal for the day. Once she got there, she stared hard at the little ice-cream freezer part of the store, feeling the need for a hot-fudge sundae to wash the taste of ash from her throat. She reasoned that she could have frozen yogurt with the hot fudge, which was mostly sugar anyway, and with going to the gym, the day could be a draw—no loss, no gain. Probably the Dr. Pepper earlier threw that balance off, but Ally was in a good mood and wanted something good to eat to go with it.

As she contemplated her options, her phone rang. She dug it out of her purse. Her good mood deflated somewhat as she read the caller ID.

"You didn't call me back," Misha said as soon as Ally said hello.

"It was a busy morning, what with the fires and all," Ally said.

"Why would you guys be busy? You don't put out fires."

Ally sighed. "We're a counseling center. People upset by the fires come to us for counseling."

"People need counseling for that?"

Ally shook her head. Sometimes she was amazed that they shared the same gene pool. Misha definitely got the shallow end.

"So about that make over," Ally started.

"Never mind about that. If you're going to throw a fit and be all against the process…"

"I never said—"

"Look, it's no big deal," Misha said. "It's just a thought we had. But because you keep asking me about it, I double checked with Julie, and she said that the costume would definitely fit. So yeah, come a little early and we'll get you costumed up right. Show up around 6:30, and bring whatever you want to drink. It's BYOB."

"Are you even considering that I might have other plans?" Ally asked.

"You don't," Misha said confidently. "Michael's doing the

kiddie haunted house, which you hate, and his adult party isn't till the next day. You have nowhere else to be."

"Maybe I don't want to go."

"Too late. You promised."

"I never pro—"

"Oh, that's my call waiting. Gotta go!"

Misha hung up, leaving Ally frustrated she didn't get to finish her rant. She considered calling her sister back, but there really was no point. Misha always got her way.

Ally went back to the menu and ordered her usual turkey sandwich and a small hot-fudge sundae with cookie crumbs. It was only after she sat down with her tray that she realized how unhealthy the sundae was. She had ordered on impulse, fueled by her feelings, and her feelings had wanted the soft-serve comfort. She wondered if smaller people ever worried this much about eating hot fudge sundaes. She dipped her spoon in and scooped out a large bite. It didn't taste nearly as good as she hoped it would.

That woman is looking at you. Ally saw the woman in the corner of her eye and turned to see her better.

She accidentally locked eyes with the woman, who had a tight perm and square glasses, and then Perm Head looked quickly away. Ally hunched herself further into the corner of her booth and stared out the window. She was allowed to eat. People needed to eat to survive. Besides, the lady was here too, eating the same things as Ally. So why should Ally feel bad about it? Ally snuck another glance at the woman. While Perm Head was clearly thinner than Ally, she was by no means thin. Still, Ally could feel the judgment waves radiating off of Perm Head. Ally imagined a little shield around herself, a fire-wall that would deflect all head-shaking at the fat girl eating bad food and let Ally eat in peace. She stared out the window and shoved another spoonful of creamy fudge goodness into her mouth.

What you really need are happier thoughts. Like Fantasy Man.

Ally took another bite and tried to focus on Fantasy Man's face. She couldn't really focus.

She went back to an earlier fantasy. She was a double agent, and she was being chased, and she was in the park, and she whirled around, and there he was, the man who trained her, the man she was betraying. She looked up into his eyes, and …

That woman really is looking at you.

Ally tried really hard to not look around the restaurant anymore and finished her meal as quickly as possible. The sandwich was bland. She didn't finish the last of the sundae. She felt completely unsatisfied by both.

The news had warned that the worse time for smoke and ash would be between 1 and 4 pm. The air was thick with both, and Ally breathed shallowly as she walked to her car and unlocked the door. She swung her purse in first, and she settled behind the wheel. She put the key in the ignition, put on her seatbelt, and adjusted the volume of her radio. Beyoncé blasted out at her. She smiled, put the car in reverse, and, only then, looked into the rearview mirror.

She should have seen what was behind the car. She should then have been able to back up, turn left, leave the parking lot, and head back to work.

Two perfectly shaped blue eyes stared back at her instead. As Ally blinked in surprise and horror, the left eye winked.

"Miss me?" Allison's melodic voice asked.

✱

Like any good Californian, Ally had perfected driving. Over the years, she had developed an autopilot, a somatic function that let her do most car-related tasks without thinking. Her hands knew where the gear shift was, how to turn on her high-beams, and her eyes did a regular rotation between her side-mirrors and rearview mirror without her ever having to give it any conscious thought.

The sight of Allison's brilliant blue eyes under luxuriously thick eyelashes that just seemed to go on and on seemed to stun even Ally's autopilot. It was as if she had never been in a car before. She tried to leave the car, get away from those eyes and that disembodied voice—"what, no hello?"—but she couldn't find the door handle. When she did manage to get the door open and tried to lunge away from the car, the seat belt threw her back against the seat. She tried to release it, but fumbled with the button.

"Smooth move, Ex-Lax," Allison said, her eyes watching coolly from the mirror.

"You have no mouth! How are you talking?" Ally asked, frantically pulling on the belt.

"I have a mouth. You just can't see it."

Ally glanced up at the mirror and Allison tilted her head back, her perfectly pink lips mouthing the next words. "Would you rather look at this?"

Ally shook her head vehemently—a mouth by itself was too scary right now. The mouth slid down, past a cute-as-a-button nose and back to those cold blue eyes. Ally quit fighting the seat belt and put her head in her hands.

"Poor thing, you're really a mess, aren't you?"

Ally looked up at the mirror, at the eyes staring down at her. The eyes narrowed.

"Is that chocolate sauce on your shirt? What did you eat for lunch?"

"Nothing," Ally said, brushing at the stain.

"Nothing you were supposed to," Allison said. "Ally! You promised—this time you would stick with it, make it work. How long have you been on your diet? A week? Did you even make it through the first day without cheating?"

"It's been a month!"

Ally tried to glare at Allison's eyes, but was too thrown off by their dismembered appearance.

"Wait, that's the rearview mirror! I can't even see myself in it!"

"That doesn't mean you can't see me. Inner reflection, Ally. You'll get it, eventually."

Ally stared hard at her hands. She noticed, idly, that she needed to clean out from under her nails. That was a reasonable thought. A sane thought. Inner reflections, on the other hand, were not sane.

She could hear Allison sigh. "You're late. Lunch hour is over, kooky. Time to get back to work."

Ally looked down at her car's clock and nodded numbly. It was then that her automatic pilot kicked in, taking her through the motions of starting the car, backing up—Allison had to tell her there was no one behind her since she couldn't see for herself—and driving the short distance back to work.

"You're not the best driver in the world, are you?" Allison's bodiless voice asked. Ally managed to get her seat belt off this time, and got out of the car, happy to slam the door shut behind her. She turned to look at her car and could just see the faint out-line of a reflection in the car window. It was Allison's. She waved. Ally blinked, hiked her purse up on her shoulder, and walked numbly to the Center's front doors.

"I'm insane," she said under her breath. She didn't nod back to Leah, the downstairs receptionist, when Leah said "hi." She felt barely conscious as she walked up the stairs, though later she would feel proud that her autopilot took her to the stairs instead of the elevator.

On the second floor, Ally walked past the people still waiting in the lobby and waved her security card in front of the little scanner by the door, made her way to the file room, put her purse away, and then started filing. *I can't screw up the alphabet. B always comes after A and it always goes ellemen-o-p. Nothing to it, nothing to mess up.*

Michael came in to check on her five minutes later.

"Hey Ally, you all right?" He stood behind her as she tried to shove a folder into a drawer.

"Yeah, sure," she said, not turning around to face him.

"Because you don't seem all right," he said, walking around the drawer to face her. She glanced up at him, then shut the drawer and reached for another file.

"I'm fine," she said. He took the file from her hands, making her look at him. "What?" she asked.

"You tell me." It was a staring contest, and Ally tried to keep her eyes very still, to not betray the whirlwind of feelings going through her. *I'm insane,* she wanted to tell him. *Everything's fine except that I'm insane.* She could feel herself start to give in under his concerned gaze, feel her chin start to wobble ever so slightly. Any moment now she was going to cry.

She turned away and grabbed one of the intake packets and took it to the copier to make more.

Michael followed her as Ally stood by the copy machine. The whomp whomp of papers sliding through its mechanisms helped Ally not cry.

"Just tell me what's wrong," he told her, his arms crossed against his chest.

She sighed. "What if the most perfect version of yourself was haunting you?" she asked. "What would you do?"

"Interesting what if. I would say that the most perfect version of myself is haunting me. We're all haunted by our own expectations of what we could be."

"Is your perfect self mean to you?" Ally asked wryly.

He laughed at her. He was treating her question just as he would any of the what-ifs they talked about, and she wasn't sure if she was relieved or disappointed.

"I think I'm mean to me sometimes," he said. "We all have that little voice inside our heads that tell us we're not good enough, or smart enough, or lovable enough. We just have to learn where those voices are coming from—our parents or people who want to see us fail. Then realize that those voices are wrong."

She stared at him. A paper got stuck in the copier and she took a moment to clear it out. Then she decided to try another approach.

"When you look in the mirror, what do you see?"

He titled his head to the side.

"Again, another interesting question. I see me."

"You as you are or you as you wish you could be?"

He looked at her, deep in thought. "If we're talking about a metaphoric mirror, then I guess I see what I want to be. But then, I try to be what I see, and then what I see is me."

Ally considered this. She had ten more copies to wait for, ten million more questions she wanted to ask Michael. *I should just tell him what's really going on.* When she closed her eyes she could still see Allison's cold baby-blues staring back at her from her rear-view mirror.

You don't want him to tell everyone else how crazy you are, do you?

No. She didn't.

"What if it's impossible to become what you see in the mirror?" she asked instead.

"Nothing is impossible," Michael said.

"You really think so?" Ally asked.

"Yes. I think anything we strive for we will inevitably achieve."

"Yeah, but do you think impossible things can happen, like in real life?"

"Of course I do."

"Like, magic?" She held her breath.

He laughed. "What, like what Sandra's into? Okay, that stuff is impossible, something out of nothing and all that, but other things aren't."

He put his arm around her shoulders.

"Are you sure you're okay? Because lately it's seemed like…."

Mercifully, the copier was done.

"I have to take these papers to the front," she said, gathering up the large stack.

Michael nodded at her as she left and Ally walked away feeling confused and downhearted. She dropped the papers off at reception. Then, her thoughts directed her feet toward Dr. Barclay's office, and a few moments later she arrived at the door.

It was closed.

Ally sighed. She wasn't sure what she would have said if Dr. Barclay had been available anyway. *Oh, by the way, about that hearing voices thing? Do you know of any good medication for that? How 'bout hypnosis, that ever work? Oh, no reason, just wanted to know because a friend of a friend was saying….*

Ally felt tired all of a sudden, and sad. It had been a long day, and it wasn't even close to being over yet. She felt the sudden urge to call her mother, though she didn't know what for. In general, she avoided talking to her mother whenever possible. She'd just want to hear how Ally's diet was going, or talk to her about some cousin getting married so that she could ask about Ally's love life, and then use that to suggest, ever so gently, that maybe Ally should look into weight-loss surgery because look how well it worked for her cousin! As if a husband was a guaranteed side-effect of weight loss.

Ally had to go to the bathroom and got as far as the little hallway just inside the door when she remembered Allison. It was a public bathroom—she wondered if that would make any difference. She wasn't sure she wanted to risk it, but as she stood there, her bladder decided to put in its opinion on the subject. It didn't care whether she was going crazy or not, it was full and didn't want to be. Ally took a deep breath and practically ran toward the stall closest to her, making a point not to look in the mirror. As she pushed on the door, a voice called out "Somebody in here."

Embarrassed, Ally dashed into the second stall, put a cover on the seat as quickly as she could, and sat down. She looked over at the shoes next to her. She didn't recognize them as anyone's from the office and felt a little better. They were open-toed—a no-no at work—and showed off brightly colored toenails that reminded Ally of Sandra.

"Actually," the voice said, sounding somewhat young and definitely unsure. And oddly familiar. "There's no toilet paper in here and…"

"Oh, no problem!" Ally said, pulling a good amount off her roll. She held it under the stall divider.

"Thanks!" the voice said, greatly relieved. "'Cuz I really didn't want to air dry."

Ally laughed. Shortly after, the toilet next to her flushed. Ally finished up herself, and flushed her toilet and unlocked the door. Then she paused, debating.

If she went out and the other woman saw Allison, Ally would know she wasn't crazy. If she went out and the other woman didn't see Allison, she would know she was. Of course, maybe Allison wouldn't be there. Either way, Ally had to know, once and for all.

She took a deep breath, opened the stall door.

"Sandra? What are you doing here?" she asked, surprised. Ally was so startled to see the light, airy woman in the sterile, cold bathroom, she forgot to look in the mirror.

"I'm meeting Michael for a late lunch. Didn't he tell you?" Sandra asked. She pushed strands of her mostly-blonde hair out of her eyes. Her roots were showing, but somehow they added to her look instead of taking away from it.

Ally shook her head. Michael probably would have told Ally, if she hadn't been avoiding him.

"It's been real busy today. I haven't seen much of Michael."

"Yeah, I heard about that. Helping out all the anxious fire-survivors. The lobby is totally full." Sandra shook her head. "Thanks for the TP save, by the way," Sandra said, smiling up at Ally.

"I think every woman's been there," Ally said, shrugging. Sandra reached out and picked a stray hair off Ally's shoulder, casually dropping it to the floor. For some reason, the small gesture made Ally feel closer to Sandra—that feeling battled with Ally's instinct to not trust the Wiccan, and then overpowered it. She felt suddenly that she should confide in Sandra, tell her all about Allison, the fact that she was most likely insane. She was a witch.

If Sandra didn't believe her, no one would.

Thinking about confessing, Ally finally turned to face the mirror. She stared hard at what she saw there, which was…herself. No one else, just plain old, non-perfect Ally. She wasn't sure if she should feel relieved or not. She didn't trust that Allison was gone for good.

"Is there something wrong?" Sandra asked, looking at Ally's reflected frown in the mirror. Ally forced a smile and shook her head at Sandra's reflection.

"No, nothing." She turned back toward Sandra. She smiled half-heartedly, walked to the sink and washed her hands in the tepid water. Sandra followed suit, eyeing Ally. Ally smiled again, drying her hands on some paper towels, pulling a few more out for Sandra, handing them over without even thinking.

"I'll get Michael for you." She followed Sandra out, glancing briefly back at the mirror as if expecting to see something there.

Michael was showing a family back out to the lobby, their hands loaded with brochures, their ears loaded with soothing words. Ally envied them their simple, rational fears of fire.

"Hey!" Michael said, and stepped forward to hug Sandra. She hugged him back, then he turned to Ally. "Everything okay?"

"Yeah," Ally said. She pulled at her shirt, a movement she could tell Michael noticed. He knew she did that when she was nervous.

"You sure?"

Sandra joined Michael in his concerned appraisal of Ally. She grew uncomfortable and guilty under the combined force of their caring gazes, especially since Sandra's seemed even more intense than Michael's.

"You look…pale," Sandra said.

"I'm fine, really," she told both of them. "I should probably get back to work though. Delkey needs fifty copies of a flier, on blue paper. You guys enjoy your lunch." Ally hurried past them, catching a look exchanged between the two of them. Somehow, she just knew that she would take up a great deal of their lunchtime conversation.

INSPIRATION POINT

The rest of the day flew by. Ally was both glad for the day to be over and scared to go home. What if she saw Allison in her rear-view mirror on the drive home? How would she drive then? And what if she was in the bathroom mirror again? Would Ally forever have to avoid her bathroom?

She heard Michael say something, but she was so wrapped up in her own world she didn't catch what it was.

"What?" she asked.

"I said, are you ready for the gym?" He looked at her expectantly. It took some more eye blinking and a thorough removal of her thoughts from their whirlpool to discover the wave that Michael was riding. The gym. That thing they did most nights after work. Which required special clothing. Which she didn't have. Because she had a strange spirit-slash-hallucination in her mirror.

"Uh, no," she said at last. "I forgot to bring my stuff."

Michael must have been more tired than Ally realized. His sigh was deep and exasperated and he didn't even try to disguise his annoyance.

"You know, you said that you wanted me to help you." His words echoed Allison's and Ally felt herself grow red. "But this is a commitment Ally. You can't just do this half-assed. You can't just go home and curl up on the couch and then complain about your life never changing."

Ally blinked again, surprised by Michael's admonition. And ashamed. And somewhere deep inside her, angry too.

"I'm sorry, it's just I was in such a rush this morning I completely forgot my gym clothes. We can go tomorrow…"

"Tomorrow is Halloween—I'm doing the haunted house thing for the kids, so not going to the gym. I'm going today, and I'll go Saturday. Not tomorrow." He stared at her, one hand on his hip. It was as good as if his finger were wagging at her. "You didn't go yesterday, and if I don't go tomorrow, you won't, because you have Misha's party, and that would mean three whole days without working out. Four, if you don't go on Saturday with me. Five since you don't usually go on Sunday. And that's a week Ally, an entire week off. You can't get into a routine by taking five days off."

"I don't live that far away—I can go home, get changed, and meet you at the gym…" she offered weakly.

"Okay! That sounds great! I'm proud of you for sticking with this," he said. "And I didn't mean to get so grumpy—it's been a long day."

She nodded with genuine sympathy, feeling guilty for her own complaints. She hadn't been the one dealing with ten million upset and anxious families today.

"We should get going before the gym gets too crowded," she said. Michael nodded and led the way out.

Allison wasn't in her rear-view mirror on the ride home, and Ally felt somewhat comforted by that. Not wanting to face the issue, she avoided her bathroom and changed into her clothes in her bedroom, putting her hair in a ponytail by feel.

The gym had already started to fill up with the after-work crowd when Ally got there, and she had a little trouble finding Michael in the throngs of people. When she did, her heart played Wipeout against her ribcage. Michael was working out right next to Fantasy Man. Having pictured the man so many times in her head, Ally couldn't face the real thing, afraid somehow he could read her mind and know all the fantasies she'd had about him. It was too mortifying. So she stood on the edge of the room and willed Michael to look at her. By some minor miracle, he did, and she waved at him. She pointed toward the women's section. He pointed to the empty treadmill next to him. She shook her head and pointed again toward the women's section. His shoulders lowered in defeat and he nodded, then smiled and gave her a thumbs up of encouragement. She smiled back quickly, watching to make sure Fantasy Man hadn't caught this exchange.

The women's section was less full than the main gym, with all the usual gang in attendance: Blonde One, Blonde Two, Spandex Lady. Ally hopped on her usual treadmill and started her usual daydreaming about how life could be, would be, if she kept sticking with her current routine.

The music swirled all around her, and she saw, in a brilliantly shot montage, her future: getting up early, going to the gym, craving crisp greens and losing the taste for chocolate, going to the gym again after work. But even a good training montage didn't feel inspiring enough to get her through the next 30 minutes on her treadmill. She didn't really want a slightly improved version of her life. She wanted a better one.

✳

Ally whirled again. Fantasy Man was already behind her, had anticipated her move. He should have. He was the one who trained her.

He charged her, knocking the gun from her hand and slamming her onto her back, holding down her arms above her head. The breath had been knocked out of her, and as she stared up into his eyes, she began to rethink her life as a double agent.

Fantasy Man leaned down toward her, and the feel of his body against hers made her want to press back against him. She forced herself to keep still. She could feel the warmth of his breath as he whispered in her ear:

"Play along, and I might just be able to get you out of this."

He was off her in a swift move, pulling her up with him so fast she stumbled slightly as he took her arms from above her head and pinned them behind her back. Startled, she felt cold metal pressed into her hands—he had given her a gun.

When she looked up, she understood why.

Black-clad figures, faces obscured by tactical masks, surrounded them. There were at least half a dozen in her view, and the hairs rising on the back of her neck told Ally there were probably a handful behind them as well. All of the figures had guns out. All those guns were pointed at her.

"It's okay," Fantasy Man told the group in a loud, clear voice. "I have her." He shoved his gun into her side to emphasize the point.

"I really don't think you do."

The figures in front of Ally and Fantasy Man parted enough to allow a dark-haired man in an expensive suit to pass through. He had gray hair at his temples, and a deep scowl across thick brows. His was the kind of face that seemed built for frowning, and his features were living fully up to their potential.

"We have her," he said. He pulled a gun from a holster his jacket had been concealing only slightly more than his sizable gut and pointed it directly at Ally. "And it ends here."

"Five," Fantasy Man said. It made Frowny Face pause.

"What?"

"Four," Fantasy Man continued. And, after a beat, "three."

"Look, I don't know what you think…"

"Two."

"Listen, if you want to die with her…"

"One."

A huge explosion just behind Ally and Fantasy Man rained sparks and metal down on the scene, and Fantasy Man shoved Ally hard behind him. There were three figures facing her, all of them staring wildly around and not paying anywhere near enough attention to her. Smoke was billowing out from the explosion as well, and she took advantage of it. She swung the gun Fantasy Man had given her out from behind her back and aimed while running, catching one figure in the thigh, another in the stomach, and the third in the chest. All three went down without firing off a shot.

Ally ran hard back up the embankment and toward the clump of trees she had passed on her way in, desperately hoping they might provide some level of cover. She flung herself around the nearest trunk and took a second to take a deep breath and peer back behind her. Fantasy Man was charging in her direction, bullets flying past him. Ally considered her options. She raised her gun and squeezed the trigger.

A black-clad figure fell hard behind Fantasy Man. Ally squeezed her trigger again, and another one of Fantasy Man's followers fell. By now he was in shouting range of Ally.

"To the street!" he yelled. She nodded and turned, sprinting back the way they had come by motorcycle, up the steep flight of stairs, taking them two at a time. As she got to the road, a black van screeched to a halt in front of her. Ally brought her gun around, unsure of what was going to come next. Fantasy Man grabbed her by the back of the arm as the van door opened in front of her. Fantasy Man shoved her forward as hands reaching out from inside pulled her in, and jumped in behind her. The door slammed shut and Ally could feel the van jolting forward.

"Well that could have gone better," Fantasy Man said. Ally, gun still in hand, pressed her back against the side of the vehicle and looked around her. There were three other strangers in the van, two men and one woman, faces open but blank.

"I thought she'd be taller," the woman said. She was tall herself, had the legs of a kickboxer, a nose that had been broken at least once, and a jawline that most men would envy. Pretty was never going to be her adjective. Scary maybe, tough, possibly homicidal, but not pretty.

"Who the hell are you?" Ally said, her gun still out and ready, finger over the trigger.

"Relax, we're on your side." The man to the left of the woman had a scar running from the edge of his dark hair line down to his chin, slicing the corner of his eyebrow. It was a good eyebrow for all of that, and the bright smile he flashed at Ally made the scar the least interesting feature on his face. She felt herself wanting to smile back, but kept her face neutral.

The third of the trio was wearing a black turtleneck and had a weak chin. He seemed particularly bored by what was happening, or else had the kind of face that just didn't know how to have fun.

"Then tell me what is going on," she said.

"I should probably start by saying that I am not who you think I am," Fantasy Man said. "My real name is..."

✳

As Ally was contemplating all the names Fantasy Man could have...*Jake? John? Justin? Why could she only think of J names?* she became aware of the voices in front of her. The Blondes had moved back to the reclined stationary bikes, peddling their legs, flipping their magazines, waggling their tongues.

"I heard she had a bad Botox session, and that's why she couldn't come," said Blonde One to Blonde Two.

"I heard it's because she had a huge zit on her forehead and had to have an emergency visit to her dermatologist," Blonde Two responded.

"Who is she with now? I know she left Doctor Brannagh after the mole he removed left a small scar…"

"Who knows anymore? She goes through dermatologists the way Janet goes through husbands."

Ally laughed along with the Blondes, catching their attention. She turned away quickly as they both turned to look at her, and stared hard at her console. They kept talking, but in more hushed voices, and Ally suspected they were talking about her. She stared down at the digital numbers on the treadmill telling her heart rate, how many calories she'd burned, how far she'd gone, how many minutes she had left, and sighed.

It never ends. The Blondes were beautiful, and probably so was the Dermatologist-holic and Janet, whoever they were, but they still weren't happy, any of them. This was what she was working toward, the chance to be thin and just as miserable? But she just didn't know any other way she could fix her life.

She took a deep breath, and tried to go back to her day-dream, and Fantasy Man, but couldn't. The momentum was lost. She looked to her left to see the clock by the doorway, see if she would make it home in time for anything good on TV. As her eyes brushed back down toward the floor, she caught her reflection in the mirror.

As before, there was bouncing. Not as before, the bouncing

was of firm breasts and shampoo-commercial hair.

Allison winked at her.

And Ally nearly fell off her treadmill.

THE READING RAINBOW

Allison ran on her treadmill like she was running down the beach, and Ally swore she could see an almost silvery-blue haze and the barest hint of a sea breeze floating around the perfectly constructed hallucination. Or ghost. Or whatever the hell she was.

Ally looked around in a panic, checking to see if anyone else was looking at Allison. The Blondes had their heads together, and Spandex Lady was watching something on one of the TVs. Ally wanted to curse. How was she going to know if she was crazy or not if no one was looking in Allison's direction?

"They won't be able to see me," Allison said, and Ally tripped on her treadmill. She had to press the stop button to keep from being dragged backwards by the belt, her hands gripping the side-bars for dear life.

Spandex Lady looked over at her, and the Blondes watched her curiously over their shoulders.

"You all right, dear?" Spandex Lady asked. Ally looked over at the mirror. Allison was still running on her treadmill.

Ally looked at the reflections of Spandex Lady and the Blondes, looked back at the real people, compared. The same. Hers was the only reflection that was different. She pointed at the mirror, and Spandex Lady looked at it.

"What?" she asked, concerned.

"Does anything look funny to you?" Ally asked. "In the mirror? Anything look... different?"

Spandex Lady looked closely a moment, as though searching out the trick question.

"I think they cleaned them," she said at last. "They were starting to get a little dusty."

Ally stared at her in disbelief. She was an old lady, she told herself, her eyes were probably bad. Ally glanced at the Blondes, who were also looking at the mirror.

"It's the same," Blonde Two said. "Why?"

"I—I don't know," Ally said. "Having an off night," she added, and grabbed her sweat towel and her water bottle. She looked over at Allison, who was doing light stretches next to her treadmill. Blonde One was staring right at that spot, but she just shook her head slowly, gave Blonde Two a significant look.

"Diet pills," she stage-whispered.

Allison giggled.

Ally glared at her reflection and hurried out of the room. With no real thought of where to go or what she was doing, Ally went to the drinking fountain, and let the cold water run over her lips. She drank a little, even though it tasted bad and she had a bottle full of better water. She needed to clear her head, but it seemed full of so many dust bunnies that no amount of Swiffering could clear it. The dust bunnies were hopping around and wriggling their noses. And Allison was something that only Ally could see.

"Hey Ally!" Michael said, making her jump. She whirled toward him, her hand over her heart. "Sorry," he said, reaching a hand out to her. "You okay?"

She nodded, smiled weakly, and shrugged his hand off her shoulder discreetly.

"I just wanted to say hi," he said again. He seemed pleased about something, but she was too distracted to ask him about it. She grabbed his arm instead and marched him to the nearest mirrored wall.

"Look," she commanded him.

"Okay," he said as she stood him in front of the mirror. "What am I looking at?"

Allison winked at Ally.

"The most beautiful woman in the world," she said, and raised her hands above her head like a Vegas show girl. Ally looked at Michael expectantly, waiting for him to react to Allison. He looked over at her even more expectantly.

"You don't see anything unusual about my reflection?" she asked him at last, desperate now. She waved at the mirror. Allison waved back merrily.

Michael studied the mirror for a long time. Allison gave him her best Marilyn Monroe, blew him a kiss. Finally he smiled.

"I see a very beautiful woman," he said at last. Allison stood up straight, surprised.

"No one should be able to see me yet," she said.

"I see someone who is kind, and smart, and gorgeous inside and out, even if she doesn't realize it."

"Oh," Allison said, and made a face. Even Ally felt her shoulders fall in defeat. Michael was sweet, but she was still crazy.

"And I see her being very brave, actually going after what she wants, changing herself. I know this is hard for you, and I'm very proud of your effort." He put his arm around her shoulder. She smiled weakly at his reflection, embarrassed.

Allison tilted her head in a "aren't they adorable!" gesture. "He would be the perfect guy for you if only he wasn't gay," she said, shaking her head. "And I bet if you lived with him you wouldn't eat as badly either."

Ally glared at Allison.

"Why are you glaring at yourself?" Michael asked. "You don't believe I see all those things in you, do you?"

Ally turned to him, away from Allison's innocuously smiling face.

"I just have a hard time believing them about myself," she said, truthfully. She felt shaky, the reality of Allison examining her nails in the mirror and Michael standing right next to her, unable to see or hear the alter-ego, sinking in. "You know, I'm suddenly not feeling very well," she said.

"You don't look that well," Michael agreed. "Maybe you should take it easy."

"Actually," she said. "I think I want to go home." He looked at her, pressed his hand to her forehead.

"Yeah, I think maybe you should…"

She brushed his hand away and then walked away from him quickly.

"Do you want me to come with you?" he called after her.

"No!" she yelled over her shoulder. *It's not like I'm alone.* She glanced over at Allison walking in the mirror beside her.

"Oh, he's real?" Allison said suddenly, pointing toward the middle of the room. Ally turned to look, winced, and walked faster.

"Never mind," she said, trying to get out of there as soon as possible.

"He's even hotter in person," Allison said. "I think you got a few of the details wrong in your daydreams."

Ally looked sideways, catching one last glance of Fantasy Man. Michael was walking back toward a machine near him, so Ally kept going, even as Allison kept talking.

"Course, probably a lot of that comes from your near-complete lack of experience with men. You never, for instance, give much attention to his package, which I have to say is quite nice…"

Ally turned the corner, away from the mirror, and Allison's voice faded in the background as she walked out the front door.

"You really need to get to that in your fantasies. A nice hard and fast—"

Fortunately, Ally couldn't hear anymore. She marched to her car, practically tearing open the door.

"—would do you wonders—even a fake one," Allison continued, her eyes hovering in the rear-view mirror.

"Go away!" Ally yelled.

"Get over it!" Allison countered. "Look, I'm here to do you a favor. I wish you would just accept me already."

"Accept what? You won't tell me what you are!" Ally said, slamming the door closed, reaching for her seatbelt.

"I tried. I can't help it if you can't understand it." Allison's eyes flashed in the mirror. "And if I have trouble explaining things, it's because you made me bad at it."

"I. Didn't. Make. You." Ally gritted her teeth and stared at Allison's eyes. She opened her vanity mirror and looked into it so she could see more of Allison. "You picked me to haunt. Or you're the symptom of an illness. You aren't real, therefore I couldn't have created you."

She slammed shut the vanity. Allison's eyes returned to the rear-view mirror, her voice bubbling up from beneath it.

"But you did. Every time you closed your eyes and pictured some faraway place, you created me. Every time you wanted to escape being you, you became me. I'm in your head, part of you, yes, but separate also."

"Why?" Ally demanded, opening the vanity again to get a better look at Allison. "Why would you show up now, all of a sudden? Why are you out of my head?"

She realized she was shouting and looked around, suddenly self-conscious. An older man looked at her curiously as he passed. She turned the car on and put it in gear.

"You can't be in my rear-view mirror," she told Allison. "I can't drive that way."

"I can tell you what's behind you, like before," Allison said, sounding hurt.

"Get out of my mirror!" Ally shouted. The blue eyes blinked slowly.

"Open the vanity."

"I can't see with that in my face either," Ally said.

"Open the passenger one then," Allison said calmly, her lip-less voice melodic. Ally reached over and flipped open the passenger vanity. She looked up in the rear-view—Allison was gone.

"Drive safely," Allison's voice said from the other side of the car. Ally gripped the steering wheel until her knuckles were white, and then slowly loosened her grip, breathing deeply. She backed the car out of the spot and turned up the radio, full blast.

Allison decided to sing along. And, of course, she had a good voice. Ally turned off the radio, but Allison kept singing, so she turned it back on.

Ally wasn't letting her automatic pilot drive today. Instead, she directed her car through the streets of Santa Clarita purpose-fully, carefully, doing her best to ignore Allison's occasional trying-to-be-helpful comments about her driving.

"You might want to slow down, Miss Lead Foot."

"Watch out for that pedestrian."

Then, there was her ability to sing along to every song, per-fectly. Ally even tried the hip-hop station. It was strange that Allison knew every word to Eminem when Ally didn't. It was even stranger that Allison knew the unedited version. Ally changed the station quickly.

After a while, Allison stopped singing.

"Where are we going?" she asked. "Shouldn't you be home by now? Or are you detouring for another scrumptious cellulite snack?"

Ally ignored her, pulled into a parking lot, found a spot, and got out.

"Hey!" Allison called. Ally just slammed the door and looked up.

Huge, stable, and the center of Ally's fantasy world, the bookstore glowed with the warmth of a small church, beckoning Ally in.

"Sanctuary," she said to herself, and smiled at her own silliness. Then she went inside.

It was difficult to decide which section to look in first: religion, self-help, or psychology. Ally started off with books on the occult. It was easier to think she was being haunted than that she was crazy. Plus, the store had put up a nice display of books on witchcraft and all that in honor of Halloween, right next to ones about ghosts and other supernatural things. She took it as a sign, and randomly grabbed at a few of the books. Arms already a bit full, she headed over to the psychology area and found one on psychosis. Finally she hit the Self-Help shelves. There was a book on killing your inner demons. Ally thought that sounded about right and grabbed it, along with one on weight loss she'd been meaning to read by a popular TV psychologist.

Armed now with a small library full of books, Ally stumbled her way toward one of the reading tables by the café. She dropped the books on the table, then went and stood in line. She stared hard at the fancy coffee drinks being made behind the counter. A double chocolate, extra-large frozen coffee drink ladled with whipped cream and sprinkles gave off a delicious smell. She sighed and ordered an iced-tea, unsweetened, and sat back down.

Calm down, she told herself. *Don't panic. These books are going to help.*

She picked up one on hallucinations, but it turned out to be about LSD. Ally tried to think about some way she could have come in contact with the drug. It would be so nice if all of this was just a bad trip. Unless traces of the drug could be found in chocolate, she doubted that was the cause. She flipped through a book that detailed hallucination case studies and got engrossed in a story of a teenager who still talked to her imaginary friend. Then that made her wonder if she was actually communicating with a childhood friend herself.

Allison reminded her too much of her mother's well-meaning "critiques" to be an old friend of hers.

Ally kept looking.

Another book was a true-story accounting of a man who'd gone into the Amazon. It was interesting, it was deep, but it was not going to help her with a very suburban hallucination, especially since she didn't eat any funny mushrooms. She didn't even like mushrooms.

She tried books on hauntings next. She found one called *Ghostly Matters* that looked promising, though she wasn't entirely sure what it was about. She put in the buy stack. There was another one written by a psychic, and that gave Ally an idea. If all else failed, she would seek professional help in the world of the occult. She knew a witch, after all. As she slipped through the books on ghosts, she realized that she was looking in the wrong place. No one had died and ghosts were spirits of the departed. So unless she was dead and this was some warped form of afterlife, then she needed something other than ghost stories.

That left psychology and self-help.

She picked up *Embracing Your Inner Critic: Turning Self-Criticism into a Creative Asset.* This one was the best of all since it started with a story about a hobgoblin. He had created an evil mirror that showed the darkness of the world. Then the mirror was broken, showering shards of it over everyone, and in the shards they all saw a distorted, ugly world.

Allison lived in her mirrors. Ally moved the book to the top of the buy pile.

A book called *Trapped in the Mirror* seemed to suggest that all of Ally's problems were her parents' fault. She liked that idea, and put that in the buy pile as well.

She added a few more to her pile, including one full of new ghost stories just for fun, and gathered her pile to take to the register. It was times like these that credit cards were invented for, she told herself. As she walked, she passed by the outside window. She didn't think anything of it until she saw something in it move.

"None of that will help," Allison said, her faint outline barely visible in the tinted glass. Ally jumped, startled by Allison's ghost-like appearance, and backed quickly away from the window, turning around in time to run flat into someone else. A male someone else. A tall, male someone else with really good arms and pale skin. She looked up, petrified, into the brown eyes of Fantasy Man, her books scattering before her in slow motion.

Her heart decided to take a cigarette break.

"Whoa," he said, and bent to help her pick up her books.

Ally's heart roared back with new enthusiasm for beating. She had an impulse to reach out and touch his hair, but shook it off, and bent with him, trying to grab the books before he could read the titles.

"*Trapped in a Mirror*," he read. She snatched it from his hands.

"For a friend," she lied. His voice was higher than she assumed it would be, and suddenly that small detail annoyed her. Thinking about his voice made her think about her fantasies, and she blushed deeply.

"It's okay, I've read a self-help book or two in my time," he said, his smile generous.

"Why?" she blurted out. In her fantasies he was not the kind of man who would ever need to read anything like that. *The Wasteland, Hamlet, The Old Man and the Sea*, but not *Trapped in the Mirror*.

He ducked his head down like a bird.

"Everyone needs a little insight sometimes," he said. He looked at her closely then, and she felt her blush spread down her neck, her chest—even her toes were red now. "Don't you go to my gym?"

She stared in new horror. No. He could not have seen her in her exercise clothes. Then she looked down and realized she was still wearing said exercise clothes, and wanted to die. All she could do was nod.

He reached out a free hand, shifting the books to do so.

"Tom," he said. She looked down at his wide hand, noticing a ragged cuticle. She looked back up at him.

"I don't feel too well," she said, and dropped all of the books in her hands and ran.

She made it as far as the bathroom sink—the stall was three feet too far—and then threw up. She shook a bit as she turned on the water, rinsing out her mouth, and then washing it all down the sink. Then Ally laughed. Borderline hysteria, really.

She'd just met the man of her dreams and had nearly been sick on him.

I'm so totally insane. With another maniacal squeal of laughter, Ally looked up at the mirror and Allison stared down at her, hands on her perfectly thin hips.

"Boo!" Ally told her, and started laughing again.

Allison shook her head. "I wish you would just accept me already," she told Ally, who was still giggling. "I can make everything so much easier for you, if you just let me."

Ally stopped laughing, put her hand to her forehead. "Leave," she told her. "Just leave me alone."

"I'm sorry," Allison said, and almost sold it.

Ally turned and walked quickly out.

Fantasy Man—Tom—was standing by the bathroom, her stack of books in his hands. He looked worried.

"You're so nice." She stared at him as though he was a specimen, and, again, fought the urge to touch him. His face was wide and open, the kind that looked like it was sculpted out of marble, with the eyebrows lifted in perfect arches of worry. "Super nice."

"Are you okay? Do you need help?"

She smiled at him weakly. "I just need to go home." She gestured toward the stack of books, and he handed them over hesitantly.

"I can help," he said.

She shook her head. "I'm okay," she said sadly.

Damn, he really was good looking. Even if his voice was more a bari-

tone than a bass, more non-fat frozen yogurt than extra-creamy homemade ice-cream. Ally walked away, but could feel him following her. She turned around, stopped him in his tracks.

"No, really, I'm fine. Just…embarrassed."

He nodded.

"Okay, then."

"Thanks for your help! I'll see you at the gym, I guess."

He didn't keep walking with her, though she could feel him watching her.

There was no line at the registers. *Thank God for small favors.*

Allison was in the car mirror on the way home. She decided to take the opportunity to tell Ally, in detail, why Ally needed her help.

"Your hair is horrible. You really need to start blow drying it. And your nails. We are well past the age where we bite them, aren't we?"

Ally zoned her out, glancing every now and again at the bag full of books next to her. She didn't consider herself religious, but sent up a silent prayer. *Please, if there is a God, let there be an answer in one of those books.*

STRIKE THAT, REVERSE IT

Ally slumped against the wall of her apartment, shoving her purse next to the Feathered Witch costume still on the entryway table. She felt exhausted and nauseated from her earlier encounters, both with Fantasy Man – Tom – and Allison.

Tom. He had a name. And he was sweet. And kind. And she could not have handled that situation any worse. *I'm just embarrassed.* Did she really admit that to him? *He must think I am so strange!*

It would be easy to blame Allison for how the meeting with Tom went, but Ally felt like she would have found a way to mess it up no matter what. She wasn't supposed to actually talk to the men featured in her fantasies. She'd learned that lesson with Billy, Michael's roommate. They weren't supposed to meet her, not as she was, still fat, still not sure what she was doing with her life, still so perfectly normal and plain and…

Not the fantasy version of herself.

If she looked like Allison. If she was Allison. But no—so far the spirit of her fantasy self had proven to be kind of mean. And super critical. And very annoying.

Ally had to find a way to get rid of Allison. And then maybe she could find a way to actually talk to Tom, like a real person and not a freak.

Ally dragged her bag of books to her couch and settled in to read.

Over an hour into flipping through books, and Ally was ready to start trying. She had been taking notes as she went, and considered her list. Then she went to the kitchen to get some supplies.

Theory One: Allison was a ghost. It was a long shot, but the way to get rid of, or at least contain, ghosts was pretty easy. Ally pulled a box of kosher salt from her cupboard, then grabbed some black pepper and a few other spices. She ran to her closet and dug around until she found an old woven change-purse, pink and blue, she had bought at a flea market. She went back to the living room with all her supplies.

She carefully combined all the spices into a bowl, and then poured them into the little change purse. This was supposed to be a gris-gris bag, which would ward off evil spirits. Ally had to make do with the limited supplies in her kitchen, but according to what she read, keeping it on her person should protect her from Allison—assuming Allison was a spirit.

Next, she took the salt into the bathroom and poured out a line along the bottom of the mirror.

Allison laughed at her from behind the glass.

"Honey, if salt was going to make me go away, your sodium level would have already taken care of that. You salt everything."

Ally flung a handful of salt at the glass, which threw Allison into another giggling fit. Ally clutched her gris-gris bag closer, and then shoved it against the glass. Allison pushed back, startling Ally so much she dropped the bag in the sink.

Ally went back to the couch and her list. She crossed off "ghost." She hadn't had much faith in that explanation anyway, and part of her was just a little relieved. Ghosts implied death.

Ally looked at the next item on her list: hallucination was written in blue ink. She wasn't really sure what to do with that one. She looked back in the book at ways to challenge hallucinations. The problem was, the most common hallucinations were auditory. Ally could see Allison. In fact, she saw Allison before she heard her. The biggest suggestion was confronting the hallucination and telling it to go away. Ally felt she had done that already, but figured it was worth another shot.

Back into the bathroom, back in front of the mirror, back to facing Allison.

"You are not real and you need to go away," Ally said in her best assertive yet calm voice.

"Uh-huh."

"You are only a hallucination, and I am asking you, firmly, to go away."

"Well since you asked firmly," Allison said. Then she disappeared. Ally blinked at the mirror. Could it really be that easy?

"Hello?"

"Hi," Allison said, popping up so suddenly that Ally jumped back. "You called?"

"Go away!" Ally's voice was not as calm and firm as she wanted.

"No," Allison said. "Try something else."

Ally glared at the mirror, and then left the bathroom. Back at the couch she put a question mark at the end of "hallucination." She still just wasn't sure.

She stared at the next item on her list. It felt like the least likely possibility.

Throughout her reading, Ally kept going back to the story about the hobgoblin and his mirror. A follow up Internet search revealed that the story was actually part of the original Snow Queen saga. As the story went, the devil had made a magic mirror that distorted the appearance of everything it reflected, failing to reflect the good and beautiful aspects of people while magnifying the bad and ugly parts of them. The mirror was shattered into millions of pieces which were blown around the world, some getting into people's hearts and eyes so that they could only see the bad and ugly in things and people.

There was a long tale of the splinters getting in a boy's heart and the longer journey of the girl who loved him. The girl saved him through the power of love and the purity of her heart.

Ally sighed. It was a good romantic tale, if overly high on religious symbolism, but not the answer to her problem. Allison wasn't ugly—she was beautiful.

Still, it was on her list: hobgoblin's mirror. Unfortunately, she didn't have a special someone trying to save her with the purity of love in their heart, so there wasn't anything she could do about that one.

In her last book, *Trapped in The Mirror*, the children of narcissists struggled with self-loathing and self-destructive tendencies because their parents made them feel that they never really had the right to exist. Ally thought about Misha and her medication for anxiety and then her own struggles with overeating. In some ways, that book was too close to her life. And it didn't help Ally deal with the perfect version of herself that was haunting her.

But it was on her list as well: "Narcissistic damage." She didn't have a cure for that either.

What she did have was the last thing on her list, provided by Allison herself: magical creation. Hadn't Allison insisted that Ally had made her? So didn't that mean she could unmake her?

Ally had a plan. The constant drone of Allison's detailed list of "constructive criticism" on the car ride home had played in her head and inspired her. It had become chant-like after a while, a steady rhythm of back-handed-compliment, degrade, critique, back-handed-compliment, degrade, critique. It reminded her of the Oompa Loompas singing their songs of morality, warning people of their wrongs. Only Allison's version warned Ally of her imperfections.

Thinking of the Oompas made Ally think of the movie, then of the chocolate factory—mmmm…chocolate—and of Willy Wonka.

"Strike that, reverse it," she said, staring at her list. It was something Wonka said in the movie. Ally marched back to the bathroom. *I have to get this exactly right or else it won't work.* She had picked her book carefully, deciding on the self-help that talked about the inner critic. Then she grabbed a towel and squared her shoulders, ready for the onslaught of negativity she was sure was going to come her way.

"What is it this time? Paprika?" Allison was smirking. It was not an attractive look on her, Ally decided.

She just nodded to Allison, the barest recognition, and walked past the mirror and turned on the bathtub faucets. She waited until the water got really hot before putting the plug in and adding the bubble bath.

"You can't even fit in the tub. Doesn't it depress you to even try? Don't you want to do something about it?"

Ally sighed ever so slightly. *Ignore her,* she told herself. *She'll be gone soon. Just ignore her.*

But it did depress her that she had to wedge herself into the tub. She undressed quickly, and as far away from the mirror as possible.

"I can help you! I will help you, if you let me. I'm giving you really great advice here," Allison called out. "It's not like anything you've done without me has worked. You need me." She sighed heavily as Ally continued to ignore her.

Ally closed her eyes and sighed. *I swear I'm not annoying in my fantasies.* She stepped into the hot water, letting her skin adjust before lowering the rest of herself in.

The overflow began to chug down the displaced water her oh-so-buoyant body pushed up. Allison sighed dramatically again, the worst kind of criticism—unspoken. Ally laid back, book in hand, and tried to read.

"Reading is no good. You need to take action. I can help...." Allison started in again.

"If you want to help me, you can shut up!" Ally snapped back. "You aren't real and you're making me crazy."

"Crazy?" Allison called from the mirror. "Honey, you're the one trying to do the same things over and over again expecting a different result. You can't do this on your own. You need me. You barely have a life—I can give you one. Your fantasy life is seriously lacking—you don't have sex in your fantasies. When's the last time you even got kissed in one? You spend all this time with the build-up, and then, nothing."

"I like romance," Ally said defensively.

"You're practically a virgin," Allison snapped back. "You don't fantasize about the rest because you've barely had sex—one guy, and how long did that relationship last?"

"So what?" Ally said. "If you are a reflection of me, you've only been with one guy too!"

She felt she scored big on that one and grinned to herself. Except Allison's voice took on a new, seductive tone. "Oh, but you have erotic dreams," she said. "And I get to enjoy *every moment of them...*"

"I don't..." Ally said hesitantly. She did. She just didn't like hearing about them from someone else. And Greg, her ex—she didn't want to share that experience with this annoying twit of a hallucination either.

"God. You are such a prude!"

Ally closed her eyes, took a deep breath, and concentrated on her plan. Then she focused on her book.

"He gently pulls me close, sliding his hand down my arm…" Allison began.

"Shut up!" Ally said.

Allison laughed. "So prim!"

Ally ignored her, concentrated on the words on the page, reading the same sentence for the fifth time.

Okay, what did I do next? I had a fantasy of Allison. Okay, so let's reverse it…a fantasy of me.

Ally pictured what she looked like. She recoiled from the image at first, then repeated the words she read. *There is nothing wrong with me. There is nothing wrong with me. So, just be me.* Her brown hair seemed to always be slightly frizzy, and her stomach rolls had a tendency to show through most of her shirts. Her breasts often challenged the support of her bras. *But still, nothing wrong with me,* she told herself firmly. Her hazel eyes weren't bad, just plain. She liked her lips, and her nose. She had a good chin. It was a start.

Now she needed a fantasy to be in.

She'd always wanted a big career, so maybe she could give herself one. Let's see, something not too active since she still wasn't in that great of shape. Ally thought about all the jobs she had rejected on the internet career test. Writer was on the potential jobs list, and writers didn't live that active of lives. Also, she could type fairly well. Couldn't be much to writing considering how many books there were. You come up with an idea, you write it down, easy peasy, as she used to say when she was little.

So, I'll be a writer.

Ally pictured it, long hours at her computer, typing away. Just for the hell of it, she pictured herself at the gym too, going to town on the treadmill. Now her image of herself had a smaller stomach roll. She pictured a few more gym montages, got the stomach smaller, and then stopped herself. *As you are dummy*, she chided. *So I don't go to the gym.* Her stomach rolls jiggled back in place. *And then I write.*

She figured out how long it would take for her to finish a book. *Four months? Yeah, four months.* And then she needed to get it published. She pictured another few weeks, another month or so at the outside. So, five months from now, November, December, January, February, March. Okay, so then by April Fool's Day, she would have her book published. Maybe not in stores yet—it probably would be a summer release—but the deal could be all worked out. So she would have money.

Ally thought some more. How much do writers make? Hell, she told herself, this is a fantasy, who cares? Her book sold for enough money to buy a really nice house in the hills, overlooking the valley, with a pool in the back, and, because she couldn't let it go entirely, a room dedicated to her own personal gym. Once she was rich it would be easy to get thin. But, she reminded herself, she would not be there yet, not for this fantasy.

This was harder than Ally anticipated. She never stayed herself in her fantasies.

Okay then, rich, with a house, not thin yet. I need more details. I need...a romance.

With someone who likes fat girls? She sighed, rotated on her hip, away from the mirror, dropping the book onto the floor behind her. Well, maybe he could see past the extra poundage to the incredible woman within? Ally thought about that, tried to tell herself how wonderful she was. Then she tried to tell herself how wonderful she would be as a successful writer. With lots of money. And a house.

Details, she needed details.

Ally stood on the stone walkway next to her lush green lawn, and looked at the large mess at the end of her cement driveway. Someone had dumped all of a man's personal belongings into the middle of the street. Clothes. Lots and lots of clothes, plus golf clubs, a hockey stick, snowboard, guitar, surfboard, all in a heap right where she couldn't get her car around it without running something over. Ally looked around at the houses nearby—the pile had to come from one of them. The door to the house next to her opened, and a woman walked out, tossed a basketball at the pile, which thudded into a pair of jeans, and turned around and walked back inside.

Well, that solved that problem. She had just mustered up enough courage to go over to the house and tell the lady off when a car drove down the street toward the pile, stopping at the foot of it.

A man jumped out, broad shouldered and with nice arms, but slightly pale, and surveyed the mess.

"Shit!" he said. He left his car and jogged up toward Ally's neighbor's front door.

"Jessica!" he yelled, turning the locked handle, pounding on the wood. "Jessica, can't we talk about this?" The reply was muffled, but the tone was definitely no. Ally could have told him that no woman who was going to reconcile with a man threw his stuff in the street. She wouldn't want to help haul it back in.

Ally watched the scene curiously, taking notes to write about later, since she assumed this was what writers did. Finally, the man turned around, and spotted Ally for the first time.

"Oh," he said, looking at the pile, Ally's driveway, and then at Ally again.

"Yeah," she said back. "Oh."

"I'll move it," he said quickly. "As soon as I can."

"Uh-huh," she said, nodding, looking again at the pile. There was a lot of crap there to move. She thought she saw a chair buried under some suit jackets. The jackets were nice though. They looked expensive. She became more curious about the man. "What did you do?" she asked, turning back to him. His face contorted into a look of anger and frustration.

"Wasn't me," he said. "She just couldn't handle the fact that I had a problem with her cheating." He shook his head. "We broke up and I said I'd come get my stuff. Apparently I didn't get here soon enough."

Ally nodded, not sure if she should believe him.

"You live next door?" she asked, nodding to his car. "I've seen that here a lot."

"I did," he said.

"Have somewhere else to stay?" she asked. He shook his head, looked angry again.

"I can get an apartment. I told her it would take a while, and she said I could keep my stuff here—just take what I needed."

"Guess she changed her mind," Ally said, leaning back against the side of her house. She studied the man. He really was good-looking, more so the way his lower lip pouted and the way he kept running his hands through his hair—helplessness looked adorable on him.

And nice, she remembered suddenly, the image of the real-world Fantasy Man—Tom—standing outside of the bathroom with a stack of books popping into her head. Ally took a deep breath and pushed past it. *House. Strange man. Pile of stuff. Focus.*

"I really will get that stuff out of here," he told Ally, looking up at her. "It's just…it will take time to get a truck and…find a place to put it and…"

Really adorable, she decided as he flopped his hands down at his sides, defeated.

"This really sucks," he said.

Ally had to laugh at him. He glared up at her for a moment, then laughed along.

"Thanks for being so understanding about this," he said, smiling at her. She nodded, then looked down, embarrassed. She was going to be sad not to see him around, now that he was moving.

Suddenly, she had an idea. She looked at her house, then back at the pile on her driveway. Why not? Brushing away the million-and-ten reasons that immediately jumped into her head—all in her mother's voice, she noted—Ally spoke before she lost her nerve. "I have a spare bedroom," she offered hesitantly. "Has its own bathroom and you can get in and out through the slider if you don't want to use the front door."

He stared at her, as though not understanding what she was saying.

"I just moved in a bit ago," she continued. "I was going to look for a roommate anyway. It could just be a trial maybe, till you find something else. Honestly, I could use the company. And the rent." She smiled shyly at him. "If you're interested, it would be a short move."

He grinned at her then. "How much?"

"How much you willing to pay?"

"Whatever it costs." Someone turned the dimmer switch of joy up on him. He was radiating happy relief. "I'll draw up a contract...you can fill in the amount, whatever it costs. Can I move in today?"

Ally smiled at his eagerness. "Need a hand with your stuff?"

He grinned back at her.

✻

See? Ally told herself as she shifted her position in the bathtub. *I'm good at this!* Although it was strange to put Tom in her fantasies after talking to him. She rolled over again, noticed her hands were all pruney. *Just like before.* She could go back to the next chapter of her new fantasy, one she was nicknaming "The Boarder," later. It was time to get rid of Allison.

Ally stood up, grabbed her towel, and wrapped it around herself. Then she stepped from the tub, just shy of being seen in the mirror. And she wished, with all her might, that when she looked in the mirror she would see herself and only herself—not Allison. She closed her eyes tight, hoping that would help.

She took a deep breath, stepped in front of the mirror.

She opened her eyes.

Nothing. There was nothing in the mirror. At first Ally was relieved, and then it hit her. There was nothing in the mirror! No sign of Allison sure, but no sign of Ally either. She had disappeared! She looked down at her hand, could still see it, and waved it in front of the glass. She could see her hand, but couldn't see its reflection. She could, however, see what was behind her, as though looking through herself. She started to panic, stepped away from the mirror, and wished harder.

Me, I want to see me, she told whatever force may be listening.

She looked in the mirror again, and again, saw nothing.

"Oh God!" she said out loud. "I'm invisible!"

The laughter started to her right, bubbled up as though coming from the bathtub. It hovered there a moment before gliding closer to her, past the toilet, and into the mirror.

It brought Allison with it.

"You are so gullible!" she said between gales of laughter. "That just totally rocked!"

Ally was almost positive she never said "rocked" in her fantasies. She glared at Allison.

"You're a total and complete bitch!" she told her.

Allison rolled her eyes at Ally. "Overreact why don't you? And if I'm a bit bitchy it's because you made me that way."

"I didn't!" Ally said. She held her towel tightly, shook her head. She did everything the same. *I should have reversed it all.* Unless she was supposed to wish and then take a bath?

"You can't get rid of me," Allison said, readjusting her own towel around herself, showing off her body as she did so. "Doesn't matter what you do."

Ally glared at her harder.

"If I made you, I can unmake you." she said. She leaned forward, toward the mirror. "Go haunt someone else!"

Allison laughed.

"Not a ghost, not a ghoul, not a hallucination too. Not a dream, not a pill, not something you can control at will. Here to stay, sorry to say, learning new tricks, every day." She smiled at Ally.

"What new tricks?" Ally asked, suddenly suspiciously. "And you said earlier…Michael wasn't supposed to see you, yet. What are you? Why are you? Why me? Why don't you just go away?"

She was close to tears now, could feel them coming, but didn't want to cry in front of Allison. Allison just shook her head at her. Exasperated, Ally whirled away from the mirror, ran to her room, and threw herself down on the pillow.

She wanted to be a million miles away, somewhere else, someone else, anything to not have to deal with the mess her life had become.

So she slipped away.

✳

She helped the stranger move his stuff into her house. It wasn't until the third trip out that he thought to introduce himself.

"Tom," he said, extending out his hand.

"Ally," she said back, extending her own, perfectly manicured one. Three trips and she wasn't even winded. She tossed her perfectly bouncy hair over her tan, toned shoulder, and smiled a gleaming smile at Tom. "Welcome to your new home."

HOME

She took Tom's hand. Suddenly, they weren't in front of the fancy house anymore, but by the silver-blue lake—the calm, still shimmery lake. Ally was beginning to not like this lake, and the way the breeze that pushed the hair off her face never seemed to touch its surface.

Beauty neighed a greeting then went back to her grass.

Tom smiled down at Ally. "Are you getting cold?"

"What?" Ally asked.

"Should we go?" he asked her.

"We were just somewhere else," she said, confused. "Don't you remember?"

He shook his head.

"We've been here the entire time, Ally. You fell asleep." His smile was warm, adoring. "It's been a long day. Why don't we go home?"

"Where's home?" she asked. She could smell his musky scent from here, a combination of sweat, hay, and something else that made her toes curl. It was filling her senses up, making her dizzy. *I never think about smell in my fantasies,* some part of her noted.

"You know where home is," he teased.

"Home is where the heart is," she said, closing her eyes, giving in to his scent, to the surreal reality of the dream. He pulled her into an embrace.

"Then my home is with you," he said in a low bass, a voice the texture of heated marshmallow goo over chocolate ice cream.

That wasn't right. His voice had been higher in the bookstore.

"Thanks for helping me with the books," she mumbled into his chest.

"What books?" he asked. "We've been here…we've only ever been here."

He stroked her back lightly, sending shivers down her spine.

"Only here?" she asked.

"Let me take you home," he said, and pushed her slightly away from him. He bent down toward her, his breath warm on her face. "Let me take you…."

She closed her eyes, went up on her toes to bring her lips closer to his…

His lips rang.

"Shit!" she said, and managed to give Tom one apologetic look before being pulled away.

She was still grumpy when she picked up the receiver.

"What?" she barked into it, pulling the towel back into place around her under the blankets of her bed.

"Ally? Did I wake you?" It was Michael. She sighed.

"Yeah, sorry, I dozed off." She looked at the clock. 10:00. She wasn't normally asleep by then. "What's up?" she asked him.

"I didn't mean to wake you. I just wanted to check on you. I called earlier, but there was no answer."

She sighed, leaning back against the mattress.

"I took a bath."

"Good!" Michael said, a little too enthusiastically. "I mean, that should help you feel better. Do you?"

She looked toward the door that led out to the bathroom.

"I think what I have may stick with me for a while," she said.

"Do you need to call in sick tomorrow?"

Ally contemplated an entire day of dealing with Allison.

"No, it's a short day because of the holiday. I think I can make it."

"And the party on Saturday?" he asked. "I wouldn't ask, it's just that….well…"

"What?" Ally said, annoyed. She could be home with Tom right now. She might not know where home was, but she suspected she very much wanted to be wherever he was going to take her.

"There's a special reason why I want you to go—I can't tell you what it is."

A new chill went down Ally's spine, something that had nothing to do with ghosts or hallucinations, but a deeper, darker fear.

"Why can't you tell me?" she asked Michael.

"It's a surprise," he said. Ally's fear was growing stronger, her suspicion overrunning it.

"What did you do Michael?" she demanded.

"Nothing," he said. It was the way he said it, defensively and guiltily at the same time. Suddenly, Ally knew. And she was not happy.

"There's a guy for me, isn't there? A blind date?"

"Not blind," Michael said in the tones of a child who knew why the window was broken but didn't want to say it. "He's seen a picture of you. And he's very interested," he added. Ally sat up, angry now.

"You were just going to spring this on me? What if I didn't have a costume, or I looked gross in it?" She thought for a moment. "Which picture?"

"The one of you and me at Vasquez Rocks."

"Head shot?"

"The other one—torso shot." Ally shook her head.

"And he still wants to meet me? What does he look like?"

"He's cute—trust me, he's totally someone you would go for."

"Michael…" she said, suddenly very tired. "I can't believe you."

"It's a good thing, really. He's a friend of Sandra's…."

Thinking of the petite blonde on top of the rest of the day Ally was having—and of Michael and Sandra planning even more things together—made Ally testy.

"He a witch too?" she snorted.

"No." He sounded annoyed now, and Ally regretted her tone with him. "He works with Sandra, has a very good job in print and web design for her company. He's very successful."

"Again I ask, and he wants to meet me?" Ally pulled at a loose thread on her bed-in-a-bag comforter.

"I told him you were funny. And smart. And nice."

Ally laughed a little, felt guilty again. "I don't mean to be bitchy about it, I'm just tired."

"I know," he said. "You've not been sleeping well lately. But you're still going to come, right?" His voice was somewhat pleading now. "You promised."

"God, it's like we're in school again," she said, and leaned back against her wall, stared out over her bedroom. "People can break promises. They do it all the time."

"You don't," he said. She brushed his statement away the same time she brushed her damp hair off her forehead. "And Ally, this is like back when we were in school. Back when you were depressed."

Ally closed her eyes and took a deep breath. She felt like crying, and didn't want to.

"I know," she said at last.

"It's been bad for a while, hasn't it?"

"Yeah," she said. "But I'll get out of it. I got out of it before. I'm doing things, making changes. I log all my calories now, even on bad days, and I've been going to the gym. Like you said earlier, it's a commitment. I've been making it, I really have."

"Look, about earlier—I really shouldn't have been so short with you. And I am not sure that counting calories…"

"Why? Because it works?"

"Because of Misha. Because she has a history of that too, and…"

"I'm not anorexic." Ally snorted. "And Misha is better." She remembered then Misha's pills with a pang of guilt squeezing her heart. "Or at least she is getting help for it."

"Yeah, I know. She's in a new support group, going to a psychiatrist."

"How do you know that?" Ally's voice was accusing.

"She told me. We talk, sometimes. And honestly Ally, Misha is worried about you, too."

"Misha is worried about me?! She's the one on pills. Look, no one has to worry about me, okay? I'm fine. I'm always fine."

"It would be okay if you weren't…"

"Look, if you were calling about the party, no worries. I said I would be there, and I'll be there. And I'll meet your blind date person. And it will be fine. Everything will be fine. Was there anything else?"

"Ally, I get that you're mad…"

"I'm not mad. I'm just tired. It was a busy day. And I'm sorry for my tone. I know I'm being short. I just…I just wish you guys would talk to me instead of about me."

"We try."

Ally closed her eyes against the truth of his statement. He had been trying. Misha, too. She just hadn't wanted to talk to them.

"I know," she said instead. "I'm sorry."

"You really don't have anything to be sorry about. It's part of it, you know? The depression? I get it. We all get it. We just want to help."

"You do help," she said, picking at the blanket. "More than you know."

"Well, let me help more." There was a touch of sassiness in his voice, and Ally knew the fight, or whatever it was, had blown over.

"Help more on Saturday. Help me with that costume. That belt is seriously so bad."

"Oh, do I have ideas to fix that! This is going to be great. You'll see." He seemed cheered up, and that made Ally more depressed.

"Sure," she said smiling, because she knew he'd hear it through the phone if she didn't. "Hey, I'm really tired so…"

"No problem. I'll let you go." But something about his tone seemed disappointed.

"Thanks for checking on me," she said. "And encouraging me."

"That's what friends are for," he said, his voice warm. "Love you. Good Night."

"You too. Good Night."

She hung up and slid down onto her back. She contemplated getting into her pajamas, but decided it would be too much effort. She pulled the blankets up over her instead and closed her eyes.

She was by the lake, with Tom. And she really wanted to know where home was.

Though she tried, her head wouldn't let her go back there.

Someone wants to meet me. He saw me—saw my body—and still wants to meet me. I wonder what he's like.

She drifted into sleep expecting to wake up at the lake with Fantasy Tom. Instead, she found herself lying in her bed, unable to move, not sure if she was awake or asleep. A figure, something vaguely human-shaped but lost to the shadows, entered and came closer to her.

Ally had experienced these kind of dreams before and knew what would happen next. She would want to move, to scream, to do anything, but would stay still, paralyzed. She would will herself awake, will the moment to be just a dream.

Michael once told Ally that these sorts of dreams usually meant that the dreamer was feeling helpless in her life, stuck. Misha once told her that those weren't dreams at all, but alien abductions.

Whatever the cause, Ally was dreaming it again. She stared out over her room, every detail exactly as it was when she went to sleep—her jacket tossed over the chair in the corner, the packaging from a pair of tights still sitting on top of the dresser, the tights in question in a shriveled pile on the floor. And there, in the doorway of her room, stood a dark figure moving slowly toward her.

Ally tried to pull her mind away from the image, to take control of her dream. *Think of something else, anything else*, she willed. The only thing that came to mind was Allison.

"No one is supposed to see me yet." What else had Allison said? "Learning new tricks." A new terror filled Ally as she contemplated Allison's words—what more could the dream-image of herself do? Such was her fear that she was able to yank herself away from her nightmare. She sat up, breathing hard, trying to take deep breaths, calm down.

Then she screamed.

Someone was in her room, sitting on the edge of her bed. Ally screamed again, crouching up into one corner of her bed, blankets at her chin. Her eyes darted wildly around for some sort of weapon. The fact that she could move was the only thing that gave her any sense that this was real.

"Relax," an all-too-familiar voice said. Ally leaned over and clicked on the bedside lamp cautiously. It took a second for her eyes to adjust to the sudden brilliance of the light and make out the shape of the figure sitting on the edge of her bed.

Allison smiled at Ally. "It's just me."

GHOSTS GONe WILD

Ally stared at Allison, her terror slowly being replaced by confusion, and a tinge of anger.

"You're my reflection," she said, holding the blanket up to her chin, a shield between Allison and herself.

"Inner reflection…" Allison started.

"But still, a reflection." Ally fought the urge to scream again. "You live in the mirror."

Allison laughed her light, tinkling-of-bells laugh.

"I'm a part of you," she said, her blue eyes flashing, her white teeth gleaming. "I live where you live."

She looked like the wolf right before he ate Grandma, and Ally felt a chill slide down her spine. She backed further away.

"If you're a part of me, why are you so…separate?"

Allison laughed again.

"You should quit trying to figure this out and just go with it. It's what you're good at, right? Going with the flow?" And now she looked like the wolf after Riding Hood complimented his teeth. Ally fished under the covers for the towel and wrapped it around herself as she stood up. She walked very carefully around the bed, around Allison, staying as far away as she could. Allison's eyes followed her.

"I have to go to work," Ally said, not having anything else to say. She got out of the bedroom and practically ran to her walk-in closet in the hallway, grabbed clothes quickly from the hangers, and then dashed into the bathroom.

Her own real-life and really imperfect reflection blinked back at her, shaking slightly. She stared at it a moment, feeling a small measure of relief to be able to see herself again, to prove that she was real. And then she got dressed as quickly as possible. She looked up from smoothing her pants legs down, and then jumped back, landing hard against the closed bathroom door.

"You!" she managed. Allison was leaning against the bathroom counter next to her, smoothing a stray curl back into place.

Ally felt a coldness creep throughout her body. Her reflection had a reflection. She stepped forward, as though dazed, and watched her real life reflection come to stand next to Allison's. However aware of the differences she was before, she was not prepared for this side-by-side comparison. She looked huge standing next to Allison, and blotchy, and there were circles under her eyes.

"I know. It's hard to look at," Allison said. "I know that some of it you can't help, but some things you could at least work on. How many diets have you been on? You'd think one would have worked. And your skin—ever hear of moisturizer? I can't even look at your hair. You need a haircut, a dye-job, and a deep conditioning treatment, in that order. And then it would take a score of products and a team of professionals to actually make it look more than just 'fine.' God, no wonder you never date." Allison shook her head, disgusted.

Ally looked away from her reflection, from Allison's perfect image standing next to it. She wasn't sure if she wanted to cry, laugh, or scream.

Allison's voice softened. "Poor thing. You just don't have a clue, do you?"

Ally turned around then and opened the door. "I have to go to work," she managed to say.

She went about her morning rituals somberly, unable to form a coherent thought with Allison floating around her. She couldn't tell if Allison was actually floating or just moved to make it look that way. So far, the former-reflection was obeying ghost rules, not touching anything, not making any kind of impression on anything but herself. Ally suspected she could walk right through Allison, and maneuvered herself to avoid that possibility. She went back to the bathroom to gather her gris-gris bag, but it didn't stop Allison from floating. She vainly threw a small discreet handful of salt at Allison's back, and it sprinkled the carpet without having the slightest impact on the apparition. Ally went back to ignoring Allison.

Her hair went up in a bun, her teeth got brushed and flossed, her face covered in foundation and blush, and the bags under her eyes partially diminished by concealer.

Allison offered unwanted tips. "You should use a clean face-sponge every time you put on foundation so you don't contaminate it. Start from the inside of the eye and brush out. You should have a lip-liner a shade darker than that lipstick. How old is your mascara anyway?"

Ally moved silently, not trusting herself to speak. As quickly as she could, she made herself ready, and without a last minute appearance check, she headed out the door. She fully expected Allison to glide out behind her, but once the door was shut, the litany of suggestions ceased as well.

It wasn't until she got to her car and saw only herself in the rear-view, side, and vanity mirrors that she realized Allison was confined to her apartment. It was then Ally cried, just a little, trying to control herself as quickly as possible.

I'm crazy and I'm being haunted, she sobbed to herself. Only haunted wasn't the right word either. She dried her eyes and focused on her reflection. It was nice to see her eyes again, even if her mascara was flaking and she probably should replace it.

As Ally drove to work, her thoughts whirled like the remaining ashes swirling around under the gray sky like snowflakes. The sky was so darkened by smoke and ash the sun seemed to give up trying to shine through it. The darkness contributed to Ally's mood.

Ally managed to get by Michael without him seeing how upset she was. The shortened day worked in her favor since everyone had a lot to do to get ready before the weekend. People were excited for Halloween and everywhere she went, Ally heard people discussing their plans.

Delkey had chosen to wear a costume to work and was dressed as a genie, belly button ring shining in the fluorescent light. Again, Ally wondered how the woman got away with it. Michael's holiday concession was a funky headband that had wiggly eyes bouncing on the top of it. He brought a pair of cat ears for Ally and called her Catwoman the rest of the day. She smiled at him whenever he did, still sensitive to their conversation the night before and wanting, more than anything, to see fine in front of him.

"That's who you should have been for Halloween," he said, helping her sort charts in the filing room.

"Sure, I do skin-tight real well," she said, then felt ashamed of how much bitterness she let come through. Michael's good cheer seemed immune to it though. Ella stuck her silvery head through the door, her bat earrings dangling lower than her short bob.

"Mike, I need your help with something," she said.

"Okay," he said, sounding chipper. He rolled his eyes at Ally and then smiled back at Ella as he walked toward her. He hated being called Mike. Ally went back to her filing, letting her mind drift over the alphabet so that she didn't have to think about anything.

Her thoughts came unheeded, and in a way that didn't even feel like her thoughts.

You would never look good as Catwoman. Even if you lost all the weight, you wouldn't have the body of someone who hasn't been fat. You will never be the kind of person who will be happy with herself. You shouldn't even try.

Shut up! she told herself. She was getting annoyed with her own thoughts. Was it just her imagination or had they been getting worse since Allison showed up? It was as though Allison's voice was in Ally's head, constantly criticizing, constantly trying to tear Ally down.

She shook her head and tried to concentrate on the files in front of her.

But her mind floated like ash in the wind.

Her back was to the door, but she felt his gaze like a wave of heat and looked up. She didn't turn.

"Ally." He breathed her name, sending cold chills down her spine so that she felt hot and cold at once.

She wanted to turn, and resisted it. "Tom, this isn't a good time." She could feel him come closer and her heart pounded in her chest, her bosoms heaving with her heartbeat. Bosoms? Some part of her wondered where that word had come from.

"I needed to see you," he said. She whirled to face him, her hand fluttering against her long, pale throat. Tom's long hair was disheveled and hung lose around his face and down to his shoulders. *But he had short hair…* His shirt was unbuttoned, his smooth chest peeking out at her. He looked fresh from the farm, and she was hungry for some country cooking.

"There are people here…" she began hesitantly, her hand sliding unwittingly down to rest on her cleavage. His eyes followed the movement, then drifted back up to her face. He licked his lips.

"No one nearby," he said huskily, and he walked closer still.

She felt her stomach quiver, her breath come faster.

"And I needed to…"

"Don't," she said, stepping forward, her fingers on his sensual and wide mouth. She pulled back suddenly from the touch, as though burned. Heat ran through her body and the quivering in her stomach began to travel through her, up to her head, then down to her knees.

He took her hand, and his larger one was warm, strong. She could feel the calluses in the palm, proof of a life of labor.

"How can you stand it? Knowing we're supposed to be together…" He raised her hand to his lips, kissed her fingertips, his eyes burning into hers.

She pulled away, not wanting to, but feeling she should. This wasn't right, this was…forbidden. It was the only word for what he wanted, what she wanted, what they couldn't have. She turned away from him. She couldn't take the want in his eyes.

"Someone could come in…" she said, her own voice husky, lower and throatier than she had ever heard it. Her heart was a staccato in her chest, her breasts rising and falling with each rushed breath.

"I don't care," he said, and pulled her to him in one violent gesture, taking her into his strong, well-muscled arms.

She tried to push him away. It was a weak effort, as weak as her knees. She could feel the warmth of his body against hers, her breasts crushed against his chest. "We shouldn't," she said, her eyes transfixed by his, drowning in their deep pools, wanting to be pulled under. He was so close. The feel of him intoxicated her.

"You want me," he said.

She didn't even try to deny it, and as he bent his lips close to hers, she raised up on her toes, reaching out for him....

When their lips met it was all Ally could ever imagine it being. She felt the kiss through her entire body, felt a need rise up in her she had never felt before. Her world narrowed to his lips, the feel of his arms, and the closeness of him.

His tongue sought hers out and she welcomed it, explored it with her own, gave in to the moment.

He lifted her in his arms, pressed her closer to him. That surprised her, and the surprises kept coming as she felt something she hadn't felt in a very long time—and boy did this feel real. And big. And hard. The feeling of him throbbing against her brought out an answering warmth and wetness in her. After that, thoughts were difficult to formulate.

Ally felt flushed now, completely wrapped up in his lips, his tongue, and his hands now exploring her body. He carried her to the table in the file room and laid her on it. Her legs wrapped up and around him, some instinct in her taking over. Her hands sought out the smoothness of his chest, her fingers scratched lightly at his skin, then slid around to his back, under his shirt.

He moved his kisses down her neck and she let out a gasp.

"You're the only one," he whispered hoarsely to her.

"Oh, Tom!" she moaned. She tore at his shirt, flung the material away from her, and he slipped hers over her head, exposing her black-lacy bra. *Didn't I put a tan bra on this morning?* He slid his hands up her thighs, leaned into her, kissed her. She pulled him close. His mouth went down her neck to her chest. She let out another gasp.

Her gasp turned into a panicked gulp as she looked up into Michael's face.

"Where do you want to go for lunch?" he asked her. Tom cupped Ally's breast, his thumb sliding under the lace, and she tried to move his hand away. Michael just smiled at her as though there was nothing unusual about what she was doing.

"Uh, I....oh..." Tom's kisses moved lower. Ally tried to push him away, tried to reconcile what she was feeling with what she was seeing. Tom was sliding her bra strap off her shoulder and she could feel his hands moving toward the clasp in the back. She tried to pull them away.

"Are you alright?" Michael asked. "You look a little flushed."

Ally finally gathered all her strength to push Tom off of her, part of her sorry to make him stop. As she shoved against him, her hands passed through air, and she found herself sitting awkwardly on the edge of the table alone.

Michael still stared down at her.

She looked around for any sign of Tom, but he was gone. Ally checked herself. Her shirt was back in place, not even mussed. She discreetly checked her bra strap—tan colored, as it was supposed to be, and where it should be on her shoulder. Still feeling warm, she stared back up at Michael, confused.

"Are you okay?" he asked, his voice steeped in concern.

"I got dizzy," she said, trying to explain why she was on the table even though he didn't ask.

Michael felt her forehead with his hand.

"You feel warm," he said. "What have you eaten today?"

"Uh..." She tried to remember.

"Have you eaten today?" he asked. She shook her head. *No, between the apparition in my apartment and the trip to soft porn land, I didn't get around to eating.*

Michael tsked her, and walked over to the filing cabinets, taking something out of his drawer. He came back with a baggie full of apple slices.

"Here," he said. "This should help until lunch. Sandra called. She said she was going to go with us, if that's okay? She has a half-day too. Only an hour left," he added. Ally took the apples and nodded at Michael. Then she looked up at him, perplexed.

"Hey, this is going to sound weird but, what was I doing when you came in here?"

Michael creased his eyebrows in concern.

"Sitting there," he said. "Looking bored. Maybe that was sick and I read it wrong?"

She stared up at him. She could still remember Tom's kisses, his hands, his...other things. She blushed. Sex with her ex, Greg, had never been like that—not...quite...like that.

"Okay," she said, getting up.

Michael grinned at her. "Why, were you thinking non-work-related thoughts?" He followed her back to the stacks of charts she had yet to put away.

"No!" she said quickly.

Too quickly, and Michael laughed at her. "Yeah right. Probably off on one of your romantic adventures."

She was about to shake her head and protest again but a moving shadow caught her eye. The shadow turned out to have bright auburn hair and wicked blue eyes.

"Oh, I think this was better than one of your regular romantic trysts, don't you?" Allison asked. Ally's eyes flew back to Michael, but he didn't seem to have heard anything. "I think it's sweet how you plan the meeting, first date and all that. But don't you think it's a lot better just to jump to the good stuff?" Allison asked, lounging against a filing cabinet. Ally tried to keep a straight face, not give any indication she was seeing a woman who was not there and who vaguely resembled herself.

"So, where did you say you wanted to go to lunch?" she asked Michael, hurriedly shoving charts into drawers to try and not look at Allison.

"I didn't. I asked you where you wanted to go." Michael grabbed a stack, started to put some charts into a drawer two over from hers.

"Anywhere is fine with me," Ally said.

"Anytime, anyplace….Oh, Tom, just like that!" Allison said dramatically, then snickered.

Ally's face went from rosy to red. A, B, C… Think of the alphabet. "How about Italian? Get a nice salad?"

"Toss a nice salad." Allison grinned.

Ally glared at her from the corner of her eye, willing her to be quiet.

"You are such a prude!" Allison said, shaking her perfect curls.

Ally turned her head so that Allison was out of view. Out of sight didn't put the perfect product of her imagination out of earshot.

"Dick. Penis. Johnson."

Ally turned on her heel and walked out of the room. Allison and Michael followed her, Allison giggling and Michael concerned.

"Forgot something," she said to Michael over her shoulder. She sat down at her desk, shuffling through the drawers and trying to reign in her temper. Allison's taunting was just cruel. And distasteful.

"Oh, Tom, I want you so badly, you and your hard co…."

"I have to pee!" Ally declared loudly, and walked very quickly from the room.

In the bathroom, Ally checked under all the stall doors for feet, then leaned against the counter, her hands crossed over her chest, waiting. She didn't have to wait long, and Allison appeared next to her, laughing.

"Cock!" she finished through gales of laughter. "Oh my, that was way too easy!"

"What do you want from me?" Ally growled, standing up and facing Allison. She was the same height as the fantasy version of herself. At least she had that much.

"Nothing that you aren't already giving me," Allison said, grinning toothily.

"What does that mean?" Ally asked. "What am I giving you?"

Allison turned toward the mirror, started to play with her hair, arranging it in different styles.

"What?" Ally asked again, louder.

Allison glanced at her. "Tell me you didn't like it, that you didn't enjoy every second of your moment with Tom."

"How did you do that?" Ally asked. "You were in my head, controlling my thoughts…"

"And do I get a thank you? No…." Allison sighed dramatically.

"Thank you? I've never been more humiliated in my life!"

"I've been in your head honey," Allison said, and shook her head. "I think we both know that's not a true statement."

Ally blushed again, and then shook it off violently. "I'm telling you for the last time," she said, and tried to speak calmly, slowly. "Leave. Me. Alone."

Allison shook her head, almost sadly. "Poor thing, you really just don't get it. I'm not the one causing this. But while I'm here, I plan on making life more interesting for you." She smiled, then winked at Ally and disappeared. Ally expected some sort of sound, some other indication of Allison going from one place to the next—*and what was the next place?*—but there was nothing. Frustrated, scared, horny, and a little sick to her stomach, Ally went back to work.

BOOK OF DaZe

"So, Italian?" Michael asked, as she returned to the filing room. Ally looked at Michael, into his soft brown eyes, his carefully styled hair, the mole on the right side of his chin. He cared. About her.

"Actually, I still have some last minute things to do before Misha's Halloween party tonight," she told him. "So I won't have time for lunch."

"It's a half day. We have all day."

"I have a lot to do," Ally insisted.

"What things? Maybe I can help..."

"No, you go have a nice lunch. Plus, you have the haunted house for the neighborhood kids to get ready," she said, smiling at him. "Worry about that. Tomorrow, I'll show up around 6 to get ready for your party, okay?"

"Ally, I'm really worried about you, particularly after our conversation last night. If you're dealing with depression again, you need help. I can help."

Ally turned to face him, and took a moment to look at him, really see the concern in his eyes.

"I know," she said. "But right now I just need a little space to figure some things out. I promise, I'll tell you if it gets too bad."

He sighed and then gave her a quick hug.

"Okay," he said. "I'm a phone call away, if you need me."

Ally nodded and had to turn away from him before she gave into the urge to tell him everything. This was her issue, not his, and she didn't want to burden him with her problems. She walked into the front office, Michael a slow shadow behind her, and went to the computer to check the schedule for next week. As she moved the chair to sit down, a blurry shape moving in front of the glass caught her eye, and she looked up, afraid to see curly auburn hair. But the hair was short, dark brown, spiky, and framed a soft round face. It took Ally a moment to recognize him. Bobby Dominguez. The boy who grabbed her, what seemed like, forever ago.

Bobby looked like a different person, calm, smiling, serene. He waved a pudgy hand at Ally, and she waved back instinctively. Dr. Barclay smiled at her as she came out to collect Bobby and winked as she passed the front window.

"Wow," Ally said under her breath.

"I know," Michael said behind her. "Ever since that last incident, it's like he completely turned around. Dr. Barclay isn't sure why, but she's going with it."

"What's his deal—why is he here?" Ally asked, looking up at Michael.

"Well, it started a few months ago, after a trip he took to Seattle…."

Ally couldn't hear what else Michael was saying. A melodic voice was singing, loudly, right into Ally's ear. She jumped up with a squeal, turned to look into Allison's grinning porcelain face.

"What?" Michael asked, looking right at Allison and not seeing anything.

"I thought I felt a bug," Ally said weakly, her voice loud, trying to talk over Allison's falsetto.

"I'm right here, you don't have to shout," Michael said. Or at least that's what Ally assumed he said. Allison's voice was going through elaborate rises and falls of some song Ally never heard before in what she suspected was French. Maybe Italian. It was hard to tell, but it was definitely one of the operatic languages. And Allison was singing it like a born diva.

The noise was deafening, and Ally could no longer ignore it. She excused herself quickly and went into the filing room. The serenading followed her, and Ally snatched up her purse and ran for the bathroom, wondering how she could explain her behavior this time. Ally barely glanced around the bathroom to make sure no one was in there, and then whirled toward Allison.

"Shut up!" she shouted. Allison laughed.

"Temper, temper," Allison snickered, leaning against the counter.

"You stupid, annoying, mean…."

"Mean?!" Allison countered, hands on her hips. "I'm trying to help you, you ingrate. You wanted a more interesting life—you got one."

"You are not what I had in mind," Ally said.

"But I am more interesting—I'm the adventure you never had, the mystery you never got to solve, the perfect distraction from your life. You like having me here. Admit it."

"Like it? Like feeling insane? Hearing voices only I can hear, seeing things only I can see? Having sexual encounters orchestrated by a figment of my imagination?"

"Oh, you loved that, don't pretend you didn't. You're just sore because Mikey interrupted you."

"Michael," Ally automatically corrected.

"Whatever…I've tried being nice…"

"Nice!" Ally squealed. "Annoying, degrading, insanity-inducing—anything but nice!"

Ally fished through the bag until she found the bottle of Klonopin and a bottle of water. She didn't think, just shook some of her sister's pills out, swallowing them before Allison could react. Allison disappeared again, as silently as she arrived. Ally stood there, breathing hard, full of pent-up anger she had no release for. It made her want to cry. She went to the sink, splashed water over her hands just to have something to do. She took her time drying them, concentrating on breathing deeply, calming herself down. She finished the bottle of water and stared down at the bottle of pills. It was a desperate action, and she knew it. Misha said she took them for anxiety—maybe they would work on hallucinations too. Ally wasn't sure if the medication was what made Allison disappear, or what effect the pills would have on her. Probably the dosage wasn't right. She had no idea what the side effect would be.

She had never felt more reckless. Or more hopeless.

Michael was waiting for her outside the bathroom, arms crossed over his chest.

"Okay, what the hell is going on with you? And don't tell me nothing."

She stared at him, trapped between the bathroom door and his short-but-still-imposing frame. Ally wanted to run and hide back in the bathroom, but she suspected he would just follow her in there. Pulling self-consciously at her shirt, she stretched it out around herself, wishing she could stretch it so large she could just hide beneath it, disappear under the folds of stiff black fabric, and not have to face any of the soap opera her life had become. *A bad soap at that.*

She realized she had been standing there silently with her thoughts for too long. Michael shifted his weight impatiently.

"I'm having a bad day," she said, because it was the truth. "My mom…" She didn't continue. Michael pulled her into a tight hug.

"I wish you could just stop talking to her all together," he said into her hair. "She is just so toxic."

What Ally didn't say is that her mother and father were out of town, and while they might call Misha while on vacation, they wouldn't call Ally. In fact, Ally hadn't talked to her mother in almost two weeks. It had been really nice, actually.

"She really is," Ally said. *And she's not the only toxic voice I've been hearing.*

"Oh Ally. I wish you saw yourself the way I saw you. I wish you could give up this idea that you have to be perfect to be lovable. I have never not loved you."

She pushed him away. The contact was too much right then, made not crying too hard.

"You don't count. I mean, of course you do, but…"

"But what?"

Ally shrugged.

"But I don't feel it. Not right now. It's just a phase. I'll feel better, I really will. I have in the past. It's not that bad. Just a hard day."

Michael took a deep breath and let it out slowly. "Look, is there something else going on? Something you're not telling me?"

Ally started to say something, tried to say something. She just couldn't. *I'm hallucinating something who stepped out of my fantasies* is just not something she knew how to tell her best friend.

"It's just…low blood sugar," she said.

"Ally," he began, but she forced a grin on her face.

"I just need to figure some stuff out, okay? And to probably eat something. I'll call you later, okay? Have fun at lunch."

She pushed past him, and didn't give him a chance to say anything else.

Ally ran into Sandra on her way out, almost literally as she was careening down the stairs.

"Ally!" Sandra said. "What's the rush?"

"Uhh… errands," Ally said. "Michael's upstairs."

"You're not going to lunch with us?"

Ally shook her head.

"Are you okay?" Sandra asked.

"I'm not feeling well," Ally managed. "Plus I have things to take care of before my sister's party tonight."

Sandra didn't look like she was going to let Ally go with such a lame explanation, so Ally rushed on. "I really have to go. But I'll see you guys tomorrow."

Sandra stared at her a moment. Ally got the distinct impression that she wasn't looking at her so much as reading her.

"Are you sure you're it's not serious?" she asked, her green eyes dark with concern. "Maybe…."

"It's nothing, just a headache," Ally said, smiling big to prove she was okay. It hurt her to do so. Something about Sandra didn't look convinced. Ally took a few more steps down. "I really have to go now—see you later!" She waved and rushed the rest of away down. She didn't want to think about what Sandra might have seen in Ally to cause such concern in her eyes.

BaSIC TRaINING

The gray sky overhead had gotten darker, and the ash-laden sky seemed water-laden too, promising another wet Halloween. Ally looked up as she drove and remembered Halloweens past and how unfair it was that in a place where it supposedly never rained, the clouds always seemed to come in at the most inopportune times. It seemed every Halloween was a wet one, and every Fourth of July, and every time her family planned a rare camping trip, the clouds would gather.

The clouds above her had yet to unburden themselves of their soggy load, but the air, still clogged with the dying coughs of smoke the fires continued to hack out, was thick with the impending torrent.

She pulled her phone out of her purse and pushed Misha's picture until the phone rang. She put it on speaker, and after a few rings, her sister picked up.

"Hey Ally"

"Those pills, the ones for anxiety. What do they do?"

"I told you, they aren't the everyday ones. You can bring them tonight. No big deal."

"Yeah, but what do they do?"

"They help with anxiety."

"But what does that mean? Exactly?"

"Well, don't freak out. But they are basically benzos. Like, valium. They just sort of calm you down."

"What if you took a lot?"

"I don't. I know you probably think I do, but I don't!"

"I didn't think you did," Ally said, pulling up to a light and taking the moment to rub her hand over her face. "It's for work. A client. What would happen if he took a lot of pills?"

"He'd get high," Misha said. "It's why you gotta be careful with that stuff. And do not drink alcohol while on it. It can really fuck you up if you do."

"What kind of high?"

"Like…high. I don't know. Euphoric."

"How long does it take to kick in?"

"With food, maybe a half hour or so. Without, maybe faster. Why? Is it that kid with the sketches? What was his name?"

"Bobby," Ally said, surprised.

"Yeah. Is he okay?"

"Yeah. I mean, he had an incident…" Ally realized she'd already shared too much, broken confidentiality. "But yeah, he's fine."

"Good. I liked him."

"He's likable," Ally agreed. She wasn't sure what to say next.

"Misha, why do you take pills for anxiety?"

"Because they help. Actually, I've been meaning to talk to you about it. I was going to on Tuesday, when we went shopping, but you seemed like you were in a bad mood. I have been…dealing with some stuff."

Ally nodded. It's what Michael had told her, too.

"What kind of stuff?"

"I'm in a group. We talk about things. I'm not sure you want to hear about it."

"Why not?"

"Because, well. I don't know. Because you think my life is perfect. You think I'm perfect. But I don't. And I'm afraid if I try to talk to you about that kind of stuff it will just, like, piss you off."

Ally stopped at a red light and took a second to close her eyes.

"Misha, I'm sorry…"

"Look, it's no big deal. But maybe we can talk more later. At the party. Tonight. I am kinda in the middle of some stuff, decorating and all that."

"Yeah, sure. I'll see you tonight."

And then Misha hung up.

Ally opened her eyes in time to watch the light turn green, and drove forward.

I've been a real shitty sister. She took a deep breath and let it out slowly as she turned left at the corner. She shouldn't have taken the pills. There was a lot she was doing lately that she shouldn't be doing, like not paying attention to Misha, not telling Michael what was really wrong, not telling anyone about her panic attacks. Things had been wrong long before Allison showed up. Ally remembered the pills again. Thirty minutes. No food, high dosage, probably the pills would kick in sooner. Ally imagined that she could start to feel the effects already.

She should probably get food. That would help. And yet…

She didn't actually feel hungry. That might be a side effect. She should have asked Misha if that was a side effect.

But hey! No Allison. Ally felt good about that. She felt good in general, actually, and realized that if she was maybe starting to feel high she probably shouldn't keep driving.

Her automatic pilot had kicked in while she drove and she found herself pulling into the gym parking lot.

That would do.

Ally felt confident as she strode into the gym—today was the day she would put all her failed ambitions behind her. Today would be the first stop on her road trip to success. She would work out. She would lose weight. She would meet a nice, normal guy and fall in love. She would be a better sister and a better friend. And she would find a career that she enjoyed.

The giddiness was spreading.

Ally tripped in the doorway to the Women's section. She looked around self-consciously, and was surprised to see The Blondes were there. Spandex Lady too. Maybe everyone was working out early because of the holiday. She went sheepishly to a free treadmill next to Spandex Lady's. She tried smiling at the older woman, but Spandex Lady's concentration was on the book in front of her—*who could read and work out at the same time?*—so Ally turned her attention to her own treadmill's panel. It took some concentration. After all, she was high. Was she high? She managed to plug in the usual information and make the machine whirl to life.

She dredged up the memory of her one free personal trainer session, which was mercifully short and unmercifully with a young, hot man Ally'd been too embarrassed to question. He had said to warm up before hitting the weights, and then do cardio after, so that was Ally's plan—today, she would lift weights.

She programmed five minutes into the machine, and started walking, focusing her attention away from The Blondes, who kept looking at her and then whispering to each other, and onto the three screens hanging in front of her.

Screen one had, per usual, music videos, full of hard bodies, tight clothes, and little musical merit. Screen two had the news. Screen three showed one of those courtroom shows with "real litigants and real cases."

The five minutes passed fairly quickly, and feeling her confidence puff her up again, Ally floated over to the first of the weight machines and slid onto the seat. Start with the legs, Hot Trainer had said, so she put her legs on the pad and squeezed down. When nothing much happened, she lowered the weight and tried again. This time she could move her legs, and felt the pull in her upper thigh muscles. Quadriceps, she read. She counted ten reps, then moved on to the next machine, whose sticker told her she would be working her hamstrings. Ten of those and she went back to the other machine, then back to the hamstrings, and by this time her legs were feeling pretty tired. She remembered her resolve, and she made it to both machines three times. Two sets of ten, one last set of eight each. It was a good start.

She moved on to the thigh machines, finding them slightly easier, then on to a bicep/tricep combo that got her breathing hard, and then a chest press with a lat pull-down combo that she had to go really light on. After that, she hit two machines that worked different parts of her shoulders. By then she was sweating and had to spray down each machine after she used it with the towel and spray stuff the gym provided members. She wondered if the sweat had Klonopin in it, if she was sweating the pills out.

Finally, it was time to get back on the treadmill. Ally was already feeling tired, and had taken three trips to the drinking fountain already. She wished she had remembered to grab a water bottle. She had finished her water earlier in the day and forgotten to refill it after taking the pills. She set the treadmill for 30 minutes and watched it begin its countdown.

By minute twenty-five, her whole world had changed.

At minute twenty-six and thirty seconds, Ally was watching a clip from Glee and wishing she could be in a musical. Allison appeared at her side with a smile, and said simply, "As you wish."

Bowing, she stood in a dancer's starting position, and then started to sing. By minute twenty-five, Ally was positive that she had entered the twilight zone.

Because the entire gym was singing along with Allison.

✳

The first verse started slow, lyrics Ally had never heard before:

"You've been sad and blue for such a long while,

Your life lacking things to make you smile.

You think you've found the cure for it all

You jog and sweat to make yourself small..."

Allison leaned against the stationary bike a brunette was using, her perfectly highlighted head next to the overly-streaked one, and sang out, "To be thin." *Definitely not a real song*, Ally noted.

Allison had sung before, so Ally wasn't all that impressed. However, she was hearing voices again, and that got her attention, because this was a new one—whispered, possibly male, and panicked.

"Stop her," it said. It said something else too, but Ally couldn't make it out—something about bake, cake, steak....she couldn't quite catch the word. As she strained to hear the whisper, her head tilted to the side. And then an unseen orchestra swelled up in slow strands of sweet harmony that went with Allison's sweeter voice. This too was new. Allison had never had an orchestra before. The apparition sang out again.

"To be thin."

Another woman turned her head to look directly at Ally and repeated the refrain.

"To be thin."

Ally began to panic.

The orchestra repeated the melody again as Allison and the brunette gave Ally identical big-eyed sympathy stares, and then switched gears as Allison twirled away from the bike, the pace suddenly more upbeat, more big-band style playing along with the musical scoring of the strings. Allison leaned back against one of the machines—for biceps, Ally remembered—in a perfect Doris Day pose.

The two Blondes leapt down from their respective machines and moved in rehearsed synchronicity toward different machines behind Allison.

"A set of ten, and I do it again, every day the same routine," Blonde One sang out as she worked. "Buns of steel, and salad every meal, anything to keep myself lean.

"To be thin," she sang.

"To be thin," Allison and the other Blonde echoed.

And, an echo only Ally seemed to hear:

"Stop her."

It was too much. Singing, whispered voices... Ally jumped off her treadmill.

As she tried to go to the door, Blonde One and Blonde Two strode forward, grabbed her arms and led her back to Allison, the three of them forming a moving triangle around her. They sang together as they walked.

"We pay a price, how we sacrifice, to keep up the shape that we're in.

If you only knew, you'd work hard too, it's just so great to be thin."

As they moved through an intricate routine, to an unseen

accompaniment, with a vision of herself that Ally knew had not, until now, been seen, she realized that there really was no logical explanation for what had been happening to her. And so, instead of finding the nearest wall to thud her head up against while drooling, Ally felt herself swaying ever so slightly with the music, humming along with the refrain, "to be thin," and envying The Blondes and Allison their graceful movements. Her distraction was so complete, she momentarily forgot the whispered voice.

The show went on.

Allison moved across the floor now, picking up her own verse as The Blondes danced back-up for her.

"You've dreamed the dream, torn at the seam, of a world you could never know.

Too little too late, to change your fate, just sit back and enjoy the show.

All that you thought, for all that you've fought, there's no way you're going to win.

You haven't a clue, how we're better than you, wonderfully happy to be thin."

And the three women posed, a Charlie's Angel tableau of thin sexiness, Blonde One showing off her arms, Blonde Two showing off her legs, and Allison showing off her whole body in a position any pin-up would have envied.

"Stop..." the voice crackled again.

Ally shook her head. She didn't want this—the musical, the voice, any of it. Again, she tried to leave.

But the music swelled up, and Allison grabbed Ally, whisking her away to the main gym. Lights rotated all around her, switching colors as they orbited the room. Blue to green, red to yellow, purple to pink. Ally turned in a circle, taking in the gym. Nothing looked the same. The equipment seemed to move all around her as though on wheels, and the people working out on the machines intensely pumped and pushed in time to the music, which was building itself up, faster, louder, more rock-edged. Ally spun all the way around, ending up face to face with Allison, who grinned at her.

"You catching on yet?" she asked playfully. "Or do you want to know what you're really missing?"

Allison took her hand, and the music sped up even more as Allison led Ally around the gym.

A group of women wearing belly-baring shirts and low-riding shorts were writhing en masse, running their hands over their perfectly flat, tight stomachs.

"Oh, it feels so good, to be thin," they sang. "Feels so good, should be a sin."

Again Ally was drawn away. "Stop her," she heard again.

Ally's panic was quickly turning to frustration. There were too many things happening, too much noise, too many lights, and a growing uneasiness gnawing up her spine every time she heard the voice. Stop who? Allison? From singing? From what? Plus, was this musical number ever going to end?

The music blared out faster and faster, and people flew by in a whirlwind of motion, doing pull ups, doing crunches, on the stairmaster, on the bike, all sweating, all smiling, all sexual, all thin.

Out of nowhere, he was there, standing in front of her, dressed in black slacks and a white shirt, the top buttons lose and showing his chest. The music stopped at the same time Ally's heart did, and everything around them grew dark. The light froze on them, a gentle glow illuminating from above.

Tom smiled at her as the room spun around them. And slowly, like the trickle of a stream over rocks, the music began again. And he sang.

"All you've ever wanted, all you've ever dreamed. All you ever fought for, all you ever schemed. It's all been just another fantasy. It's all been just a way for you to be...."

His voice was low, dark and thick like devil's food cake. He stepped closer, so close she could feel his breath against her.

"Anything and anyone but you. And there's only one thing that can make your dreams come true...."

Allison appeared next to him, draped herself over his side, his arm wrapping around her waist.

Ally felt an urge to tear the perfect version of herself away from the perfect version of her fantasy man, but couldn't move.

Allison and Tom smiled at each other, and then Allison faced Ally, and sang out, pronouncing each word like its own fog horn, holding the last note out, loud and long, a diva's power chord:

"To. Be. Thin!"

And slowly, the faucet was turned up, the water flowing fuller, faster, cascading down to crushing notes.

Tom and Allison began to dance to it.

He pulled her close to him, let her spin away. In unison, Ginger Rogers and Gene Kelley, they moved away from Ally, and all the lights came up, filling the gym. Ally looked around and everyone was coupled up, hot-body to hot-body, and they were all dancing, big-band style to go with the music.

Ally felt very conscious of the fact that she didn't have a dance partner, that she was the only audience to this entire spectacle. More than that, she was overly aware of how nicely Tom and Allison moved together, how great a couple they could be.

And then there, at the corner of her vision. Just a flash, a shadow really, and already lost to the light…someone, or something, alone. Ally tried to head toward it, but the lights shone in her eyes, the sound filled up her ears. Suddenly hands were pulling her away, into the dance. She found herself kicking and twisting, her body taken over by the music and the people around her. She was twirled, swung, dipped, and passed so quickly from partner to partner she couldn't tell if they were male or female, let alone what they looked like. And then, again, Allison and Tom were in front of her.

They danced side by side, holding hands. Tom pulled Allison around into a dip, picked her up out of it, and placed her on the other side of him. She leaned in and they pressed their cheeks together, facing Ally.

"Oh, it's even better than you could ever imagine it to be," Allison sang.

"You get lots of attention from guys that look like me," Tom joined in.

Dancers moved in all around them, and the music kept building, and Ally realized she was in for the big finish any moment now. She held her breath.

"You're the most beautiful thing that I have ever laid my eyes on," sang Tom, looking at Allison. "I'm enthralled, I'm so charmed, man I'm totally gone."

And then Allison was pushed forward, everyone moving to make her the center of a half circle, Tom right behind her.

"I've got the world on a string, and I give it a spin…" she sang, another note held out for everyone to admire, the unseen orchestra falling away to silence beneath it. The music came back with Allison's words, and she teased them toward the end of the song.

"All you want to be," and the whole gym moved forward with Allison's steps. Ally backed away from her, from all of them. "All you've longed to be," and Allison came forward again, and again, Ally stepped back. "What you so envy," she sang, the music rising up with her voice, "to be just like me…" and everyone moved around to their final poses, showing off an Olympic array of hard bodies. "Oh to be better than you've ever been…" and one last musical pause as Allison and the whole gym seemed to take a breath. She let it out with her final words, drawing them out and up:

"To be thin!" The orchestra pulled out all the stops, the drums, the symbols, all leading to the last "da da daaaaa!" and the last sound of Allison's held-out note.

Allison tossed her hands up and the music ended with it.

And then they were all gone.

Ally blinked, and stared confusedly around her. She was standing in the middle of the gym floor. The gym had less people in it than the musical, but what people were there were just working out, like normal. The overhead speakers played some alternative rock that involved a lot of screaming and shouting.

And Ally was alone.

The change was so swift, and so dramatic, that she felt her knees crumble beneath her. She fell hard on them, fighting the urge to cry. She knew now. Understood. Her life was no longer her own.

IN THIS WEEK'S EPISODE...

"Work a little too hard?" someone, a male someone, asked Ally, and she looked up. Maybe the voice in her head had been his? He was pleasantly round faced, and his front teeth were crooked. He showed them when he smiled, which was what he was doing now.

But with concern.

"Did you say something?" she asked.

The concern deepened. "I, uh, just asked if you maybe worked too hard? Are you okay?"

She could see it in his eyes, the worried crease between them speaking for him.

"I'm okay," she said suddenly, and pulled back her lips in what she hoped might pass for a smile.

In his current state of near desperation, the round-faced man accepted her flash of teeth as a sign that she, as she said, was just fine.

"Just stretching," she added, because she felt she needed a reason to be on the floor. He nodded, smiled, and she could see he didn't believe her.

Ally got to her feet, trying very hard not to shake. The man seemed ready to catch her if she fell, and that was some small comfort, but he looked too weak to actually be able to, which made her legs find enough strength to pull herself together and stand by herself. She flashed her teeth at him again, knowing it looked more like a grimace than a smile, and not caring.

"I think I've had enough for the day," she said, and tried to put some false-cheer in her voice. Again, because it was the thing to do, he accepted what she offered.

"Yeah, maybe it's time to call it quits." He seemed relieved he didn't have to persuade her of the fact.

She wished she didn't think he was right.

She took a breath, put one foot out to test herself and then slowly shifted her weight to it. She half expected to fall, or to float, or to hear more singing, and when seconds passed without any of those things happening, she took another step, then another, like a foal finding her legs. Round Face smiled more encouragement.

"There you go," he said, and if Ally had had any energy left to blush with, she would have. It was taking everything she had to play this game of normal, and so she just made a vague nodding motion, and concentrated on her feet. She should be mortified to have someone give her his best sympathy stare, but then, she should be able to go to the gym without it turning into Hello Dolly too. Things weren't going the way they should go.

She kept walking, and Round Face hovered near her, a fearful mother following a toddler. Ally made her way back toward the women's locker room, and Round Face faltered, not wanting to let her out of his sight, but not able to follow her either.

"I'm okay," Ally said with more conviction than she felt. "I feel much better now. I'm just going to grab my stuff and head home. I live real close, not a long drive or anything."

His eyes creased again, his face as readable as before so she smiled at him again, this time able to make it feel more natural, and gave a little wave as she headed into the locker room.

She felt much better once there was a door between her and Round Face's concerned eyes. She sat on one of the benches by the lockers, her legs happy to give up their burden. She leaned her head back against the wall behind her and closed her eyes.

After all the dramatics, she had to admit that insanity didn't feel much different than anything else. Her heart still beat more or less steadily in her chest, and her lungs still took in and blew out air. Ally looked at her hands and saw that the palms were still lined, the tops still freckled. She touched them to her face and felt all her familiar features. There was no outward sign to show that she had snapped the thin line between sanity and insanity. There probably would be no way for anyone to know how crazy she had become, if she could manage to keep her "episodes" in check.

Ally decided that's what the musical was. She'd had an episode. That's what they called them at the center when patients would have outbursts of emotion and start yelling or breaking things. Some patients could track their progress by having less episodes in a week than the one before it. If an episode got bad enough, there was a special room doctors could take them to. It wasn't padded or anything, but it didn't have anything terribly breakable in it and the kids could lose control as violently as they needed to.

She wondered if anyone else witnessed dancing and singing in their episodes.

"Stop her," she whispered to herself. She wondered briefly if she had imagined the voice. *Any more than she had been imagining Allison?* She shook her head. She could either question everything, or nothing. Trying to figure out what was real and what wasn't…she wasn't capable of that right now. She was, after all, officially insane.

No. Not insane. She felt that, deep down. This was beyond anything she had read about hallucinations. This was beyond anything she had read about anything. She had actually changed locations. And sure, maybe she was high, maybe that was part of it.

But the voice, the second voice. It was too real, too….scared.

It had to be something. Allison had to be something, something real, something Ally could fight.

You made me. Okay, so then there had to be a way to unmake her.

Okay, think back. She tried to rewind the events of the last few days, and ended up back in her bathtub. She had wished to see the most perfect version of herself, and then she had.

But that wasn't it. She had tried reversing the wish and it didn't work. This was not a fantasy caused by a wish, there had to be something else—and there was, just before, a vague image, a slippery memory, something silvery....

A loud knock on the door interrupted her thoughts, and Ally squinched her eyes up.

"Hello?" she called out, confused why anyone would knock. The door wasn't locked. It was an open locker room.

A male voice called through the door. "Everything okay?"

Ally did a mental head slap. Round Face! She had told him she was just getting her stuff and coming right back out. His face was probably all squished up with the uncertainty of entering no-man's land or just walking away. The knock had probably been his compromise.

"Everything's great!" she called out to him. And, having rested and adjusted to her new status as an insane person, Ally did really feel that things might end up being okay, eventually. *A long eventually that would probably require many years of therapy.*

I was just stretching? Had she really said that? And now this poor man was worrying himself sick over her. She got up quickly, grabbed her things from her locker and headed out the door.

The causes of her insanity would just have to wait.

In her car, Ally had time to contemplate her problem more

fully. Her cell phone sang a song on her drive back to her apartment, but she ignored it, frustrated. She didn't need another distraction right now. What she needed, she decided, passing a sign and quickly merging into the right lane to make a last minute turn into a parking lot, was food. She pulled up to the Taco Bell drive-thru speaker and managed to spend eight bucks on a single order. Probably she didn't need the Mexi-fries, Mexican pizza, taco and a burrito, and most definitely she should have ordered a diet drink. If she was going to be insane anyway, she might as well stay fat. And suddenly, Ally felt starved. The pills were likely out of her system by now. Or else, making her hungry.

She drove home quickly, eating the Mexi-fries on the way. Then she took her things up to her apartment and sat on the couch, sipping at her drink furiously and opening the pizza. Finally, her mad eating rush subsided, and she pulled back from the coffee table and flopped back on the couch cushions.

"Hungry much?" asked a voice to the side of her, and it was a symptom of the state Ally was in that she didn't even flinch.

"Did you want something, or are you just here to pester me?"

"I don't pester—" Allison started to say, but Ally cut her off.

"Save it. I don't have time for you right now."

And with that Ally got up and headed for the bathroom.

Allison was waiting in it for her. "What's with the attitude?" she demanded, one hand on her perfect hip.

Ally sighed. She turned to Allison, and spoke with a tone reserved for impertinent toddlers. "I have to get ready for Misha's party. Can we go over all the ways you are superior to me later?"

"I don't get you," Allison said. "Defensive and depressed at the same time. And clueless too."

Ally shook her head. She didn't feel clueless anymore—in

fact, she felt as though she had just finally gotten a clue—the biggest of all. Her reality wasn't something she could trust anymore. What was there left to be afraid of?

"Allison," she said. She smiled coldly at the ghost. "Tonight is my little sister's Halloween party, and I have to be there at six to get dressed in some godmother costume I have never seen and probably won't fit me and then cavort with all her beautiful friends while I try to avoid the chips and dip. Don't you think that is enough torture for a night? Don't you think you can, I don't know, find something else to do? Brush your hair a hundred times, file your nails, bathe in virgins' blood maybe?"

Allison did not look amused.

"Why don't you go work on your next musical number then—I think you have real Broadway potential."

Ally turned her back on the ghost. She wavered for a moment before taking off her shirt, and then, with a shrug, stripped naked. What was the point of caring anymore, anyway?

"So I take it you don't want to go to the party tonight," Allison said.

"Wow, you know me so well—it's almost like you are a part of me. But separate. Me, but not me." She smiled sweetly at Allison and stepped into the shower.

"Okay wise-ass, I get that you're upset. I don't get why you're upset with me."

Ally leaned around the shower door to stare at Allison. She opened her mouth, and then shut it decisively. There was no point. There. Was. No. Point.

She turned on the water.

"So now you're going to ignore me?"

Ally didn't say anything since that was exactly what she was doing.

"I can help you."

Ally ignored that too and pulled the plastic door closed behind her with a whack.

And then Allison was in the shower with her.

"What the hell!" Ally said, pulling back against the wall, looking at Allison through the cascade of water. Allison was, of course, naked.

She shook her mass of reddish curls, curls that the water had failed to frizz out. "I can help you."

"So you keep saying," Ally said

"You'll see," Allison said. And then there was just the water, the steam, and Ally.

Ally washed, dressed in black jeans and a black shirt, her costume alternative when the fairy godmother one didn't fit, and scrounged in the kitchen for a glass of milk and a few cookies, taking them with her to the dining room table.

The furniture in Ally's apartment was mostly hand-me-downs and bargain specials. The entertainment center was a chipped black lacquer from her aunt and uncle, her coffee table was from an Ikea sale, and her end tables used to be in her parents. Her dining room table was new—the one new purchase she made for the apartment. It had a glass top supported by metal curved legs that matched the chairs that came with it. Ally ran her hands over the smoothness of the cool glass and wondered what on earth she was thinking when she bought it. The table was too modern, too stylish for the rest of her apartment.

It didn't surprise her when Allison suddenly appeared on the other side of it, casually running her hands along the edge of the glass. She felt like nothing could surprise her, anymore.

"I agree," she said to Ally, and Ally nodded at her. "It doesn't fit you. But it suits me just fine." She smiled.

"You're not going to sing a song about it, are you?" Ally asked. "Another hit from the Hallucination Hussy?"

"I keep telling you—I'm not a hallucination." Allison crossed her hands over her perfect chest with perfect irritation. "Not a ghost, not a dream—not anything you can name or label or anything else."

"Then what?" Ally asked, leaning forward, her elbows on the table. She liked the feel of her chin digging into her hands, reminding her that she was alive, and real. Even if she didn't feel real, her chin did.

Allison leaned back in her chair.

"You really want to know?"

"I want to know how the entire gym got involved in my fantasy if it wasn't a hallucination. And I want to know how come I didn't wake up where I started to daydream, and I want to know what more is going to happen to me. And to you. Yes, I really want to know."

Ally stared at Allison, a steady stare, a calm stare, and Allison stared unflinchingly back. She didn't even blink, and so Ally tried very hard not to either.

"I am you," Allison said at last. "I am a part of you—the best part of you—realized, made real. By you."

Ally leaned back against her chair, pulled her knee up to her chest, rest her chin on it. "Bullshit," she said.

Allison laughed. "I didn't think you would understand. I'll try to explain it anyway. You created me."

"You keep saying that," Ally agreed.

"Because it's true. You created me to be the perfect version of you. To be, as you would say, all your potential realized. I am you, as you see yourself capable of being, but only in your dreams. In your daydreams you can transform into me, become me at any time. Thus, as I am you, you are me."

Ally blinked at Allison. "O-kay…" she said at last, slowly, drawing the word out. "We're the same person."

"No—we're made from the same person, but we are, as you can see, two separate people." Allison gestured to Ally, sitting hunched into herself on her chair, and then back to herself, sitting gracefully displayed on hers.

"Is this like that episode of Buffy where that thing shot Xander and he became two people—the good him and the goofy him—and if you killed one you would kill the other?" From Allison's look Ally could tell that her fantasy self didn't watch TV, and didn't have much tolerance for people that did. "There was an X-files episode kind of like that, only it ended up being a shape-shifter," she added, just to annoy Allison, and was pleased to see the crease between Allison's eyes that proved she did.

"Like I said, this is unlike anything you have ever heard of. I am unlike anything you have ever heard of."

"But you're me. I've heard of me." Ally was getting a perverse pleasure from making this explanation as difficult for Allison as possible. The perfect version of herself was getting perfectly irked.

"Look, it's all mysterious and shit, okay? It's supposed to be—I can't explain it to you."

"You can't or you won't? Or you just really suck at explanations?"

Allison stood up and in a display of temper, paced across the dining room.

"Look Fatty, I don't know what little game it is you think you're playing, or where the sudden appearance of your spine came from, but I'm here to tell you it's too little, too late. It's done, okay? This ball is rolling and there isn't a damn thing you can do to stop it."

Ally stared up at Allison, the memory of that voice floating in her head. *Stop her.*

"Too late to stop what?" she asked quietly.

And Allison grinned. "You always wanted to be me," she said lightly. "Well, now you're going to be able to."

Ally shook her head, confused. "I'm going to turn into you?" she asked.

Allison tilted her head to the side, her hair cascading nicely down her shoulder. "In a way. As far as your friends will think, or at least, all the people around you anyway, you will have become me. But, actually, all that will really happen is that we'll switch."

"Switch what?"

"Lives," Allison said, opening her arms, gently letting her hands point to the sides as though gesturing to the fabric that made up the room, the apartment, the universe.

"Lives," Ally repeated. "But you don't have a life—you're just a fantasy."

"Hole in one," Allison said. "And that's what you will become—a fantasy."

Ally shook her head. "I'm a real person," she said. "I can't become a fantasy. People know me. I'm going to a party right now at my real-life sister's, who is my real-life flesh and blood. She'll wonder if I just disappear and you show up saying that you're me. No one changes that much that fast."

"But they won't see a change. Just as no one but you saw the little musical performance I gave earlier, no one will notice that you are not how you have always been."

"You'll look like me?" Ally asked, wondering if in the bargain she would get to look like Allison, and wondering also if Allison would have as much trouble losing weight as she did.

"No," Allison said derisively. "I will look like me but they will think that I am you. That is, they will think that you have always been thin, and beautiful, and successful."

"I don't see how people would not know something changed."

"I can show you. We can do a trial run, tonight, at the party."

Allison's eyes lit up and the look in them made Ally feel wary. Her hair, still wet, stuck to the sides of her face, and she brushed it away. This sounded dangerous. But it also sounded like her best chance to understand better what was happening, and what it was she was supposed to stop. "How will I see?"

"Just as I can be here and only you can see me, so you can go with me to the party, and no one will see you. You will be able to watch, unobserved yourself, how everyone reacts to me—to Misha's prettier, sexier, more successful sister."

"I still don't understand," Ally said. "All our lives she has been the prettier one—the golden child. You can't suddenly change that."

Allison smiled. "I think you'll be amazed to know just how easily what you think of as reality can be altered. Just say yes, Ally, and you'll be able to see, to understand. And better yet, you won't have to go to the party."

Ally nodded slowly. A trial run. A chance to understand.

"But just for tonight," she said. "I want my body back when all this is over."

"Really?" Allison said incredulously, looking Ally up and down.

"Really," she said firmly. But even as she said it, she felt her own soft flesh soften her firm resolve.

OH MICKEY, YOU'RE SO FINE

Allison made Ally drive to the party. She told Ally that she was not quite sure how long the exchange would last, and she didn't want to waste time en route. Ally kept glancing in her direction, wondering about her. Why wouldn't Allison know how long the trade-off would go? Why did she seem nervous? Was Allison really able to "take over" as she had said? Maybe she was bluffing. Maybe she wasn't as sure as she seemed. Maybe there was still a chance to stop her.

The sky had finally let go of its burden and was happily making lakes and ponds of the roads, pissing off trick-or-treaters everywhere. Some determined candy-gatherers had their parents follow them around with umbrellas rescued from the backs of closets, and Ally passed them as they huddled together against the weather. She envied the children their futures—the parents their reason for staying in the here and now.

The present is a gift. Ally found the phrase running through her head, but couldn't place its source. Yesterday was a gift she wanted to return. Tomorrow was a gift she hadn't registered for. She didn't know if she would get a day after tomorrow, the way things with Allison were going.

She looked over at the hallucination/fantasy/ghost sitting quietly on her side of the car, a small smile bending her lips upward in an evil arc—or maybe Ally was just imagining it. Allison did seem pleased, if a little anxious. Ally wasn't sure what she felt herself. She turned her attention back to the trick-or-treaters, people having happier thoughts than her own.

Misha lived in a large two-story house up in the richer part of Santa Clarita, Stevenson Ranch, one of a series of properties that one of Misha's rich friend's parents' owned. The friend in question went to Cal Arts, the prestigious arts school in Valencia, and his parents bought the house for him to stay in. He rented out rooms for a very reasonable rate, not having to pay the mortgage himself. Misha and three others lived with him, Real World style—there were constant parties, drama, and messes.

As they pulled up to the house, Ally almost turned the car around. The entire place was decorated for Halloween in a hap-hazard way—webs, ghost lights, paper cutouts, and huge, blow-up versions of Frankenstein, a pumpkin and a ghost. They'd planned to outdo all the neighbors, not with creativity, but with sheer volume of decoration. Every type of Halloween thing that could be put in the yard had been placed there, none of it coming together in any kind of theme—scary ghosts and friendly ghosts swung from the trees. Evil witches and childlike witches stared out from windows. The yard was a mish-mash of decorations, not sure if it wanted to intimidate, amuse, or just confuse people passing by.

Ally could see Allison eyeing the house with disgust.

"And you are intimidated by the people who decorate like that?" Allison scoffed.

Ally shrugged. Today she wasn't intimidated by anything. Nothing was real anymore. Everything was real. She was operating with new rules.

"So now what?"

"Give me a moment," Allison snapped. She closed her eyes and seemed to concentrate very hard. Ally watched closely, waiting for something dramatic to happen. There was a slight shimmer around Allison, so faint Ally wasn't sure she was actually seeing it. It was silvery blue, and reminded Ally of the lake. And the lake reminded her, oddly, of the voice she had heard in the gym. "Stop her." Now that it was too late to stop whatever she was supposed to stop, she felt something pass through her, and felt her stomach drop out from under her, her head spin slightly. She looked up at Allison and shook her head, confused. Something wasn't right. The perspective was…wrong. And then Ally realized that they had switched spots in the car. Allison was now sitting on the driver's side and looking more solid than Ally herself had ever felt. Allison was wearing what Ally had been, only different. Her black jeans were skin tight, her black shirt low cut.

Ally was surprised. Somehow she thought that the clothes would be too big, that they would be Ally's clothes. She looked down at herself and saw the outfit she was wearing before. As Allison kept saying, she was the same, but different. Ally took another look at Allison and was surprised again by how small Allison looked. Tall, sure, but so thin, and shrunken looking, like there was hardly anything to her. She was actress-sized, and away from the big or small screen, looked too frail for real life.

And Ally…Ally felt hollow and scared. She looked down at her body, and though it looked real enough, she felt as see-through as she assumed she now was. Allison turned and smiled at her.

"Ready to see how the other half live?"

Ally had to turn away from the gleam in Allison's eyes as she nodded.

Allison swept from the car, tossing her radiant curls over her shoulder, excited energy flying off the ends of each strand. Ally wasn't sure how the rules of her new status worked, and she stared at the door handle apprehensively. She realized she probably couldn't turn it, that her hand probably would go through it, and she felt the panic that can only come from realizing you are a ghost. If her heart could beat, it would have. When she actually did feel it beat, Ally was confused. *Like a ghost,* she mentally reclassified herself. It was still incredibly unnerving. But she also realized that if she still had a heartbeat, Allison probably had one in her ghost-like form as well. Things with heartbeats were alive. Which meant they could be killed.

"Just think yourself out of the car," Allison commanded, turning back to her, clearly annoyed. "That's how I go from place to place—I think of the place I want to be, and then I'm there. Like a dream," she added.

Like a dream. Ally thought herself outside of the car, and, quicker than a blink, was there. Just like how moments change in a dream, she decided, and filed that in the "things I know about Allison" file.

Ally was able to walk to the door with Allison and was thankful she didn't have to think herself inside. Misha answered the door, wearing an Arabian princess costume, all in red, and smiled out at Allison.

Ally was shocked by the sight. Her sister, naturally thin, had become skeletal. Her shoulders jutted like a coat hanger, and her normally perky breasts were non-existent, even with a push-up bra trying its best to make mountains out of the tiniest of mole hills. Her color was off—her hair was limp. *Anorexic,* Ally realized. Suddenly she remembered that Misha wanted to talk to her about something at the party and wondered if this was it. *Anxiety pills, a group. Maybe Misha was fighting an eating disorder in both realities.* If so, she was losing the battle in this one, and Ally felt ashamed that she had agreed to the trade-off, and wasn't there to talk to her sister. She vowed she would make it right when she got back to her real body, her real life.

"Ally!" Misha cried, and Ally was startled to hear this new version of her sister call Allison by her own nickname.

"Come on now, Mickey," Allison said. "You know I hate being called that." Misha smiled shyly, a self-conscious look that the Misha Ally knew would never have had.

"Sorry, old habits die hard. Just like how you're the only one who calls me Mickey," she said. *I would never call her Mickey. Misha suits her so much better.* It was almost easier to think of this new Misha as Mickey, as someone different. This was not her sister. This couldn't be her sister. She wouldn't have let her sister become a shrunken-in shadow like this.

As Ally worked her best denial skills, Allison glided into the house, and Ally had to scuttle through the door so that she wouldn't have to think herself through it.

As thin as Allison was, Misha almost made her look thick by comparison. Ally had to look away and gazed around the house instead. Misha and her roommates had decorated the inside of the house as garishly as the outside. It was as though they had bought out a small party-store's supply of Halloween items. Ghosts, skeletons, witches, black cats, mummies, Frankensteins, vampires and any other scary things that could be pasted to a wall, hung from the ceiling, or put on a table were scattered overwhelmingly throughout the room. And then someone had come along and covered each item with fake spider web, fake spiders crawling over almost every surface.

There was also food everywhere—chips, chocolate, cheese and crackers, all arranged on holiday platters and trays so that anywhere you stood in the room you were within arm's reach of some sort of snack.

"Allison," she whispered, trying to get the fantasy-girl's attention "This isn't real, is it?"

Allison ignored her and was taking in the house and decorations with a humoring air. Ally took Allison in with a suspicious glare. "What have you done to my sister?" she asked. Allison didn't even allow her eyes to flicker Ally's way, and turned her attention onto the incredibly-small Misha.

"Mickey, everything looks great!" Allison said, lying through her pearly whites. Misha beamed under the praise, and excitedly pointed out which parts of the Halloween explosion she was responsible for. Ally felt like crying, watching her sister's emaciated frame bounce around like an eager puppy trying to please her owner.

"The spider webs were my idea," she said proudly.

"The perfect touch," Allison said, smiling. Ally wanted to scratch the smile from Allison's face.

"This is Julie," Misha said then, and Ally had to blink again— Julie of the costume donation. Julie was Ally's size, if not larger, and Ally had to wonder if it was Allison's influence that made Misha have a plus-sized friend, or if this was the real Julie.

Julie put her hand out awkwardly and Allison took it as though it were a dead fish.

"Nice to meet you," she said in a way that took all the niceness from the phrase.

"Yeah, you too," Julie said self-consciously.

"Julie is my friend from school," offered Misha. "And hers is the costume you'll be wearing."

Allison looked Julie over, taking in her butter rolls and thunder thighs. Ally could hear the judgment as harshly as though it were aimed at her. And it had been, many times before.

"It's my sister's costume, actually," Julie said quickly, and Ally couldn't help but think this was a new addition to this reality, the reality of a thinner Allyson Smart, and terrifyingly skinny Michelle Smart.

"I'm sure it'll be great," Allison said. Misha stepped forward then and took Allison's arm. It was getting more and more painful for Ally to look at her little sister. As the shock of Misha's appearance wore off, Ally's anger was beginning to grow.

"Come on, I'll show the costume to you," Misha said, leading Allison toward her own bedroom. Allison stayed close to Misha in a cozy, almost intimate way. It was false, and cold. And again, Ally felt her rage build up.

Misha's room was full of black cat decorations: paper black cats on the walls, porcelain black cats on the dresser, stuffed black cats on the side tables and bed. One of the stuffed cats turned its head and Ally nearly screamed.

Misha's cat Mort did not look happy.

"The fairy godmother," Misha said, pulling the plastic draped costume out of her closet. "You're sure you don't mind being her? Everyone else already picked and…"

Ally realized how nervous Misha was. Suddenly it occurred to her that it would be extremely hard to live with perfection as an older sister. It was hard enough to have near-perfection as a younger sister, but with Allison around all the time, picking on Misha, offering all those cruelly-helpful tips like she'd been offering Ally—it was no wonder this reality's Misha was sickly thin. It would have been like having two versions of their mother, with one of them young enough to be around Misha all the time. Ally shuddered.

Allison took the costume and smiled, her teeth glinting like the Candyman's.

"No, I think I will really like being a fairy Godmother," she said, and there was almost a sinister sound to her voice. Ally was suddenly reminded more of the evil queen from fairytales instead of the fairy godmother. What new curse was Allison going to "gift" Misha with? Hadn't this new Misha suffered enough already?

A low growl came from the bed, and Ally realized that Mort didn't like Allison's tone either. In fact, the cat was standing now, his back arched and mouth hissing. He was mimicking the cut-outs on the wall but the reality was much more menacing than the cardboard could ever be. Mort seemed to grow three sizes as he glowered at Allison.

"Mort!" Misha said, and swept the cat up into her arms. "I don't know why he always gets weird around you," Misha said, apologizing. "I'll put him in Alex's room and let you change in peace." She left the room, trying to shush the still yowling cat, and closed the door behind her.

Misha's cat loved Ally in her reality, but couldn't stand Allison. It was another interesting tidbit.

"Allison," Ally tried again, but again she was ignored. So Ally settled for warily watching the former-ghost instead. The panic was rising in Ally's throat, and she had to keep telling herself that this was a trial run only and that she was going to be able to get back to her reality to make this right…somehow. She had to find a way…

In the meantime, Allison changed quickly into the costume Misha had given her, but in doing so she seemed to change the costume as well. Allison's version of a fairy godmother was not the matronly version Ally had pictured, but the sexy knock-off version. The corset waist was cinched so tight it came in like the neck of a vase. The corset had also contributed to Allison's already impressive cleavage. The skirt of the dress was shorter than custom dictated, and Ally was almost positive it shouldn't have slits down either side.

"What're the slits for?" Ally asked, almost surprised by her own voice.

"So I can dance," Allison said, rolling her eyes in a "duh" fashion, and Ally was more surprised by the response than anything before.

"About Misha," she started, but Allison waved her off.

"Mickey looks fine. You worry too much." And with that dismissive comment, she admired herself in Misha's full-length mirror.

The color of the outfit was appropriately pink and blue, and there was a bow pinned just under all that cleavage, little shimmery wings attached to her back, and a wand trailing glitterized ribbons. Allison's hair was up in an almost-matronly bun, though Ally didn't actually see her put it up. Strategic hair tendrils had been allowed to escape and brush against her long, pale neck. And there was a bow in her hair as well, matching the one on her dress.

She looked like Playboy's version of a fairytale character.

Ally looked down at herself, surprised to see a version of the costume where her jeans had been—her costume looked as she imagined the original had before Allison's alterations. The skirt was long and billowy, the corset more generous, although it still hitched her cleavage up to a surprising height which made Ally a little uncomfortable but also somewhat impressed. Actually, the plus-sized version was way better than she would have imagined. She actually liked the way she looked in it.

Ally shook her head. "I don't understand."

"We've already established how wanting you are in that department," Allison responded.

"She's going to know that's not the costume she gave you."

"She will know what I want her to know," Allison countered. "Bibbidi-bobbidi-boo," she said, waving her wand around gleefully. "Let's go in to the party!"

Almost as soon as Allison emerged from the hallway, Misha's friends gathered around her, oohing and ahhing about her outfit. Alex, the spoiled homeowner, was the only one still able to act cool in the presence of such perfection.

For a moment, Ally got caught up in just how much attention Allison was getting. The kind of attention Ally always assumed she wanted. The boys at the party made room for her, did their best to show off in front of her. The girls circled around trying to find a way into the group to get closer to her. Then Ally saw that the dance to win Allison's favor was one of stumbling insecurity. No one seemed comfortable, or all that happy. Except for Allison.

Alex, dressed as Tarzan and raised in the kind of confidence wealth and good looks breeds, managed to play it cool and looked almost bored with Allison's presence. A pack of skinny blondes and brunettes—a Pixie Fairy, a Red Riding Hood, and a Mary, of the little lamb variety—were almost able to keep up with battle of one-upmanship Allison was waging. Misha, the usual center of a group like this, was struggling.

"So, what kind of music do we have?" Allison asked, sweeping over to the computer and the playlists displayed there.

"Every kind," Alex said, and smiled.

"I made some party playlists," Misha said, clicking on one. The first song was Thriller, and she looked at Allison expectantly. The way she wilted under Allison's indifferent smile was heart-breaking—what had happened to Ally's sister?

"Nice," Allison said dismissively.

"I have others," Misha said, scrolling through the webpage.

"This will work," Allison said. "It's too early for dancing anyway."

"This is the dance list," Misha said, but quietly.

Allison had already moved on, staked out a corner of the couch and sat with her perfect legs crossed. Misha stared at her a moment, and then went into the kitchen. Ally followed her, still feeling sick by this new, insecure Misha. She watched her sister take a shot of tequila, close her eyes, and breathe deep. Suddenly Ally wanted to reach out and touch her, to tell her what a bitch Allison was, to comfort her. She felt ashamed for ever wanting to one-up Misha—not if it looked like this. As Ally tried to walk toward her little sister, she attempted to move aside a chair in her way.

Her hand slipped through where the wood was supposed to be. She waved her hand through the back of the chair, and again, felt nothing.

She had no mass. She had no...depth, substance, weight. Ally had spent her entire life, or so it felt, trying to minimize herself, to disappear in to the background and take up as little space as possible. And now, here she was, taking up no space at all, with no one able to see her, no one able to hear her.

She wanted to sink to her knees, but was afraid she would sink through the floor—*and why hadn't she done that already? Oh, God, please don't let me sink through the floor.* She put her hand to her chest and was relieved that she could still feel herself. She felt solid to her hand. Ally touched her face, and all her familiar features were there. She could move her hands through her hair. She could pinch her arm. But she could not touch the chair, or the counter, or her sister.

Ally looked around for Misha, but her little sister was gone. Panicked, Ally rushed out of the kitchen, walking through Pixie Fairy as she did so. She barely noticed.

Misha was sitting near Allison, a lowly shrinking violet against Allison's vibrant rose bush. She was putting on a brave face though, and Ally doubted anyone else could tell how unhappy Misha was. Ally felt proud of her sister for that. But unsubstantial, and feeling useless, there was nothing Ally could to do to help Misha now, except wait out this experience and hope it would end soon.

Ally moved closer to Allison, so that she could hear better, and purposely caught the fantasy's eye, just so she could feel like she existed. Allison looked at her briefly, the smallest recognition, and then looked away.

"Oh, but the best was when we were in cheer together," Allison was saying, clearly continuing a discussion theme. "We were only together the one year, my last and her first, and Mickey was trying to do a bow and arrow on a lift, lost her balance, and fell. Her bases caught her, but one of them nailed Mickey here in the face, split her lip right open. And there's all this blood everywhere, and Mickey is just screaming and screaming like a banshee. I finally had to slap her to get her to stop."

Roars of laughter greeted her comment, and Alex mimed a slap at Misha, who flinched and sunk further into herself.

"There was no slap," Misha said. "And this guy Michael drove us to the hospital."

Ally's ears perked up. *Michael!* Where was Michael in the world where Allison was real?

"Who?" Alex asked.

"He was one of the spotters."

"A male cheerleader?" Alex scoffed.

"Is he the one that killed himself?" another of Misha's friends asked. Ally didn't see who it was. Her eyes bore into Allison. *Killed himself? Michael? No. I mean, he went dark, but he got through it. I helped him get through it…*

"No, I think he just ran away or something," Allison said, avoiding Ally's gaze. "Anyway, Mickey had to get stitches," she continued. "If you look really close, you can still see the scar."

People leaned in toward Misha as though they could see it, and she put her hand up by her mouth, hiding her lower lip.

The scar was real, as was, for the most part, the story Allison had told, but Misha had always been rather proud of the scar, a reminder of just how dangerous cheer could be, and a symbol that cheerleaders were not just pom-pom wavers. It was one of the few times in her life Ally had felt close with her sister, holding Misha's hand while Misha got stitches. Michael had driven them to the hospital. He'd stayed too, calling their parents, taking care of the insurance and all the details. He'd been as protective of Misha as Ally had been.

At the time, Misha had been miraculously calm, but later she'd whispered to Ally that she'd been really scared. And Ally had been proud of Misha for getting back up there and doing the lift again. In her world, it was a good memory. For all three of them.

But in Allison's world, it had all gone horribly wrong. In Allison's world, Michael didn't have support and…Ally didn't want to think about him not existing. Run away, she decided. Michael must have run away. And Misha…living with that perfection—real perfection, and not the kind Ally imagined Misha had—had taken a terrible toll on her little sister. It took the spark out of her eye, the bounce out of her step, the vitality from her body, and the softness from her name.

"Stop it," Ally said to Allison, feeling her protectiveness overtake her. Allison ignored her.

As Allison launched into another embarrassing Misha story, Ally couldn't take it anymore.

"STOP!"

Allison flinched slightly at the shout but kept talking.

"Fine," Ally said, "but you asked for this." She began to sing "Oh Mickey You're So Fine," waving her arms around like a cheerleader from the music video that went with the song. As Allison shifted in her seat, Ally sang louder, getting up to fully throw herself into the dance routine she was making up.

Allison stood up suddenly, brushing past Red Riding Hood as she marched into the kitchen.

"What do you think you're doing?" she demanded as Ally followed her.

"Don't treat Misha that way."

"What way? I was just telling stories."

"You were trying to embarrass her."

"I was doing exactly what you wanted me to do. You always wanted to take her down a peg, right? To show her up? To be the prettier, more charming one? Well this is what that looks like. It's your fantasy – don't blame me if you don't like it."

Ally felt her face redden with shame.

"You're right, I don't like it. I don't like this reality at all. I want to stop, switch back."

"No," Allison said, her hands on her hips. "It doesn't work that way. You agreed to this. You can't back out now."

"I can. I want my life back."

"Oh really?" Allison scuffed. "Are you sure? Look at you."

Ally glanced down at her outfit, the same one she had liked on herself earlier in the evening. This time all she could see was the way the material of the dress clung to her belly, and how wide her hips looked in the skirt.

"Stop it," she said again, less sure of herself.

"Face it, Ally, I am only giving you what you want. What you deserve. Stop being a little bitch about it."

With that, she flaunted out of the room.

Ally crossed her arms over her body in a self-hug. What had she created? She followed Allison out into the hall.

"Look," she began. Allison tossed an evil grin over her shoulder, and then made her way over to Alex, who was looking bored in the corner, his bare chest gleaming in the light.

Allison sauntered up close to Alex, and said something in his ear that Ally couldn't hear. Alex grinned back at her and leaned forward. After a few moments of flirting, Allison took him by the hand and led him down the hallway toward the bedrooms. Ally couldn't bring herself to follow.

Allison wasn't real. Ally kept floating back to that. Allison wasn't real and this couldn't really be happening, and somehow it was all going to be okay. There was no way that Allison could be real. She didn't have any visible pores. She was a walking pho-to-shopped fashion ad, with that same magazine-glossy look to her. Alison was something else. Something not good. Something maybe even evil.

But, if what Ally was experiencing was anything like what Allison was, she had a heartbeat. She had mass, at least to herself. She followed some sort of rules of logic, like being able to travel as if in a dream. Ally just needed more information, and then she would be able to figure this out. She had to figure this out.

Suddenly, Ally felt a pulling in her stomach, a lurching that made her head spin. She gasped and bent over, panic rising like bile in her throat.

It's happening! I'm dying!

SISTERS

Ally reached out, panicked, her hands falling through a nearby table. She whirled around, stumbled forward, and through sheer will managed not to fall to the floor. Or through it, as she was sure would happen. Then the lurching in Ally's stomach increased, making her double over again. It was as though the pain was building up toward something.

And then, Ally felt a snap.

She was back in her body. Only, her body wasn't alone. Alex had his arms around her, one hand tangled in the stray hairs at the nape of her neck and the other squeezing her upper thigh. His mouth was at the side of her neck, lips sucking in a way that was likely to lead to a hickey. There was a lot going on under his loin cloth, and Ally was very aware of how nearly naked he was.

Ally shoved him away and stared at him. His eyes snapped open and he froze, looked down at her, back up, back down. His hands let go and she fell slightly back against the dresser he had her pressed against.

"I," he said. "Um."

"Yeah," Ally said. "Strong punch. Really strong. Woo!" She offered up a fake laugh. He just stared at her another moment.

"Nice tits," he offered with a shrug.

"Thanks," Ally said, glancing down. Her cleavage was really impressive at that angle.

"What's your name again?"

"Ally. Misha's sister."

"Huh. Okay. Well, I'm going back to the party. I'll, uh, see you later."

Ally watched him walk out, the back flap of his loin cloth bouncing merrily over his ass.

She blinked and looked around. The ghostly—and she looked very transparent indeed—form of Allison was leaning up against the dresser next to her. While Ally was still in the more conservative version of the Fairy Godmother outfit, Allison's had changed. It looked more like Ally's than the sexy creation she had worn throughout the party. The lines of reality and surreality were certainly getting twisted together.

"I thought…" Ally began, then shook her head. She didn't want to share her panic with Allison. Upon closer inspection, Allison wasn't looking too good anyway, very shaky and pale, and not anywhere near as powerful. Ally felt a small rising of hope.

"You okay?" she asked.

"Like you care," Allison snapped. "I thought that would last longer." She shook her head. "Doesn't matter."

"I don't want to do that again," Ally said, shakily.

Allison flipped her see-through hair over her transparent shoulder. "I already told you; you don't have a choice, not anymore. Soon…it will happen soon."

"What will?" Ally asked, alarm pumping the blood more loudly into her ears.

"You'll disappear," Allison said, exasperated. "Into a fantasy world."

"How? Why?"

"It doesn't matter anymore and I'm tired of trying to explain it."

"Do I get to pick the fantasy?" Ally asked, thinking of possibilities "Oh, it won't just be one," Allison said, smiling her lupine-smile again. As pale as the smile was, it seemed even more terrifying.

"And I'll be me in them?" Ally said, thinking out loud.

"Yes," Allison said. "Just as you are now—doing all the things you had me do in them."

And that, right there, was the extra catch. Ally felt a chill spill down her spine and creep out over her skin. Not only was her reality going to be ruined by Allison, but Ally was going to end up in her own fantasy world.

"All the things I do in my fantasies?" she asked, mind racing.

"Oh yes." Allison grinned wider.

Ally could see through her teeth to the flowered wall-paper behind Allison.

All the things Ally was in her fantasies: spy, dancer, vampire-slayer, witch, singer, empath, model, astronaut, time traveler, Amazon, Bionic woman, jewel-thief, actress, spiritual leader, mercenary, and princess of a small exotic country. In being these things, she had taken herself on many a dangerous adventure, the kind that would make Indiana Jones want to stay home. She would just barely escape, brush against death in a dance and then move on to the next partner, and she did all those things because she was able to, because she was Allison in her fantasy life.

Up against the same odds, in the same situations, the real Ally—hell, any real person at all—wouldn't stand a chance. Death would give her the final dip, and that would be it, all the music that ever played.

"Could I die?" Ally asked, her voice barely above a whisper.

"Yes," Allison said. "Painfully. Over and over again, losing more and more of yourself each time, until finally everything that is you fades away, and all that is left is the pain."

Ally swallowed hard.

"And then Misha, that's what she'll become?"

"You mean Mickey? Always trying to compete with her older sister…" She sneered. "Didn't you always want her to envy you?"

Ally felt sick again. "And Michael?" she whispered.

"What do you really care? I'd worry about yourself. It's what you're best at."

Ally could feel bile rising in her throat and her words came out hoarse:

"How long?" Allison's grin lit up like an electric Jack-o-lantern's. A translucent electric Jack-o-lantern's.

"Soon," she said. "Soon enough."

And before Ally could think of anything else to ask, Allison disappeared.

Ally tried, very hard, to believe that this was all just a hallucination. It was a futile effort, because even she couldn't be that delusional. The fear that lodged itself like an anchor in her stomach told her that this was all too painfully real.

Allison was going to take over. Misha was going to shrink away. Michael would disappear. He might not even be alive. Perfection would enter the world, and no one would ever be the same again.

Ally left the bedroom feeling weak and transparent herself. She went to the kitchen and checked the time on the microwave.

Two hours. Allison had been able to take over for two hours.

"Ally!" Misha yelled, appearing suddenly by her side. "We're going to do an apple bob. You have got to join us!"

Misha's eyes were bright, her hair falling out of its careful ponytail. Her blonde hair looked golden against the red veils, which added to the rosy glow of her cheeks.

Ally smiled, seeing her totally normal, totally happy sister again. Her body was back to normal, back to the healthy and lean build that meant that Misha could still outrun, out-jump, and out-athlete most everyone Ally knew.

Ally pulled her into a tight hug.

"What the...?"

"I'm sorry," Ally said. She pulled back and looked her sister in the face. "I am so sorry. I have been so selfish, so caught up in myself."

"It's okay," Misha said, her voice soft, young sounding.

"You wanted to talk to me about something. Earlier, on the phone..."

"Yeah. I...well promise not to get too weirded out, okay?"

"Sure," Ally said, smiling at her sister. "I have a pretty high tolerance for weird anyway."

"I'm in a group for people who have eating disorders. I don't meet the criteria for anorexia – not yet. And I don't want to. There's this thing called disordered eating. It's like when you have massive issues with food. Like you can't just eat food without worrying about how many calories you're eating, and you avoid anything that can be remotely considered fattening, and, well, it's like the first big step toward stopping eating."

Ally nodded.

"And my friend Julie? She has it too. Disordered eating. You don't have to be like super skinny or anything. She's the one that told me that maybe I had it, and maybe I should get some help. I haven't told mom and dad yet. I'm not sure how."

Ally nodded again, feeling numb.

"I had no idea."

"I haven't really wanted to talk about it. I mean, who wants to admit that they have an issue? This is like a real mental illness, you know? Or at least on the way to one. And it's not about food. Not really. I mean it is, but... It's just like—I don't feel in control of my life. Like all this stuff just keeps happening to me and I don't have any real say or anything. And I just wanted something that I could control, you know? So I controlled my food. My body. Tried to be perfect..."

"I know the feeling," Ally said, and pushed a stray hair behind Misha's ear. "I kind of always thought you were perfect."

"Yeah. Everyone thinks that. I mean, if you're thin, and if you dress the right way or whatever. Like people just expect you to love your life. But that's not always the case. I...am not always happy. Or very often happy, actually. But I'm working on it."

"And the pills..."

"Help. I get panic attacks."

"I think I get panic attacks, too."

Misha nodded.

"I wouldn't be surprised. Mom... Well let's just say that I bet the same voice in my head that tells me I'm not good enough exists in your head too."

"I don't know how you could not feel good enough."

"I don't know how you could either. You're so smart, and funny, and kind, and have awesome people like Michael in your life. A real friend—not just someone who uses you to be popular."

Ally sighed.

"It's a really powerful voice," she said.

Misha snorted.

"Anyway, I still don't know if I want Mom and Dad to know. But I did want you to know. I...kinda already told Michael."

Ally nodded again. "He told me. Not all of it. Just that he

talked to you about stuff. He's good to talk to about stuff."

Misha nodded.

"Somehow I thought you'd be more weirded out by all this. Mad, or something."

"Why would I be mad?"

"I dunno. Like maybe you thought I was faking it? Or that you'd think it wasn't that big a deal?"

"But it is a big deal," Ally said. "And the big deal is that you felt like something wasn't right, and you got help. That is huge, and I am so proud of you for that! You don't even know. It takes a lot to seek out help. You're very brave."

"I don't know about that," Misha said. But she was smiling slightly. Ally gave her another half hug.

"You're very beautiful," Ally told her sister, suddenly struck by the truthfulness of it.

Misha seemed taken aback by the unexpected compliment. "You are too, you know," she said. "You don't know it, but you are."

Ally stared at her sister for a long moment, and wondered why she couldn't just accept the compliment.

"Did anyone ever call you Mickey?" she asked suddenly.

"Hell no!" Misha said, shaking her head. "That's way too guttural a name for me."

Ally laughed.

"See? I know words like guttural. This school thing is working great!" Misha grinned, and suddenly looked like she did when they were kids, racing leaves down a gutter in the rain. "Especially with Julie's help. She's a great tutor. I wish you guys had been able to spend more time talking…" Ally was wondering if Allison ever raced leaves with "Mickey." She shook her head. *No, of course she didn't.* Just one more thing that would be taken away from Ally. From Misha too. She felt a wave of nausea wash over her.

"Whoa, you okay?" Misha asked.

Ally shook her head.

"Not really feeling that great."

Misha gave Ally an appraising look. "You're pale. Have you eaten?"

"I'm just tired..." And suddenly, Ally felt very tired indeed. "I hate to leave early..."

"No, that's okay. You look super tired. Can I get you something maybe? Should I see if someone can drive you home? I would, but I've had a few shots..."

Ally shook her head.

"I can make it home. I really had a good time at the party though. I loved the decorations."

Misha beamed.

"We had so much fun doing them. We wanted it to look like Halloween just threw up all over the place."

"Mission accomplished," Ally said, running her hand over a nearby pile of fake spider web, and pulling at a plastic spider hidden inside.

"Take care of yourself Ally. You're the only big sister I got, and I like having you around."

"I will," she said, not sure if she could keep the promise. She felt drained.

Misha pulled a piece of web off Ally's shoulder and smoothed down the material.

"I told you the costume would fit."

Ally grinned.

"Yes, you did. I really should have just trusted you."

Ally felt something brush against her ankle and looked down to see Mort. She swept the cat up in a hug, buried her face in the purring, soft fur.

"I swear he'd rather go home with you," Misha said.

Ally shook her head.

"He loves you. He just knows I'm a sucker for green eyes." Mort patted Ally's face with a paw, and she laughed. He felt very heavy in her arms, and she felt another wave of weakness pass through her. She handed the cat off to Misha.

"I really need to go," she said.

Misha nodded. "Be careful okay? You…don't look well."

Ally nodded. She went back to the bedroom to gather her bag of stuff, and, not bothering to change from the costume, made her way through the throngs of booty-loving party-goers—early Destiny's Child was pumping from the computer's speakers—and out into the cool, damp air outside.

It was her own thoughts that chilled her as she got into her car. How would Ally ever be able to stop Allison?

SaVInG DOUBT

The rain fell over the Santa Clarita Valley, and as it fell, it washed away the remnants of the fire, dissolving the ash, smothering the smoke, and dampening the flames. It left the roads slick, and Ally had to focus as she took the wet yet familiar roads home. She wished the rain would wash her worries away as easily as it had the fire.

"Stop her." It had been a warning, from who or what, Ally wasn't sure. She was scared. She needed to find that voice, ask questions, and get answers. She needed help.

As Ally pulled into her parking spot, her cell phone rang. She didn't recognize the number. She answered with an unsure "hello?"

"Ally? It's Sandra. How are you?"

"Sandra?" Ally shook her head. "Is Michael okay?" The night with Allison was still in her head, and her heart felt heavy.

"He's fine and taking another group of kids through the haunted house," Sandra said quickly. "I guess this does seem a little odd—me calling. I just…how are you?"

Ally's eyes flickered to her rearview mirror, but wherever Allison had disappeared to, Ally had a feeling she would be there for a while.

"I'm okay. Maybe a little tired."

"Did you go to your sister's party?"

"Yeah. I left early though. Just got home in fact."

"Are you not feeling well?"

Ally cocked an eyebrow at her phone. "What's up, Sandra?

Why are you suddenly so concerned with my health?"

She could hear the blonde sigh on the other end of the phone. "Your aura is off."

"You can see my aura through the phone?" Ally looked at her cell with new wonder, then another idea occurred to her. "You can see auras?"

She heard Sandra sigh again. "Today, when I ran into you on the stairs…"

The day seemed so long to Ally that she had to think back to that moment. "I was on my way out," she said, confirming, remembering the reading look that Sandra had given her.

"You're aura was just…way off. It was off yesterday too, but today—it was, like, drained."

Ally thought about that and wondered briefly what her aura must look like now, after her switch with Allison.

"What color is it?" she asked. "My aura…what color?"

"Sort of purplish-blue. They aren't really just one color. Only lately yours has had a silvery-blue undertone to it—especially today. It was like the silver-blue was taking over."

Ally remembered the shimmer she had seen around Allison as Allison was doing the switch. It had also been silvery-blue. "Do auras normally change color?"

"Hues maybe, depending on mood, or health. But not full-fledged colors. Unless…"

"Unless what?"

"You said you're home now. Can I come over?"

Ally stared at the back of the little car port, and the drip of water trailing down the brown painted wood. Sandra, come to her house? Sandra, who could read auras? Sandra, the witch, who could, maybe, tell her what Allison was?

"Please? Just for a while?"

Ally nodded, and then made her affirmation into the phone. Sandra had been to her house once with Michael, and unlike Ally, had a good memory for directions. Ally told her to park in her second parking spot and reminded Sandra of her apartment number and then hung up. She sat in the car for another moment before she had the presence of mind to panic about something else entirely hallucination and aura unrelated—how clean was her apartment?

Ally had just finished washing the last of her dishes when she heard Sandra's sharp knock on her door. She glanced at the clock on her microwave as she rushed out of the kitchen and was surprised by how early is still was—just past nine. She had been getting more and more anxious while waiting for Sandra, and as she started walking to her door, she felt her breath get shorter and shorter. By the time she got the door open, she was practically hyperventilating, and shaking.

As soon as she opened the door, Sandra pulled her into a tight hug. Ally let the smaller woman take her weight. The action surprised her, and a wave of emotion overcame her. She began to cry, hard and uncontrollably. She still struggled to breathe. Sandra seemed prepared for it though, and gently guided her to the couch, hooking the door closed with her foot. Once on the couch, she held Ally in her arms, rocking her back and forth, and making calming noises.

"Just breathe," she said over and over again, "just breathe."

Finally Ally got a hold of her emotions, and embarrassment made her blush.

"I'm sorry," she said, sniffling. Sandra pulled a pack of tissue from her over-sized purse and handed it to Ally, who took it gratefully.

"Nothing to be sorry about. Whatever has been going on with you, it's taken its toll. You look so drained, even worse than before. Something else happened, didn't it? It's getting worse."

"What is?" Ally asked, looking at Sandra in new wonder. "What do you think is happening to me?" She wasn't sure yet that she could trust the green-eyed Wicca with her secret. She was so unsure of so many things, it was hard to find confidence in anything, especially the tentative friendship between them.

"I think...now, don't take this all weird or think I'm psycho or anything, but I think you may be...possessed."

Ally laughed then, and, so rickety were her emotions, she lost control of her laughter too, and shook with it, new tears coming to her eyes. Sandra was worried about sounding crazy. Sandra thought she was being possessed. Sandra was staring at her with hurt and confusion in her eyes. Ally pulled it together.

"Michael said you were a skeptic," Sandra began, pulling her purse toward her in a protective manner, although whether the purse was supposed to protect her or she was protecting the purse, Ally couldn't tell.

"Were, as in past tense," Ally said. "After the week I've had, there's no room for doubt anymore. Or rather, there is so much doubt, why bother with specifics?"

"Ally," Sandra said carefully. "Why don't you tell me what's been going on?"

"You said it," Ally told her, flopping back against the couch cushions, automatically pulling a pillow from the side to put over her stomach. "I'm possessed. Or something."

"Why don't you start from the beginning?" Sandra suggested, tucking her legs under her and settling into a more comfortable position. Ally stared at her a moment, waiting for some sign that this was not the action she should take. Sandra's face was open, trusting, believing. And so, as matter of factly as she could, Ally began.

Her story was a jumble of images that somehow added up to a meaning she couldn't fathom. She hoped Sandra was better at interpretation than she was. Ally laid out all her theories anyway: the wish, the self-help, the dream. Something had to cause this. She showed Sandra her list, particularly the last part: magical creation.

"I did something to cause this." She leaned into the cushion at her side, pressing her shoulder into it as though trying to burrow into the couch and away from the statement.

"No, you didn't," Sandra said, too confidently for Ally's taste. *How could she be so sure?* "There's no way you could have, I swear. I think I know what's haunting you."

Ally stared at Sandra, not wanting to get too excited, but feeling hope bloom up in her like a lily, beautiful and pungent.

"I think it's a spirit," Sandra continued, "and I think I even know a spell that can get rid of it."

"It can't be a spirit. I tried that already." She got up and got the gris-gris bag and showed it to Sandra. "And salt didn't work either."

Sandra appeared to stifle a grin.

"Yeah, that…was a good attempt. But you're several ingredients short of a real gris-gris bag. And salt only works on ghosts. I think this is a spirit, not a ghost."

"They're different?"

"Yes. I mean, this didn't come from like, an extinguished life. But I think I know a spell that can get rid of it."

"A spell?" The petals of Ally's hope-lily began to wilt. "Magic isn't real," she said.

"And fantasy versions of yourself haunting you is?" Sandra asked, almost hurt. "I believed you. You need to believe in me too."

Ally stared at her.

"I'm sorry," she said at last. "I believe in you. I'm just not sure I believe anything can help me now." And then she turned away, her eyes falling to her glass dining-room table. "I'm not sure I deserve help."

Sandra reached out her hand, took Ally's chin and turned it forward, staring into her eyes.

"You deserve your life," she said. "And there is nothing you did to cause this, or make this happen. You are a sweet, smart, funny and wonderful person. I want you in my life. I want to help you stay in yours."

Ally looked up at that, the lily in her stretching its petals a bit more toward the sun. But then doubt blew a cloud across the light. "Allison is so much stronger than me."

Sandra sighed, frustrated. "I know it seems that way, but it's not true. Any strength Allison has came from you."

"She keeps saying that I made her. That she came from me."

"In a way, maybe. Like she took her form from your dreams. I am not sure why she picked you…"

"I don't like my life," Ally said, and was shocked by her own honesty. "Or I haven't. I've been depressed. More depressed than I've been willing to admit. And I think that's why…why Allison, whatever she is, picked me."

For a moment they just stared at each other, the words hanging heavy in the space between them.

"I need you to hear this, really hear this. This was not your fault. Even your depression—that's not your fault. Not anything you caused."

"But if I didn't cause it, how can I fix it? I keep thinking if I lose weight or get fit, or do something… There has to be a way to feel better. I just need to change, I just need to…"

"Ally," Sandra said. "It doesn't work like that. Depression is a mental illness. It's something that has to be managed, professionally. You need help. This isn't something you're gonna fix with a cleanse or something like that."

"But if I don't change, how can I fight Allison? If she takes over…. Sandra, Misha, in her reality, she is so sick. And Michael. I think…I think maybe he's dead. I have to fix this. I have to do something!"

"Not alone. This isn't something you can fight alone. I'm here with you now. And Michael—he'll help. I promise. We will find a way to fight Allison. Your depression and anxiety—that's going to take longer. But we can find a way to help you with that, too."

Ally nodded, choking back more tears.

"Tomorrow is Dia de los Muertos. The spell will work best tomorrow night with all the mysticism in the air."

Ally nodded. Sure the day of the dead was a good day for a spell. That made sense. As much sense as anything had made so far, anyway. She felt another wave of weariness wash over her and closed her eyes.

"You need to rest," Sandra said. Ally opened her eyes and stared at Sandra. She had told her secret, and Sandra had believed her, wanted to help her even. She felt a wave of gratitude wash through her, and her eyes watered up again.

"Sandra," she began.

The Wicca just shook her head and smiled. "You've been through so much, and all on your own. I wish you would have come to me sooner, or Michael even. Especially Michael."

"I didn't think he would believe me. And then I didn't want to burden him and...and I don't know. I just...didn't."

"Your life is being taken over by a malevolent spirit—your best friend needs to know." Sandra tugged at a lock of Ally's hair. "I'll tell him. He'll believe me."

Ally nodded. She closed her eyes again, way too tired for this.

"I'll go now," Sandra said.

Ally made a motion to get up, walk her to the door.

"No. Straight to bed for you."

"Won't pass go," Ally said weakly, with an equally feeble smile. Sandra smiled back at her.

"Take care, Ally."

She hugged Ally tightly again, and again, Ally felt a wave of emotion wash over her. But she was too tired to even cry any more. She hugged Sandra back, and watched her leave with some new feeling in her that she tentatively called hope. Sandra knew a spell. Sandra was going to help her. Sandra was going to save the day.

Because Ally needed someone to save her. She just didn't feel capable of saving herself.

LaDY OF THe LaKe

Ally couldn't fall asleep. Every position she tried to settle into felt wrong, and her mind kept racing with everything she and Sandra had talked about, everything they were planning. She kept picturing all the ways it could go wrong.

She needed to picture something else. So, she did:

✳

"I should probably start by saying that I am not who you think I am," Fantasy Man said. "My real name is…"

"Tom," Ally supplied. It was the only name that fit.

"We've got company!" someone shouted from the front seat. The van veered wildly, tossing the people inside around. Ally went flying and landed hard on Tom, who caught her easily while bracing himself against the side. Ally's gun got knocked away.

"Hold on!" Scar Face shouted.

"Get down!" Turtleneck countered. The sounds of bullets against metal, and everyone complied, crouching low against the floor.

Something slammed into the back of the vehicle once, then again. On the third hit, the back door flew open.

Ally could see one of the black SUVs from before directly behind them. Gunfire was coming from the passenger. Tom managed to get a gun up and fire back. He shoved Ally behind him, keeping her away from the bullets.

"My gun!" Ally shouted at the woman. She watched as the woman turned slowly toward her, and grinned. The grin looked terrifyingly familiar. The woman's roots started to turn reddish, and as Ally watched, her eyes changed both shape and color, becoming a sparkling bright blue.

"No!" Ally screamed. "You can't!"

"I can!" Allison said in return. "You can't escape from me. I am everywhere!"

"No," Ally said again. "This is my head. We're in my head. It's just a…"

"Fantasy?" Allison grinned. "Scene change!"

There was no van. There was no SUV behind it. All sensation of moving ceased.

Ally looked around. She was in a large warehouse, tied to a chair. Tom was in a chair next to her, his mouth gagged with a bright red bandana, his arms bound to the chair by thick white ropes in a way that managed to make the muscles in his arms pop out.

"Better, don't you think?" Allison came up behind Tom and ran her hands down the sides of his arms, which just caused him to struggle more, and the muscles in his arm to somehow look bigger. "He makes such a sexy prisoner. I can't wait to make him scream."

"You can't!" Ally said. "I never—this isn't one of my fantasies."

"No," Allison said. "But it's one of mine."

"But…we're in…I…"

"You never are going to get this, are you?" Allison said. "This is my world. Always has been, always will be. You're just going to have to…"

But the scene changed again.

✳

"Ally, are you getting cold?" Tom asked, and Ally felt his hand on her back, his arms surrounding her. She was shaking slightly, still confused, still scared. Was she dreaming? Was she awake?

She looked around. There was Beauty, and the grass, and beside them, the lake, its calm silvery surface shimmering in the soft light. Ally felt goose-bumps rise on her arms.

"It's connected, isn't it?" she asked Tom. "The lake, and Allison, and this place." She pushed him away and stepped back. "And you."

A flicker of something passed over his eyes, and he turned away for a moment. When he turned back, his face was open and handsome, his smile sexy.

"Why don't we go home?" he said, his voice as alluring as pistachio caramel ice-cream. He tried to wrap his arms around her again. She could smell his musk, the field, hay, even the sweet smell of the flowers around her.

"This place smells," she said, taking in the scents. "I don't smell things in dreams. So, this isn't a dream. Is it?"

"This feels like a dream. Being with you always feels like a dream to me…" He tried to pull her closer for a kiss, but Ally shoved him back.

"Stop it! This isn't real!"

"Yes, it is," he said, and there was an undertone of sadness to his voice.

She walked away from him, felt the grass under her feet, the sun on her skin.

"What is this place?" Ally asked, wrapping her arms around her, feeling the comfort of her own skin beneath her hands. She looked down at her body, Allison's body really. Not very comforting after all, and she let her hands drop to her sides. "And who are you?" she asked Tom.

"Ally, honey, it's me. Don't you know me?" He looked so concerned and hurt Ally wanted to run to him, fling her arms around him, and comfort him with her kisses. But the smells of flowers, earth, even her own perfumed skin were still strong in her nose.

"Why here? Why do you always ask me if I'm cold? What is this place?"

She felt Tom's hand on her arm, turned to him.

"You don't want to be here," he told her. "You want to be home, where it's safe."

"Where is home?" She put her hand over his. "Why are you always here?" He pulled his hand out from under hers.

"There's no time," he said, his voice deep, fudge-ripple ice-cream smooth, and so unlike the real Tom's. "You don't want to be here."

"I know I don't. I just don't know how to leave, how to fight. Tom, what do you know? Help me!"

She reached out to him again, but there was something off about her arm. She stopped and stared at it, then looked down. Her body had changed. Her legs swelled up, her stomach overflowed into rolls, and her breasts hung heavy. Tom recoiled from her.

"It's starting," he said. Ally looked up at him, suddenly terrified.

"Tom," she said. "Can you help me?"

He shook his head. "I'm not real." His shoulders fell, and he looked very tired. "She's going to win, you know," he said. "It

218 | J.M. PHILLIPPE

always wins."

Ally stepped toward him. "It was you…the voice. 'Stop her.' How Tom, how do I stop her? What is she? You can tell me…"

Beauty neighed a warning, and then a shot rang out of nowhere and silenced the black horse forever.

Ally screamed, her body shaking and heart pounding.

Tom lunged for her, knocked her to the ground, shielding her with his body.

Just over his shoulder, Ally could see their assailant. Allison rose from the lake holding her own Excalibur, an M-16, the bullets pumping out of it with sharp cracks of explosion which lit up the evil grin on Allison's face. She was dressed like Rambo, and seemed to be walking on the very surface of the lake toward them, firing all the while. The bullets pummeled into Tom's back, jerking him against Ally as he absorbed the shock. His brown eyes stared up at her and blood pooled from the corner of his mouth.

"It was a great fantasy," he said, and gently touched her face. He dissolved then, became someone Ally had never seen before, a shorter, bald man, maybe ten years older than Ally, his gut pressing into her. She tried to move away from him, but his weight on top of her pinned her down.

"I found refuge in you, in your fantasies," he told her. "Even still, I tried to warn you. She'll overtake you. It will overtake you. You'll feel cold. Always. If you're lucky, you can find a fantasy, hide in it, ward off the inevitable pain for a little longer. You have to find someone, someone with real dreams….your dreams were so vivid. But dangerous."

He laughed, and it turned into a choking cough. He was dying, here, in her arms, this strange man with the same eyes as Tom's. "The voice is my own," he said at last, and tried to smile at her. "But the rest was all you. Thank you for letting me have that, and this place." He looked around one last time, the light beginning to fade from his eyes. "Wake up Ally," he whispered. "While you can. Wake…" A final bullet exploded into the back of his head, and he coughed blood out onto her with his last breath.

Ally screamed again. Over his shoulder she could see Allison advancing. She had ceased firing, but still smiled that evil, insane grin. Ally was stuck under the body of not-Tom, and couldn't move. Allison raised her gun again, almost saluting Ally with it. And then she aimed.

Ally screamed again, until a whisper caught her attention. A familiar ringing, a sound that bounced off the surface of the lake, and made Allison look toward it. Ally focused on the sound, willing it to wake her up, to shatter the fantasy world around her. Allison looked back at her with anger that turned her perfect features into something grotesque. She ran toward Ally now, pulled her trigger….

Ally sat up, gasping for air. There was no body slack against hers, no blood on her face, no demonic woman with a gun running toward her. She was in her bed, in her apartment, and her phone was ringing.

She reached for it like a drowning person reaching out to a life-saver.

"Hello?" Her voice sounded shaky, even to her own ears.

"Ally? Are you okay?" Michael's voice. Ally could have cried she was so relieved to hear him, hear the familiar concern and the calming tones.

"No," she said at last. "I'm not okay."

"I'm on my way," he said. And then he hung up. She could picture him leaving the house, his determined stride, his brisk, efficient movements. He would be there soon—maybe fifteen minutes or so. She could hold on until then. Ally made her shaky way to the bathroom, was amused to see that she was still wearing the fairy-godmother costume. It was wrinkled and twisted around her body. Less amused now, Ally tore it off. She turned on the sink faucet, let the water work up a steam, and then held her hands under it. They turned red.

He died. She watched a man die. She tried to tell herself it wasn't real, that it was a dream, that it didn't mean anything. She could remember the smell of the flowers, of the grass, of the man she knew as Tom. She could still feel his wet breath against her cheek. She could remember the smell of his blood too, and the glazed look in his dead eyes. His death was as real as anything she had ever experienced.

It wasn't a dream. It couldn't have been. Which meant that Ally had truly watched a man die, felt him die, saving her.

From Allison.

Ally slumped against the counter. Her sobs came violently, like a sudden storm. They passed just as quickly, a numbness settling over her, closing her heart, her mind.

Allison had tried to kill her. One, as she has promised, of many deaths. Again, and again, she would hunt Ally down, until all that was left was the pain.

Ally washed her face, because it was something to do. She scrubbed at her skin, still feeling numb. Turning all the hot water off, she splashed the freezing cold against her. Even that couldn't shake this new deadness from her. She moved faster then, threw on a pair of sweats and a loose shirt and twisted her hair up into a clip. Then went to the living room to wait for Michael to arrive.

She felt cold.

Her apartment didn't look like her apartment. The couch had changed into a tufted high-back gray couch with jeweled bright purple and red cushions. All the hand-me-down items had been replaced by new items, all in the same style as the dining table— metals and glass, and so many shiny surfaces. Ally could picture Allison's face in every one.

She knew her time in this world was coming to an end.

Michael arrived with a pounding at the door, and when Ally opened it, threw himself at her, hugging her tightly, pushing her back to look at her, and then pulling her closer into another hug. Ally let him, feeling disconnected from the movements, from her friend, even from herself. It wasn't until Michael dragged her to the couch that she saw that he wasn't alone. Sandra waved hesitantly at Ally, her eyes full of worry. Ally guessed her aura wasn't doing very well by the alarmed look on Sandra's face.

"Tell me what happened," Michael said, regaining his therapist composure. Ally nodded. Events, she could tell them the events. What were they now?

"Wait, did you redecorate?" he asked, suddenly staring around with wonder. "When? How?"

"It was her, wasn't it?" Sandra said, and Ally nodded. "What happened?" Sandra asked.

"Allison killed Tom," she said. "And then she tried to kill me."

Michael looked horrified, possibly more so than he should have, and Ally quickly shook her head.

"No, it was a dream. Only, it didn't feel like a dream. And it wasn't the real Tom... He changed, he was...not Tom."

Ally shook her head. *How to explain?*

"Start from the beginning," Sandra said. "Last night I left, and then…"

Ally nodded. *Yes. The beginning.*

"I have this dream—there's this lake, and a field and a black horse. When I'm there, I look like Allison, and I'm with Tom, this guy from the gym. I don't really know him, but I…" she faltered, her embarrassment cutting through the numb shield she'd erected around herself.

"You have fantasies. Everyone does. So, lately they've been featuring this guy named Tom." Sandra smiled at Ally encouragingly. "Go on."

"Anyway, Tom was there. And we were talking. And then… and then Allison showed up, right out of the lake, and shot him."

Ally felt the blood against her face once again. She knew she was missing details, that there was so much more she should tell them. How Tom was the voice, how he turned into someone else, how the lake shimmered with an unnatural light. But all she could see was the hole in the front of not-Tom's forehead, the blood all around her, and Allison's evil eyes. Her cracked numb-shield was splitting, her emotions threatening to blow it apart. She stood up suddenly.

"It wasn't just a dream." Sandra put a comforting hand on Ally's shoulder, and Ally held it there.

"I'm sorry Ally, I really am. It sounds terrible."

Ally nodded.

"Not-Tom," Michael said. "What do you mean by that?"

Ally looked at him. She shrugged.

"He changed. He didn't look like him anymore."

"What did he look like?"

Dead, bloody, corpse-like. She shuddered.

"He was this other guy, someone I've never seen before.

Maybe ten years older than us. Bald. Heavy. He was so scared."

She turned away.

"Ally, I think..." Michael began.

"It is a spirit," Sandra said, with more emotion than Ally had heard her use toward Michael before. She watched as the two of them faced off, Sandra's body-language closed off, Michael's carefully open. "Ally isn't making this up. And a chemical imbalance doesn't drain your aura like that."

"But you said yourself that illness can drain a person's energy, which is what the aura is, and so illness drains auras."

"It's a spirit," Sandra said. "No illness can cause what Ally has been describing."

"That's not exactly true," Michael corrected. "Mental illness..."

"She isn't crazy!"

"She has been exhibiting symptoms for a long time now. Depression. Manic episodes. Your spirit has only been here the last week. She's been struggling for way longer than that. She's just only recently getting worse."

"She is right here," Ally said.

Michael turned to her.

"I'm sorry Ally, I don't mean to make light of what you're going through."

"How do you explain the apartment changing?" Sandra asked.

"Ally bought new stuff," he said, looking around. "And... painted the walls." His voice became uncertain.

"I was here last night. It didn't look like this. And when would Ally have had time to do all this?"

"A manic episode..."

"Michael," Ally said. "I didn't do this. I didn't."

"Maybe you don't remember doing it." He took her hand. "I mean, mental illness, it can mess with your memory."

"Michael," she said, and got up, walking him to the kitchen. There were bright new shiny appliances in the kitchen, which was also about two feet wider than before. Michael stared.

"I…"

"Shared delusion?" Ally offered. "That's a thing, right?"

Sandra put her arm around Michael's shoulders.

"It's a spirit. Magic. I'm sorry you don't want to believe. But it's real. Ally is not crazy."

"I am not so sure about that," Ally said. "Because Michael is right. I have been depressed. For a while. Longer than a week. That's what opened the door, let this thing, whatever it is, in. It's my fault."

"No!" Michael pulled Ally into a hug. "I don't fully understand what is happening here, but I can tell you that there is no way this is your fault. Absolutely no way."

"She keeps saying I did this," Ally said into his shoulder.

"You didn't. You couldn't. This isn't your fault."

Ally pulled back, nodded weakly.

"The spell has to be done tonight to work right," Sandra said.

"The spell sounds dangerous," Michael said. "Maybe unnecessarily so…"

Allison appeared out of nowhere, her self-satisfied smile wiped clean as soon as she saw Sandra and Michael.

"What the hell are they doing here?" she asked. Ally glanced quickly in Allison's direction then looked significantly at Sandra.

"Well, thanks for checking on me," she said with a false lightness to her voice. She walked from the kitchen to the front door, motioning for Sandra and Michael to do the same. Sandra looked around the room wildly as though she could spot where Allison was hiding. Of course she couldn't. Michael just looked confused.

"No problem. I was worried," Sandra said. "My friend had that flu and it hit him really hard."

Michael opened his mouth to say something, but Sandra pinched his arm, giving him a significant look as well. She pushed him toward the door, and then turned toward Ally when they got to it.

"I am positive about that cure I told you about. It will work, and it's more than worth it."

Ally nodded toward Sandra.

Michael still looked confused, but at least had picked up on enough to keep his mouth shut.

"Thank you," Ally told Sandra. "Both of you, for coming by. I'll call you later—and of course, see you tonight, at the party."

"If you're...ill," Michael said carefully, "maybe we should cancel it?"

Ally shook her head.

"I can't let you do that. I'll be okay."

"I think you should come tonight," Sandra said. "I have the stuff for the cure at the house. We can go from there—to get the other stuff we need."

Michael looked like he wanted to start arguing again. This time Ally pushed him out the door.

"I'll call you later and we'll talk about it then," she said. She quickly hugged first Sandra and then Michael, holding onto Michael a little longer.

"You take care," Sandra said. And then she left, dragging Michael along with her.

Ally closed the door quickly, pressed her forehead against it.

"What the hell was that about?" Allison asked.

"Where've you been?" Ally responded, glancing at Allison.

"What do you care?" Allison asked. And then her look turned darker. "Have any nice dreams last night?"

Ally whirled toward her, her own eyes as dark as the thinner woman's.

"Why did you do that? Why did you kill him?" she demanded.

"I have no idea what you're talking about," Allison said. She reached over and swept a stray hair back behind Ally's ear, letting her fingers gently brush against Ally's face as she did so.

Ally felt the touch like a burn and jumped back.

THE LYING, THE WITCH, AND THE WARDROBE

Ally spent the next hour doing her best to ignore Allison as she went around touching all the things in the apartment. Allison continued the transformation of the décor as well, changing curtains and flooring. So far the bathroom and bedroom remained more or less the same, and Ally retreated there until her bed suddenly grew and sprouted a headboard.

She grabbed her car keys and purse and left Allison stroking a chenille throw. Ten minutes later, she finally felt there was enough distance between Allison and herself to breathe.

Southern California was never as pretty as after it rains. The sky above was a crystal blue, the sun shining with a new energy through a smog-free sky. Some white fluffy clouds, stragglers from the weather system that had already moved over the hills, stretched themselves out and waved playfully to the people below, the wind moving them slowly across the sky.

It was a beautiful day, and Ally soaked up every moment of it, her windows down, her stereo up. She turned onto White's Canyon, drove down to Bouquet Canyon, and turned right. She drove past the pumpkin patch where she and Misha would hunt for the perfect-shaped jack-o-lantern face when they were kids, past horses she used to daydream about owning one day, and past the last signs of normal civilization, on up into the Angeles National Forest.

In the summer, it wasn't much of a forest. Wasn't much in the winter either, but in the spring, after the rains, and in the fall, when the leaves turned, it was as beautiful as any other forest.

The wind whipped past Ally's face, brushing leaves against her car. A stray gold leaf flew in her window and rested on her passenger seat for a moment before flying out the window again. Ally wished it luck on whatever journey it was off on.

Ally drove along the twisty road, and let her thoughts twist with it.

Why am I like this? Why do I continue to be like this?

She watched a bird fly off the side of the road, and turned the wheel for another twist. Her car was climbing higher now, the trees starting to thin out. The fires had reached up here, and she could see the black scars they had left behind, the damage a few days of flames could do to something once beautiful and wild. Here the land was barren now, dejected and ugly. And yet, now and again, Ally could see small sprouts of green, the tiniest flickers of some fast growing weed taking advantage of the rain and ash to make its claim on the earth. She couldn't help but think of the mirror shards in the Snow Queen tale, how they made everything look ugly. Even in the ugly scars of fire, there was something beautiful trying to emerge. Ally realized she hadn't been able to see the beauty in things for a long time.

Michael had said it. She was depressed. For a long time. And Ally had to agree. She just didn't know why.

Ally's car continued to climb up the hill. She would be at the lake soon. Thinking of the lake made her think of the other lake, and again she felt the blood dripping off her chin, the last, wet breath of Tom-turned-short-and-bald.

She kept driving, past the lake and into the hills beyond. If she kept taking this road, she would get to a T—one way would lead to Palmdale and the other to Lancaster. She was at a T in her life as well. With the situation being what it was, Ally could no longer keep going forward. She had to turn, one way or the other. In one direction was the inevitable outcome Allison had promised her. In the other was a great unknown, something that could happen only if Ally would try to fight against the current taking her over this waterfall of death.

As Ally crested the top of the hill and looked over the valley, the sun shone off the fields on either side of the road and glowed golden in the yellow light. It was images like these that Ally assumed was why California was called the golden state. She didn't think of the gold in the hills, but of the sun shining on them. Ally pulled over to the side of the road and smiled at the sight, touched by it, and wondered suddenly if Allison would appreciate beauty like this. She suddenly wanted the apparition with her, to share this sight with her.

"Allison," she said out loud, as though saying her name could conjure the gorgeous redhead to her. Then louder. "Allison." She put all her will behind it, imagined the word floating through the ether to land lightly in the perfectly shaped ear. "Allison!"

Allison appeared suddenly and irritated next to Ally.

"What?" Allison asked sharply, arms crossed over her chest. She was a much less happy passenger than the leaf was, and Ally wondered briefly if Allison would float away on the wind too.

"I just wanted to talk to you," Ally said, staring out at the beautiful fields around her. *See? Look how pretty.* She thought it hard, and in Allison's direction, expecting the thinner woman to read her mind again.

"What do we possibly have to talk about? You want to ask me more pointless questions about your pointless demise? It's coming, there is nothing you can do about it, end of story." She stared out the front window, and Ally was sure Allison would see the fields, have to comment on their gold color. "Where the hell are you?" Allison asked instead.

Ally stared straight ahead very carefully. Allison couldn't read her thoughts. She tested her theory, and said very loudly in her head, *you're the meanest, most vile creature I have ever met and that makes you incredibly ugly.*

Allison just looked bored.

"Were you going to start talking soon?" she asked.

"Never mind," Ally said. "My mistake."

"Fine," Allison said. "Don't call me again. I'm not a puppy you know." And then she disappeared in that same unnervingly silent way she had.

Allison was separate from Ally. That meant something. Ally wasn't sure what, but it was better than the nothing she had before. She waited for the little tingling of hope she had in her heart to die out, for one of those super negative thoughts to pop up in her head.

But the hope endured.

Ally picked up the phone and called Sandra.

✴

Later, Ally strode into her apartment with confidence she was only mostly faking.

"Allison!" she called out. The apparition in question emerged and sauntered to the couch.

"You're not going to get weepy on me, are you? You might try to embrace the end of your life with more dignity than you lived it."

Ally sat on an arm chair that hadn't existed before with some trepidation, but it stayed solid enough.

"What happens, after?" she asked.

"After the switch?"

Ally nodded.

"I don't get just any life. I get a version of yours, one of your fantasy ones. Most of the same people will still be in it. You have so many fantasies, it's hard to see which one will emerge as the winning one, as the one that will become my life. I just know I will be rich, and beautiful, and respected, and successful. It will be a very good life. You always had such good daydreams."

"You won't have my life," she said.

Allison nodded slowly. "Uh-huh," she said even slower. "I will have my life."

"What about Michael, and Sandra, and people at the Center?"

"They're never in your fantasies, except as people you used to know."

"Michael is in them all the time!" Ally said defensively. Allison arched her perfect eyebrows and Ally's face grew red. "Not in that way. He usually introduces me to whatever hot guy I'm fantasizing about."

"Maybe he used to, but has he been in them recently?" Allison's voice was accusing and Ally withered under the tone and the realization that no, he hadn't. Lately Ally hadn't imagined anyone real in her life. She hadn't wanted to taint her fantasies with even a brush of reality. Because it was easier.

"So, no then. They won't be part of my life."

"What about Misha?" Ally asked softly, thinking of her little sister's shrunken form at the party.

"Well, she's family. I can't get rid of her. Besides, she's pretty, and popular—she'll be great to have around, looking up to me, wanting to be me. That is what you always wanted right? Your sister to envy you?"

Ally remembered the look on Misha's face at her party, the hurt in her, the self-consciousness that looked so foreign on her little sister's unusually narrow shoulders. No, that was not what she wanted. She would never want that, even if she had been "the pretty one." And she knew that Misha would never want anything like that for her either.

"There has to be a way to stop this," Ally said, wishing as hard as she could that Allison would just go away.

"There isn't," Allison said cheerily. "I'm rather looking forward to my new life actually—you always remembered to put in great details—the main reason why what's his face liked being in them so much."

Ally knew she meant not-Tom, and felt a new anger rush through her. "And you took him out of them. You killed him."

"No, honey," Allison said, standing up from the table. "You did. You invited him in, gave him a character to play, and he paid the price for that. Don't worry—it's not the first time he's died. It won't be the last."

Not-Tom's words haunted her. *Your dreams were so real, but, dangerous.* Ally shook her head. "I didn't know...I..."

"You." Allison walked over to Ally, bent down over her shoulder so that her next words were said mere inches from her face. "You caused this." Then she smiled, and disappeared.

Ally tried to shake off the words, the memory of not-Tom, this feeling of doom that was threatening to overcome her. She was going to fight. There had to be a way to fight. She had a plan, and allies, and she was going to defeat Allison.

With nothing else to do, Ally went into her bedroom and

contemplated her costume.

A witch.

If only.

Not sure what to do with her time, and feeling too jazzed to just sit still or watch horrible Saturday TV, Ally dug through her cupboards, now real wood—*walnut?*—and found a cake mix. Measuring cups and spoons had always calmed her, gave purpose to her energy, her actions. Baking was precise, like math. She stirred batter and put Allison, and the last several days, out of her head. Baking was a soothing science. She didn't want magic right then. She greased the cake pans and concentrated on getting an even coat of butter on the round non-stick surfaces that still tended to stick. Her thoughts were as greasy as the pan and kept sliding all over themselves, refusing to come together in any cohesive whole, or to leave her completely.

Ally poured the batter, dropping the pans on the counter with a loud bang to knock out any air bubbles, then setting the pans in the oven. And, again, her hands were idle, and she didn't have anything to do. She rummaged in her cupboard some more and found a can of tomato soup, and plopped the reddish glob into a pot. She slowly added just-under-a-can of milk, mixing it in thoroughly. She grabbed bread, a cheese slice, butter and a frying pan, and put together a sandwich, heating it over a medium heat so that the bread would be browned and the cheese melted at the same time. Stirring the soup with one hand, and nudging the grilled-cheese sandwich with the spatula in the other, Ally focused on her tasks and tried not to look at the clock.

She ate slowly, dipping the crusts into her soup, sipping the hot liquid cautiously.

Hurry up, she mentally called out to the clock. *Tick faster.*

Ally was afraid Allison would show up soon, somehow sense what was going on, and Ally wanted to leave for the party before the apparition arrived.

The cake came out of the oven and Ally put the two halves on racks to cool. She started pacing, and walked a circular track around her apartment, through the kitchen, the dining room, living room, back into the other side of the kitchen. She grew steadily more and more nervous and worried about having another panic attack. She realized then she forgot to give Misha back her pills, and wondered if maybe she should take one to calm herself down. She thought of the gym musical and decided against it.

Finally, the cake cooled enough and she frosted it. It was when the cake—chocolate with chocolate frosting—sat on her counter that Ally realized why she had wanted to make it. She wanted to leave something behind. It was a silly thing to pick to leave behind, but Ally imagined that Allison would see the cake and remember Ally and how she got to have the life she was living. Ally rummaged in her cupboard again and emerged with a green frosting tube, perfect for writing on cakes. She contemplated her final message to Allison, to the world, and after much consideration scrawled out the words:

Eat me.

She added a green heart and her name—*Ally with a y, because it was prettier*—and stood back to admire her work.

She was glad when the phone finally rang.

"Is she there now?" Michael asked, and Ally knew it took a lot for him to take the idea of Allison seriously enough to ask about her.

"No, not now."

"Was she there before? This morning?"

"Yes," Ally said.

"I didn't see—" he started. "But then, I wouldn't have, would I?"

"You will eventually. But you'll just think she's me. Although, actually, she says that the version of my life that she'll have doesn't have you in it. So then, it would be just as though we were never friends."

"God, I don't even want to think about that. I can't imagine my life without you. I never would have gotten through coming out, my dad's death, or anything without you."

Ally shook her head.

"I don't want to think about my life without you either" she said. "Michael, if she wins…"

"She won't win."

"But you believe me now? About her? About what's happening?"

He took his time answering.

"I can't explain the kitchen," he said. "I keep trying. I keep trying to make sense of any of this. It would be easier if…"

"If I was just crazy? Yeah, I'm with you on that."

"The idea of this being real is too scary, you know? I want something medicine can cure, not magic. I want to be able to help you. But this time, I can't."

"Believing me helps," Ally said. "Just being there for me helps."

She was quiet for a moment, wrapped up in too much emotion to speak.

"She made me live out a porno," she offered.

"What?" Michael's voice broke into a startled laugh.

"At work. When you found me on the table in the filing room?"

"No! Seriously?"

"You showed up in the middle. Not part of it—just there. I was so terrified you could see what was actually happening."

"Oh, God, that's why you looked so weird. Was it at least good?"

"Honestly? Yes. It kinda was."

Michael laughed, and Ally smiled.

"And don't get me started on the musical."

"Oh, my God, you have to tell me!"

"I will. All the details."

"Come over now. No reason to sit and wait alone."

"I've been alone a lot lately, haven't I? I mean, even before."

"Yeah."

"Michael? Did I cause this? Am I...? Did I...?"

"I'm going to keep telling you until you believe me. No. Never. This is not your fault."

Ally let out a breath she wasn't even aware of holding in.

"I'm on my way," she said. "Love you."

"Love you too," he said.

"And Ally?" he asked.

"Yeah?"

"Can you pick up some ice on the way?"

Ally laughed.

MYSTERY DaTe

With her costume in a bag, and three bags of ice trying to melt in her back seat, Ally made her way to Michael's. She drove with her hands gripping the wheel tightly, taking in as much as she could on the way—the streets, the houses, the setting sun glinting off the clouds on the horizon painting everything pink and orange. This could be her last sunset, her last drive.

She shouldn't think like that, Ally told herself. She should be positive, visualize the outcome. All she could see was Allison rising from the silvery-blue lake, gun in her hands and a gleam in her eyes, firing away.

Ally could hear noises coming from behind the garage doors of Michael's house as she found a spot on the street and walked to the front door. She figured that the haunted house was getting some upgrades for the older crowd due to tour it this evening. Compared to the Halloween explosion of Misha's place, Michael's house looked almost tame. Compared to most houses on the street, it reeked of the Halloween spirit. Michael and his roommates had decorated the place with carved pumpkins, fake spider webs, and hand-made ghouls pasted to the windows. A set of ghost lights hung under the eaves, and as Ally stepped on the front mat to knock on the door, it screamed out at her and made her jump back.

Michael opened the door with a grin, his face all painted up in Devil glory. His eyebrows were peaked, a pencil-thin mustache graced his top lip, and his face was both supernaturally pale and red-sheened at the same time. His horns looked glued to his temples, and as he swirled a cape around him, a forked tail covered in scales poked out beneath it. He looked fantastic. No store-bought outfit for him.

"Thank God!" he said, seeing her. He pulled her into the house with a hug and took two of the three ice bags from her. "You should have asked someone to help you with these."

"Thank God?" Ally asked, smiling.

"I need someone sane here—Sandra and Billy are driving me crazy." Ally laughed at the irony of Michael calling her sane. He seemed to get the joke and grinned at her again.

"Where's the costume?" he asked.

"In the back pack," she said, patting the strap on her shoulder. "With everything I could possibly think of to help transform me."

Michael nodded, distracted by Billy hanging a dancing skeleton from the ceiling in the kitchen.

"You need to hang it higher or we'll be hitting our heads on it all night."

Billy grunted a response, which went well with his cave-man ensemble. Ally admired his legs and wondered if he was wearing anything under his animal-patterned tartan. Michael caught her look.

"Like any good cave man, he's going commando," Michael said with a wink.

Ally raised her eyebrows with a grin.

After dumping the ice in the kitchen, Michael grabbed Ally's hand and led her to the master bedroom, where the decorations extended in the form of mysterious candles and charms scattered about. Staring at them, Ally suddenly realized that they were probably real, and probably belonged to Sandra. She wondered if there was power in any of the things around her, if they protected against evil spirits—if they would be used the spell.

Ally hugged Michael on impulse as he dug her costume out of her bag. He hugged her back, then held her at arm's length, stared into her eyes.

"It's going to be okay," he said quietly.

She nodded back.

"We don't have to do the costume thing, the party. We could leave right now, go somewhere, do whatever."

"I want to," she said. "I want to be here, with people. I want a party. I want something that's mine." He nodded at her.

Sandra came in then, dressed in a flowing skirt with bells on her feet; she made a perfect gypsy and Ally smiled at her.

"You look great!" she said. Sandra shook her hips in response, making the charms on her belt jangle.

"And now it's your turn." She turned to Michael who was holding up the dreaded purple belt. "Oh, my God!"

"Oh, this is just horrible," Michael agreed. "No wonder you were feeling depressed about it." He held up the rest of the outfit, the shapeless black V-neck dress, the bell sleeves trimmed in feathers, and the traditional witch's hat, also trailing feathers. "But the rest is workable," he said to Ally.

She gave him an encouraging smile. "If a gay man and a practicing Wicca can't make a decent witch out of me, then I refuse to believe in anything good anymore."

Michael and Sandra laughed and Ally smiled. This could be her last night in the real world. She had made up her mind to enjoy it.

With the help of some scissors, some black thread, and a creative use of scarves, Ally's feather witch was transformed into a stylish full-figured outfit that hugged her curves in a way she didn't think would have been possible. Michael did her make up like back in their Rocky Horror days, and Sandra found some appropriately witch-like jewelry from her personal collection. The end result was very nice indeed. Ally looked like a modern-day Wicca going out for a night on the town, feathers accenting her goodness and sense of fun. She stood in front of the full-length mirror and did a slow turn, taking in the entire outfit and feeling sort of like a fairy-tale princess, if the princess was Goth. And a witch. And going to a much less formal party.

"Thanks!" she said to Michael and Sandra, and as she looked at their smiling faces, she felt a sudden rise of tears. She turned away quickly in case they saw. No need to upset them, too. There was a knock on the door, and Billy poked his head in, saying that some of the guests had arrived. Then it was a hustle and bustle out to the party, where people milled around; Michael taking them on tours of the garage and back yard so that they could scream and moan, as their natures decided, over the cheap scare tactics.

As the welcome mat screamed another person's arrival, Ally shrunk back into a corner, watching all the people around her with new eyes, eyes that knew these could be the last real people she would ever see. She felt like she was being over-dramatic, and like she was not being dramatic enough.

Allison appeared, wearing the sexiest looking witch costume Ally had ever seen.

"Double, double, toil and trouble, fire burn and cauldron bubble," Allison said, rubbing her hands together maliciously.

Ally schooled her features to remain blank.

"How now, you secret, black, and midnight hag! What is't you do?" Ally countered. "You know Macbeth because I do," she added.

"Whatever. My reading was better." Allison swished her skirt around her knees as though annoyed. "Oh, here comes that friend of Michael's you like to think likes you."

"You're going to give witches a bad name if you don't start dancing," Sandra told Ally. "We're not known for being wall flowers."

Allison looked over Sandra. "I like her style," she announced. "When I'm you, I think I'll keep her as a friend."

"I'm not much of a dancer," Ally told Sandra. "I even mess up group clapping."

"I'm an amazing dancer," Allison commented. She looked over at Ally. "By the way you look like a black hog in that outfit." Ally looked away, her jaw grinding.

"As one witch to another, I'm telling you, you have to dance. We dance. It's what witches do."

"She's a witch?" Allison asked, looking over Sandra's costume again.

"I thought Wicca didn't buy into that dancing naked in the moonlight bull?" Ally said.

"Wicca?" Allison asked, and Ally wondered idly why Allison, who was supposed to be her, didn't know that.

"You know, dancing actually sounds pretty good," Ally said, her annoyance giving her new courage.

Sandra just smiled. "Have I told you how awesome you look in that costume yet?" she asked Ally.

"What is she, blind?" Allison remarked.

"Yes," Ally said to Sandra. "But tell me again." She grinned at the Wicca-turned-gypsy and followed her out onto the area of the living room cleared as a dance floor, looking back briefly to notice with satisfaction Allison's look of disgust.

It was a party, and she was dressed up as a witch and dancing with another, while the penetrating gaze of her most critical, if unseen, critic bored into her, and Ally felt something she hadn't felt since she was nine years old—freedom. What did she care if Allison mocked her? Allison mocked her anyway. And what if the people all around her were going to judge her? She was going to die soon and would never have to see any of them again. Her upcoming demise was giving Ally the kind of giddy carefree attitude she had long envied in other people.

As Ally felt the heat of the other bodies all around her, and the pounding of bass vibrating in her chest, she let go of something she didn't even know she had been holding onto all this time. She let go of her fear, and just danced.

She swung her butt around, raised her hands over her head, twisted her torso and hips in time to the music. Ally let it all hang out, and for once didn't care what was hanging or who was looking.

Allison appeared in front of her, her own witch's costume shorter, tighter, and flashier, and danced the dance of a pop music starlet.

Ally felt the stirrings of doubt in her mind, and closed her eyes to the image in front of her. *No, I'm going to dance. Dammit! I'm going to dance!*

And she did. Eyes closed to everything else around her, she moved through the song, opened her eyes to smile at Sandra, who grinned back at her, and sang along with the chorus of House of Pain's "Jump Around." And she did as the song told, going as low as she could, shimmying her way back up. Sandra clapped at Ally, moved in close to dance next to her, and they matched their wiggles, danced side-by-side, back-to-back, banged hips together, faced each other and laughed.

Ally couldn't remember the last time she'd had this much fun. She felt, for a moment, completely in love with the world, and all the people in it.

Not getting the reaction she wanted by strutting her stuff, Allison began to whisper in Ally's ear.

"Your stomach rolls are showing," she said as Ally raised her arms above her head again. Ally felt them falling to her sides and tried to play it off like she wanted to do that.

Allison laughed. "Do you know how huge your ass looks when you move it like that? Big, and wide, and shaking with all the glory of a tub of pudding."

Ally's movements grew smaller, tighter, less loose and a lot less free. She made eye contact with Sandra in an attempt to find that feeling again, to block out Allison's voice which stayed in her ear regardless of how she moved.

Sandra smiled at her, then moved her hips in a way that made her charm-laced belt jangle like any good belly dancer's.

"She dances next to you to make herself look better. She doesn't really like you, except that you make her feel better about herself. Look how she flaunts her body, knowing you can't, knowing you're so ugly compared to her she must look like an angel from heaven compared to you." Allison's words dripped their bitter poison in Ally's ear, and she looked away from Sandra and her perfectly flat stomach.

And that's when she realized. She had heard Allison's voice before. She'd been hearing Allison's voice for longer than she knew about Allison.

You don't deserve love.

You aren't good enough.

Everyone is judging you.

Ally made her way as quickly as possible to Michael's room. Since the beds were too high to flop down on, she settled for collapsing on a chair. She was putting the pieces together. And the picture they were making was terrifying.

"Ally?" a tentative voice said from the doorway. "Ally, what happened? One moment we were dancing and having fun, and the next you…left." Ally heard her move further into the room, heard the jangling of her ankle-bells, the clanking of her belt. "It was her, wasn't it? She was there."

Ally turned toward Sandra.

"Tell her to go away," Allison demanded, suddenly appearing in front of Ally, glaring at Sandra. "Tell her you feel sick, have your period, something. Make her go away."

The anger pouring off of Allison was overwhelming. Ally stared hard into Sandra's eyes, alarm rising in her. Allison couldn't know what they planned.

"Do you ever get that voice in your head?" she asked, "that voice that tells you how awful you are?"

"If you tell her anything, she'll think you're insane. You don't want to tell her anything." Allison's voice was a razor-blade, and Ally could feel it cutting into her. She also knew that Allison didn't know what was going on, and that was a comfort. Sandra picked up on Ally's clue immediately.

"We all have that voice," she said, nodding, kneeling in front of Ally. "The best thing you can do is to ignore it, not give it any power."

"She doesn't actually care about you. She can't help you. It's too late. No point in talking to her about it all. She won't remember you in a few hours anyway."

Ally turned her head away from Allison's tirade and searched around the room. Maybe one of these things was a talisman that could make Allison go away?

"Are you okay?" Sandra asked.

"I need some water," Ally said.

"You want to come with me, or stay here, alone?" Sandra emphasized the last word, clearly concerned.

"I'm fine," Ally said. "I just really want the water." Sandra nodded. She left quickly, closing the door on the noise of the party outside.

"What do you think you can tell her?" Allison asked, pacing the floor of the bedroom. "What do you think she'll do with the information, besides think you're crazy?"

"You've won already. Must you keep haunting me, ruining the few hours I have left?" Ally sat back in her chair, pushed her knees under her chin, and wrapped her arms around them.

"You poor thing," Allison muttered. "Maybe I owe you one night after all."

It was a subtle change, the passing from reality to fantasy, but Ally could feel it coming on. The air had a filtered look to it, the texture of things became less defined, the smell of the air muted. And Ally pictured quickly what it would be like to have another musical-style fantasy here, with these people, people she knew and cared about moved around like puppets, acting out roles cast for them by Allison's malicious mind. It was more than she was prepared to deal with, so Ally jumped up and ran from the room.

She ran right into Michael and another, significantly taller, man.

"Whoa! Where you rushing to?" Michael asked with a grin.

He was in good spirits, the Devil in him having a hellishly good time. His friend, tall, narrow-shouldered, and what could best be described as lanky, had suitably dressed himself as the Scarecrow, straw poking out of a stuffed shirt and overflowing a large hat. He gave Ally a goofy grin and crossed his arms over his chest, pointing his fingers in opposite directions.

"You could go that-a-way, or that-a-way," he said, looking in each direction in turn. Ally laughed despite herself. The Scarecrow smiled again and shrugged his shoulders self-consciously, making him look even more in character.

"I'm Seth," he said, and offered a gloved hand, straw poking out of the bottom of his sleeve. Ally took it tentatively.

"I promise not to set you on fire if you promise not to throw any buckets of water at me," she said and smiled. And then immediately blushed as he gave her a quizzical look. Michael laughed.

"We'll call you the as-yet-unseen Good Witch of the South. The movie only has the one from the North in it, right?"

"Right!" Seth said, finally catching on. "No buckets of water. Sorry. I'm a bit slow," he added. He patted his head. "Just straw you know. Ally, right?"

Ally nodded shyly, charmed. And then, as Michael stood there beaming at her, she had a terrifying thought. Maybe this was all just a fantasy. She was meeting a cute—as far as she could tell underneath all the make-up—and funny guy who seemed interested in talking with her. Maybe this was all Allison's doing. She looked down at her body, checking to see if it looked changed at all. She sniffed the air, trying to see if there were any strong scents in it which would prove it was real life and not a fantasy. And then her face grew hot as she realized that both Seth and Michael were staring at her, confused at her behavior.

"Uh, thought I smelled something funny," she said.

Seth shrugged again. "Might be me—real hay. Seemed like a good idea at the time, but then I wasn't counting on getting water dumped on me. Wet hay has a very distinctive odor." He seemed embarrassed, and as Ally inhaled, she became very away of the odor he was talking about. It didn't smell bad though.

"It smells like when it rains in August, and everything is so dry it just soaks it all up, all the water." She leaned a little closer in to Seth, enjoying the smell and the memory of long ago summer days.

He grinned at her. "Yeah! That's what I've been thinking all night."

She smiled back at him. "Who dumped the water on you?"

Sandra arrived then with the promised cup of water for Ally.

"Me," Sandra said, shaking her head. "I was emptying an ice bucket and ran smack into him; I can be such a klutz sometimes."

"Sandra," Michael said, motioning her closer. "Look who we finally got together." Sandra smiled at the Scarecrow while he and Ally looked flustered.

"He thinks she's hot. He'll forget all about you now that Sandra is here." Ally tried to ignore Allison's voice.

"I'm glad you two got to meet," Sandra said, and smiled at Ally and Seth.

"Sandra's told me a lot about you," he said to Ally with an embarrassed smile.

"Because he's Sandra's friend. He's just being nice, just humoring her. Really, he wants her, not you," Allison told Ally.

"All good things of course," Sandra said, smiling warmly.

"And she wants him too. She could have anyone, but she's taking him just so you can't have him. Not like you really had him in the first place. Look at how they stand so close…"

The smell of August in the rain was fading, and Seth and Sandra seemed to be standing very close indeed. He reached out and touched her arm, and she gazed longingly into his eyes. They seemed unaware of the world around them. Ally tried to shake off the feeling—this wasn't real, she had to fight this. Her reality was slipping away.

"The Monster Mash," she said suddenly. "Who wants to dance?" She moved back toward the dancing section, trying to hold onto reality, to push Allison away. So startling was her announcement, and her action, that Allison let the fantasy go.

"I don't even have to ruin this for you," she said. "You'll ruin it for yourself."

She disappeared, and Ally turned back to Sandra, Michael, and a confused Seth, who was not standing very close to Sandra after all.

"Gone?" Sandra asked. Ally nodded.

"For now."

"What was happening?" Michael asked. He and Sandra both seemed to have forgotten about Seth, who was becoming increasingly bewildered by the conversation, but Ally's eyes were glued to him. She tried to smile warmly, but wasn't sure that she succeeded.

"I just really love this song," she said, hoping that if she focused on the first part of the conversation Seth would forget about the second.

"Yeah, sure," he said.

"Dance with us?" she asked, and tentatively offered her hand. He took it in his, a piece of straw poking her in the arm. He smiled at her then, and Ally felt her heart lighten. *Let me just hold onto this moment. Let me just once have a moment like this. Let this be real.*

Seth followed her to the dance floor, Michael and Sandra trailing behind. Michael seemed to want to pull Ally aside, but Sandra stopped him.

"Now, when you do the Monster Mash," Seth said, "the important thing to remember is that it's actually a ceremonial dance in the Monster community."

"Really?" Ally asked with a smile.

"Yes," Seth said. "It's a celebration of all things Monster. You must perform it exactly or else it's an insult to the community."

Ally laughed.

"And what is the exact way to perform it?" she asked. He took her hands, pulled her a little closer, than began twisting, doing the mashed potato.

"Like you're grinding down the ripped-out hearts of the people you just maimed and killed."

Ally laughed and ground her own heel into the floor, imagining Allison's shriveled heart beneath it.

Seth grinned at her zeal. "And don't forget your Monster face," he said, glaring at her. She laughed and glared back before erupting into another set of giggles. He laughed too, and they continued to mash.

Long before midnight though, and long before she wanted it to be, Ally had to give up her real-life fantasy-like evening.

Sandra caught her eye from behind Seth, and Ally nodded back.

"I'm going to have to go," she said. He glanced at his watch.

"Really? Why so soon?"

Ally hesitated. She didn't want him to think she was making an excuse to get away from him.

"My sister," she said quickly. "Misha—she asked me to cat sit and I have to go get the cat tonight."

She smiled and inwardly cringed at her own lame excuse.

Seth just nodded. "Well if you have to go—it was really great meeting you."

Ally blushed and smiled. "It was great meeting you too," she said, feeling suddenly shy. And then sad. She'd finally met someone fantasy-worthy who actually wanted to spend time with her, and in all likelihood she was never going to see him again.

"Can I call you sometime?" he asked, and it was his turn to be shy. Ally was charmed by the nervous break in his voice. He cleared it. "So that maybe we could get together again? When you maybe have more time?"

"I would really like that," she said honestly, looking into his eyes. He grinned at her, looked into her eyes. The moment stretched out between them.

"Ally?" Sandra said, breaking the spell. She came up next to her, pulled lightly on her sleeve.

"Right," Ally said, turning away, her face flushed.

"Right," Seth repeated. "Your sister's cat."

Sandra gave Ally a quizzical look.

"Why I have to leave," Ally explained quickly.

Sandra nodded.

"So then, I'll call you then," Seth said, and then shook his head. "And we'll get together and I'll see you... then."

Ally grinned at him. "Until then, then," she said and he grinned back.

As Sandra walked with her to Michael's room, where she was going to change, she hooked her arm through Ally's. "You guys are so cute together," she said.

Ally's grin faded. "We would have been," she said quietly.

Sandra squeezed her arm. "You will be. We're going to beat her."

Ally nodded, but couldn't muster much enthusiasm for it. She turned back quickly for one last look at Seth, his head bopping to the music above the crowd.

Michael emerged from his bathroom, face freshly scrubbed, horns gone, and Sandra pulled out her own clothes to change into. Ally took her bag into the bathroom, closing the door behind her. She stared at the tile, the frosted window blurring the light of the moon beyond it. She looked in the mirror above the sink, tried to see what Seth had seen in her.

Brown hair curled under the witch's hat, colorful scarves accentuating her curves, a necklace dipping into her cleavage. Ally smiled at herself sadly. *Sure, just as I'm about to die I finally like what I see in the mirror.* She shook her head, and changed as quickly as possible.

Joining Sandra and Michael, who carried a bag full of supplies, Ally wordlessly snuck through the back door of the house and into the backyard. From there they went through the gate and up the street to where Sandra had parked her car. The sky was clear, the moon was out, and hope wrapped itself around the three of them. They had a date with a hallucination they didn't plan on being late for.

SHaTTeReD

It was a long drive out to Vasquez Rocks, or at least it felt long to Ally as Sandra drove her VW Bug up the 14 Freeway. Finally, Sandra got off at Agua Dulce Canyon, turned left, and made her winding way down the dark road. Ally stared silently out the passenger window, feeling the hiss of the air sliding in over the top of the glass, just slightly rolled down, and watched the scenery pass as quickly as her thoughts. She shouldn't be doing this. She should be doing this. This would work. This wouldn't work. She was going to die. She was going to live. She deserved to die. She deserved to live.

"Almost there now," Sandra said, slowing to an almost-stop at the stop sign. Ally looked ahead, and could just make out the towering shapes of Vasquez Rocks' most famous outcrop in the moonlight.

"Why here again?" Michael asked from the back seat.

"It's a very old place," Sandra said. "A native tribe, the Tataviam Indians, used to live around here, and they would perform their rites and ceremonies at the rocks. Mexicans used to come here too, and some grave sites are scattered, hidden, around the park. Actually, the whole place was named after a Mexican outlaw."

"Really?" Ally asked, frowning at what she could see of the rocks. "They wouldn't name a park after an outlaw."

"But they did," Sandra said confidently. "Tiburcio Vasquez. He was the Robin Hood of his people, and was eventually hung in 1875. But when he would hide here, it was said that the magic in the rocks themselves protected him from the sheriffs."

"Protected an outlaw?"

"He was a thief, sure, but he gave to the poor families, and they prayed for him. There are all kinds of magic Ally. This place is home to many of them."

"Enough magic for the spell to work?" Michael asked.

"Definitely," Sandra said.

Ally wished she felt as confident.

Sandra drove past the entrance of the park a little ways and pulled up to the fence that was supposed to keep people like them out. "We'll have to hike the rest of the way in," she said.

Michael took the bag from Sandra and signaled for the Wicca to lead the way.

Vasquez Rocks were large layers of yellow-gray sandstone with some areas of shale, basalt, and reddish-brown conglomerate, and tilted up as much as fifty degrees from the ground, the highest rock almost a hundred and fifty feet.

Ally looked up at the familiar formation—their destination, Sandra had informed them—and decided she liked it better on TV than in real life. It'd been featured on all kinds of TV shows, including Star Trek and CSI. She'd been to Vasquez Rocks before on school field trips and with out-of-town family members, but they had always just driven to that famous rock and climbed only it.

"Do we have to climb up it?" she asked Sandra, nodding toward the rock.

"Not all the way," Sandra informed her. "It would be too windy for the candles."

Ally nodded as though that made sense, and watched Sandra head for the fence.

"Don't you have a flashlight?" Ally whispered anxiously at Sandra's back.

Michael walked behind her, and that gave her some small comfort.

"Our eyes will adjust better without one," Sandra whispered back. "And this will draw less attention."

Ally thought the sound of her screaming as soon as something crawled near her would draw a lot more attention than a little flashlight beam, but kept that to herself. Instead she concentrated on making out the darkness of the ground from the darkness of the, well, dark. Then she hurried to keep up with Sandra.

They climbed over the fence, Michael helping Ally balance as she made her way over, and then set out at a brisk pace toward the largest rock in the park. Ally couldn't help but look around and imagine what shapes were lurking in the shadows. She pictured rattle snakes all around them, and spiders, and lizards, and kept looking for the glowing eyes of a bobcat or mountain lion, right before it decided to make a meal of them. Sandra found, and then kept to, a trail, and every now and again, they would pass a small plaque that, if they could read it, would have told them about the geological interests of the rocks, or possibly of some historical fact.

The air was a lot colder than Ally would have imagined, and the wind whipped at her clothes. After only a few minutes of hiking, a sheen of sweat coated her face, and her breath came quick, so she forgot to imagine what was in the dark all around her and concentrated on keeping up with Sandra.

Coyotes called in the distance, and Ally looked up, startled, suppressing the scream that jumped into her throat.

"They're a ways off," Sandra said, and Ally wondered briefly if coyotes ever took down people. They traveled in packs. There would certainly be enough of them.

"They like rabbits," Sandra said then, as if reading Ally's mind. "A lot of rabbits live out here."

"How do you know so much about it?" Ally asked.

"I like it here," Sandra said quietly and kept walking.

Ally followed quickly after. "Are you sure you know the way?"

"I've been here at night before," Sandra said. "They do moonlight hikes, about once a month, if they can. The rocks are beautiful in the moonlight."

Sandra's voice had gone all wistful and dreamy as she talked about the park, and Ally envied Sandra a connection with nature that would make her want to take a hike at night. She tried to look at the park through Sandra's eyes, see the moon lighting up the rocks, the stars twinkling in the clear sky ahead, their light shining brighter, free from the competition of city lights. Agua Dulce was too rural to have any lights at all, outside of those few that came from homes.

Everything felt very real to her then, the feel of the ground beneath her feet, the way the sandy earth gave way slightly with each step she took, Steps that kicked up a small batch of dust into an eddy around her legs, drifting slowly up to her face so that she could breathe the scent of it in. She felt the wind sharp and cold against her cheeks, chilling her nose, and drying the light layer of sweat on her forehead. She felt her heart beat, the blood pumping through her body. Ally felt too the warmth and nearness of Sandra ahead of her, and Michael behind, heard them both breathing, heard their footsteps echo in the silence of the park.

Finally the trail gave way to the large open expanse of a dirt parking lot. They jogged across it, anxious now to get to their destination. Sandra led the others up the rocks, just a little ways, where they were still mostly flat and the highest peak stretched out away from them.

Michael took off the bag and handed it to Sandra. She rummaged through it, pulling out jars of colored salt-like substances, powder maybe, and candles. She pulled three cushions out too, the kind you use for bleacher seats, and they were so unmystical, Ally couldn't stop herself from giggling.

"We may have to be here a while," Sandra said with a shrug. "They'll make us more comfortable." Ally nodded, fought her face into a more serious expression. She caught Michael's eye and had to look quickly away. He too seemed amused by the cushions.

When Sandra took out a long knife, the serious expression came to Ally without her having to try at all. "That doesn't make me more comfortable," she said.

"Me either," seconded Michael, and he and Ally exchanged a look that had nothing of their earlier mirth in it.

"It's ceremonial," Sandra assured them. "The stones in the hilt help focus power." She pulled more things from her bag: an old book, a long lighter, a bunch of incense, an incense burner, a couple more stones, and a small square mirror.

Something about the mirror caught Ally's memory, and she struggled to pull the connection free. It was as if something was purposely pushing it out of her mind, and Ally let it go for the time being.

Sandra opened the book and told Ally to hold it. Ally grabbed the leather spine and shook her head, still trying to place the memory of the mirror. She watched instead as Sandra used the colored powdery substances to draw a shape on the rocks while she directed Michael where to place the candles at various intervals all around. He lit them carefully. When they were done, Ally could see a pentagram made out of Sandra's powder, Michael's candles at each of the five points of the star. Sandra put the cushions across from each other. They formed a triangle inscribed in the middle of the star which lay in the middle of the greater circle. Sandra put the mirror in center of the triangle, the extra stones on each side of it and the knife in front of it, presumably on Sandra's side.

"Wait here," she said to Ally and Michael, then scrambled back down the rocks. She scooped something up from the ground and put it in a small pouch, then climbed back up. Finally, she pulled out a small metal dish. "Spit," she told Ally, holding the dish out to her.

"In there?" Ally asked. "Why?"

"You're the one being haunted. We need to connect you to the spell. It's your blood or your saliva, your choice. DNA, you know?"

Ally looked at Michael.

He shrugged and she could tell that he was as out of his element as she was.

Ally spit quickly and clumsily into the dish, wiping drool from her lips afterward.

"More," Sandra said, and Ally spit again. Sandra nodded her head, satisfied, and opened her pouch. She poured the dirt she got from the ground into the dish and used a small spoon-like instrument with carvings on it to mix the dirt and saliva together. Then she wiped the spoon onto Ally's forehead.

"Hey!" Ally cried, moving away from her.

"It's part of the spell," Sandra said. "Stay still—I have to do your cheeks now." She smeared more of the muddy mixture onto Ally's face, and Ally had to fight the urge to wipe it all off. Then Sandra wiped some onto her own face and Ally shook her head. At least it was her own spit on her face. Sandra was wiping on someone else's.

Michael stepped forward to get his own spit swipe, and Sandra marked him as well. Finally, Sandra took out another jar and motioned for Ally to sit inside the shape on one of the cushions. She gestured Michael toward another.

"Don't step on the pentagram," she warned the others, and they nodded.

Sandra took the cushion next to the knife, and placed the little dish of spit-mud in front of her. She mixed some of the powder from the newest jar in with the dirt, then sprinkled more of the powder onto the mirror.

"You said she showed up in a mirror, so," Sandra said, and then shrugged again. It occurred to Ally that Sandra might not really know what she was doing, that the spell was bigger than anything Sandra had tried before. Ally went from thinking witch craft wasn't real and they were just messing around to believing whole heartedly it was and that maybe they should leave the spirit realm alone. She shivered and hunched into herself, saying a silent prayer to all that was good in the world to look out for her and Sandra and Michael and not let anything possess any of them. Well, anything new, at any rate. Her fate may already be sealed, but she didn't want the same for her friends.

And it was thinking of possession, and watching the wind stir the powder on the surface of the mirror, which glinted in the moonlight, that made Ally finally break through the block in her head and remember.

"Bobby," she said out loud and Sandra and Michael looked up at her, startled.

"Who's Bobby?" Sandra asked.

"From the Center?" Michael asked.

Ally looked up at him, self-consciously rubbing her arm.

"He touched me," she said. "He touched me, and that's how it all started."

Sandra stared at her blankly, but Ally didn't care. She could feel it then, the shudder that had gone through her body, Bobby's bruising grip. And she could hear the sorrowful panic in Bobby's voice. "You!" Bobby had shouted. "It's on you, it's you! I can't take it anymore—I'm sorry." His eyes had been filled with tears. "He'll let me go, he'll go to you." And then, something had. Something had left Bobby and gone to Ally. "You!" Bobby had said. "Not me anymore."

"I remember—he had a mirror," Michael said. "He had said he was being haunted…God, I should have connected that before!"

Sandra still seemed confused, but Ally felt a sudden surge of clarity. The voices, the extra cruel voices that had been haunting her the last few days, they showed up after then. They were Allison, had to be. Only the last few hours, they had been gone as Allison had become more real. It was all making a sick kind of confused sense—as much sense as any of this made. And more importantly, if Bobby could get rid of it, so could she. Whatever it was that Allison was, she was something else before, something that had haunted Bobby. Bobby who wouldn't let go of his mirror. She looked at Sandra and Michael excitedly.

"I'm not the first person this thing has haunted," she said. "But I'm damn well going to be the last."

Michael nodded. "After he touched you, Bobby got better. If he could get better, so can you." They explained Bobby as quickly as they could to Sandra, and then all stared at the mirror thoughtfully.

"Then we have to trap the spirit in the mirror," Sandra said at last. "A binding spell. It's what I had planned anyway. The crystals will help bind it. And then it won't be able to haunt you, or anyone else, ever again."

She looked up at Ally and smiled, but Ally could tell she was afraid. Ally smiled back anyway.

"Then let's get started," Michael said, more bravely than Ally herself felt.

The coyotes cried again, and Ally couldn't help but feel there was a tone of warning to their cries. Sandra picked up her knife, unsheathed it, and cut herself quickly. The movement shocked Ally, as did the reality of watching Sandra mix her own blood in with Ally's spit-mud with the knife tip, then smear the mixture over the mirror. Michael seemed just as surprised. He and Ally looked at each other nervously. What had they agreed to be a part of? Sandra began to speak then, something in another language, *probably Latin*, and the wind picked up around them, making the candle flames dance.

This is a real spell. Goose bumps rose up on her arms.

Sandra spoke her words again, louder, and again, louder still. Her eyes were closed, and she concentrated on her words, her hands gripping the hilt of her knife tightly. The wind seemed to be all around them then, and Ally felt genuine fear, fear like she had never experienced before, go through her.

This is a very real spell. And then, as Sandra chanted, knife still in hand, the Wicca began to glow. The glow was faint at first, and Ally thought it was some trick of the candles, the candles that managed to keep burning despite the wind blowing up all around them. Then the glow got stronger, took on a greenish tone.

Suddenly Sandra opened her eyes and stared straight at Ally.

The eyes that Ally stared back into were not the light green-ha-zel full of humor that belonged to Sandra, but a dark, fiery color Ally couldn't place, filled with something Ally didn't want to name. Sandra stared at Ally with her changed eyes, and then spoke in a deep voice not her own.

"It has begun."

And then the eyes looked away, looked at a shape starting to form above the mirror.

Ally looked down at her own hands, and was surprised to see that same odd greenish glow coming from them. She looked at Michael and he had it too, but he did not look right. He seemed too still, focused on the shape forming in between the three of them, above the mirror.

Ally felt it then, the buzz of energy all around her, cours-ing through her, connecting her to the rock beneath her, and the moon above her, to Sandra and to Michael. There was an energy to the very air itself, and she felt it converging in one spot, pooling together and writhing into shape.

The shape grew a head, and arms, and legs, and fiery red-dish-brown hair, and cold, piercing blue eyes, and Allison glared at them, her face full of fury, her teeth clenched, her features con-toured into ugly rage.

"You stupid bitches!" she called out, her form wavering ghost-like above the mirror. "You have no idea what you're deal-ing with! You think you can bind me? You think you're strong enough?"

And she laughed, and it was evil, and the coyotes in the dis-tance felt her laugh and cried out in alarm.

Ally wanted to run away, wanted to scream, wanted to faint, wanted to do anything that was not sitting there glowing in front of an angry evil spirit.

Sandra's gaze was steady as she stared at Allison, who turned in the air to glare at her.

"You are not welcome in this place," she said in her un-Sandra voice. "You will be banished from it." And then she said something in Latin that Ally couldn't understand, something Michael picked up and repeated in a voice unlike his own, and Ally wondered why everyone else seemed to be taken over and not her. Then Allison shrieked with rage. Her ghost-like form writhed, as though in pain, and Ally gasped.

Suddenly her entire body felt like it was on fire. Ally's skin felt tight all around her, as though it was shrinking, pulling on her, trying to collapse in on itself. At the same time, her blood felt too warm in her veins, and pounded too loudly and hard in her head. She reached a hand out toward Sandra, tried to speak, but her voice was locked inside her pain. Ally felt like she was going to implode.

Allison laughed. Sandra saw Ally then, and understood, and said something else in Latin, which again Michael echoed in a voice too deep for him. Allison shrieked again, this time in frustration, and Ally felt a great releasing of her body, and hunched forward, breathing hard as though she'd been holding her breath, and concentrated on making her heart slow down.

She looked up and saw that Sandra's glow had taken on a different taint—it was as if the new color, silvery blue, was fighting with the old color, the bright green. The colors tangled around Sandra's body, and the Wicca closed her eyes and concentrated, as though she was the color green itself. Ally realized then that Sandra was that verdant color, and that Allison was the silvery blue. This battle of auras was as real a battle as Muhammad Ali versus

George Forman. This rumble in the jungle was for life or death.

And Sandra was losing. Ally looked over at Michael. The same green, bolstered by a reddish glow that seemed to be Michael's own aura, and silver-blue encompassed him, and Ally understood that somehow he was tied into this battle too, this battle that Allison was winning.

"Allison!" Ally called out, and tried to will her own energy into the fight—the purplish-blue that Sandra had told her was her own aura—tried to do something to help Sandra and Michael fight off that silvery blue, the same silvery blue as the lake in her dreams. "Allison!" she called again. "Take me! It's me you want!"

The apparition turned her dead-cold eyes onto Ally then, and again Ally felt the constricting of her skin, the straining of her heart. She understood what it was then, could see the silver-blue interlace itself around the purplish color spreading out from her hands, and Ally fought back the only way she knew how. She imagined the greenish glow staying, willed her own purplish-blue to blend with it, envisioned it overtaking the other poisoned aura, and concentrated as hard as she could on the colors as though her willing could make it so.

"You're not strong enough for this fight!" Allison snickered, and the tightness in Ally's chest increased. She heard Sandra, with Michael's echo, speak another Latin phrase, and the pressure building in her slackened a bit. It didn't go away, but Ally didn't feel like she was being compressed anymore. She looked over to Sandra and saw that the silver-blue light was on her too; her hand reached out for Ally's. Ally understood, and grabbed Sandra's hand, interlacing their fingers, concentrating on putting everything she ever was into that hold, giving Sandra all that she had to give. She turned and saw Michael's outstretched hand, took his, saw that his other hand was holding Sandra's, the knife now sitting in front of her, the stone in its hilt glowing.

Now Allison must fight all three of them, her energies divided, strained. The greenish glow started to spread, interlaced with Michael's red, Ally's purplish-blue, forcing the silver-blue back, back into Allison who shook with fury.

"You can't win!" she called out, but her voice was strained, and Ally concentrated harder, picturing their colors spreading more, watching with a thrill as they did so, and she knew then that they were going to win.

Allison shrieked again and gave a last push forward. Again the choking feeling came over Ally, and she almost gave into it, almost let it take her over, but Sandra's grip was iron on hers, Michael's stone, and they demanded that she fight back. Ally did and the choking subsided. Ally sensed then that Allison was all used up, had given all that she could give.

When the pressure was all but gone from her body, Ally watched as Allison slowly shrunk into the mirror, the silver-blue light being pulled into it like petals closing in on themselves. Finally, all that was left of her was the glow on the mirror's surface.

Ally looked up at Sandra, wanted to grin at her. She found Sandra shaking, the greenish light around her frantic and fevered looking. She was chanting. Had been, Ally realized, the entire time, and her gaze was locked on the mirror. Ally wanted to get up, to go to her, but she was too scared to break the spell, to in any way cause Sandra more pain. Her hand felt clammy in Ally's, and her grip weakened. Ally held onto it harder.

Michael too seemed to be aware that Sandra was in danger, the other-ness of him gone as he stared with horror at the Wicca's struggle.

The greenish light was pouring into the mirror now, the silver-blue surface swallowing it up, and Ally felt then that Sandra was being swallowed up with it. She looked around helplessly, and her eyes caught on the still-glowing hilt of the knife in front of Sandra.

Sandra was convulsing now, and Ally felt her own energy starting to slip away as well. Allison's mirror was going to drain all of them, kill all of them.

Unless Ally did something to stop it.

She let go of her friends' hands, lunged forward and yanked the knife up, plunging it blade first into the surface of the mirror.

The air screeched all around her. The mirror shattered, shards flying everywhere, and the force of the explosion blew Ally out of the geometric shape. Michael flew away into the dark, his body crashing hard into rock. Sandra was blown away on the other side to fall limply, like a doll, against her own boulder. Only Ally was knocked off the rocks entirely, and felt her body land hard on the dirt below. She tried, for a moment, to move, to think, to stay conscious. Then the moment passed, as did she, into darkness.

Dreams to Remember

Juxtaposition.

Ally had never liked the word, but, again, it was the first to come to mind as she stared into the swirling surface of a silver-blue substance that had been the lake of her dreams, a mess of blue-grays and silvers, whirling together, liquid, and yet very unlike water. And, as before, floating on top were two images, juxtaposed. Ally as she was, and Ally as she had dreamed herself to be. They circled each other, overlapping at times, morphing into different poses and angles. The distinction was clear.

Plain Ally. Beautiful Ally.

Fat Ally. Thin Ally.

Round, soft Ally. Hard, athletic Ally.

Smart Ally. Sexy Ally.

Round and round they spun, until, finally, only one image remained—Ally as she was. She reached for that image of herself, reached out to pull it closer, to merge with it, become it again.

Something held her back.

Round cheeks, frizzy hair, not-perfectly-white teeth. It wasn't what Ally wanted to be, what she wanted to claim. But it was all there was to claim, the image of Allison, of perfection, gone from the lake's surface.

And then the image of herself—her own reflection, she realized—reached its hand out and took hold of dream-Ally's arm, where Bobby had grabbed her, and pulled Ally into the liquid silver of the lake.

Last time, she'd swum through it. This time she fell, fast,

spinning, feeling the rush of air all around her, watching the ground rise up to her faster than she could think. She opened her mouth to scream.

Ally sat up, her heart pounding, her eyes opened, and stared around. She was awake now, and that was all that let her know that she had been dreaming before. She hadn't really fallen. And then, as she looked at the dirt all around her, the looming shape of the rock above her, and the predawn light of a sun that had not quite made it up over the distant hills, she remembered. She had fallen, and fallen hard. Ally looked to her side and saw Sandra's knife, the knife she had shattered Allison's mirror with.

Sandra! Michael! Ally scrambled to her feet, stiff and sore muscles protesting and her right knee popping loudly. She tried to move quickly but could only limp her way to the rock and drag her body up and over it.

The first one she saw was Michael, who had landed against the rock opposite the one Ally was now scrambling up. She limped to him as quickly as she could. He was awake and moaning, holding his head.

"Michael!" she squealed when she got to him.

"I'm okay," he managed, opening his eyes to look at Ally.

"Stay still," she told him.

He sat up, much to Ally's chagrin.

"I'm okay," he said. Then he touched the back of his head, bringing his hand forward to reveal blood on his fingers. "Well, mostly," he amended.

Ally peered around his head to the wound on the back of it. It wasn't a deep cut, but it had bled a decent amount, matting Michael's hair.

"I don't think it's too bad," she told him.

"I'll be okay," he assured her. "Sandra!"

Ally turned wildly, searching for the Wicca.

She could see Sandra lying on the far side of the rock, and her heart pounded louder. *Let her be okay, let her be okay,* she chanted as she made her way cautiously toward the small crumpled figure. She wanted to touch Sandra, to say her name, but she was too terrified. So she just stared until she could see the slight rising and falling of Sandra's chest that meant she was breathing.

Ally collapsed next to her friend and grasped Sandra's hand.

"Sandra, Sandra wake up!" she said, choking back a sob. "Please wake up and be okay."

Sandra stirred, letting out a quiet moan.

"Don't move too much," Ally said. "Something might be broken." She looked at the hard rocks that Sandra had landed on and realized how lucky she had been to land on the much softer dirt below.

"Ally?" Sandra blinked her eyes up at her, and Ally smiled, patting her hand.

"I'm here."

Sandra nodded, blinked some more, then slowly looked around, moving as little as possible.

"Michael," she managed, and then spotted him. He gave her a weak wave, and Sandra waved even more weakly back. She nodded again, recognizing where they were, and why. "I don't think I'm seriously hurt," she said, and she wiggled her fingers in Ally's hand. "I can wiggle my toes too," she told Ally. Ally helped her sit up, and Sandra closed her eyes then, as though fighting off a wave of dizziness.

"You might have a concussion," Ally told her. Sandra nodded, took a deep breath, and then carefully stood up. She winced as she put her weight on her right foot, and grabbed onto Ally for support.

"I think it's sprained," she told Ally. "And my back doesn't feel that great either."

Ally looked to Michael for help. He had managed to stand up by himself, but he was holding onto a nearby rock as though staying upright was a new challenge for him.

"Can you walk?" Sandra called out to him.

He took a tentative step.

"My knee hurts," he said. "And my head."

Sandra nodded and looked at Ally. "You'll have to help us," she said.

Ally swallowed hard. She was used to her friends helping her, not the other way around. But Sandra had already moved on, the matter, for her, decided.

Sandra looked at the supplies scattered around the rocks by the explosion, the candles scattered, the jars cracked open. She sighed.

"It was more than I thought it would be," she said quietly. "I figured I could handle it, but I should have had more help. You helped," she smiled at Ally. "You and Michael both, but I should have had more people here too, more Wicca."

"Is it over?" Ally asked.

"You tell me?" Sandra said, studying Ally's face. "How do you feel? Your aura is back…weak still, but that's probably from last night. But it's pure, or at least, all you."

Ally nodded as though that made sense to her. When her nodding went on too long, she realized how drained she actually felt and stopped moving her head. She tried a smile instead, but felt it came out more like a grimace.

"I'm okay," she said. "I had another dream, of the lake. Only this time, I went back through it to where I started from. Or, at least I think I did." She remembered the falling feeling, and shuddered slightly in the morning air.

"We need to go," Sandra said. "Help me get what we can salvage. It's going to be a long hike back to the car." She reached for her bag and winced slightly. Ally made her lean against the rock side and direct while Ally gathered all the things. Michael tried to help, but looked so much like a newly-born calf trying to do so, Ally banished him to Sandra's rock as well. Ally took the bag on her own shoulder, the one Sandra leaned against, and held onto Michael with the opposite hand. As graceful as three-legged race contestants, they made their slow, careful way off the rocks, then across the open dirt area, and up the incline to the trail they had taken in. *It all looks different in the light of early morning, cleaner and less scary.*

Finally, the three of them made it back over the fence. Ally drove back to the house and transferred Michael and Sandra to their couch under the care of Billy, who fussed around them and seemed completely unsatisfied with their tale of a prank gone wrong. Ally promised Michael she'd call when she got home, and resisted their efforts to make her stay. She just wanted to go home.

Her parking spot looked the same, and that was a small comfort to Ally. She got out of the car as fast as she could trying to maintain momentum, and headed for the stairs. She took her time going up the steps though, partly because as she came closer to her destination she wanted to put off the inevitable, and partly because her sore muscles wouldn't let her go much faster. Finally she got to her door and unlocked it. She sucked in a breath of air and held it as she swung the door away from her and peered into the apartment.

Beige walls, hand-me-down couch, table by the entryway. Ally walked into the apartment and looked around. Black entertainment center with pictures on top and glass dining room table—it was all there, all the way it was supposed to be, all hers. She smiled, finally feeling the great relief she had been holding back on since waking up. She went to her phone and called Michael, and as she did she glanced into the kitchen and saw the cake sitting on her counter, its message still glaring out from it, and smiled at that too.

Michael sounded happy but tired on the other end, and Ally told him to call her later and tell her how he and Sandra were, but that she was okay and that they shouldn't worry. After she hung up, Ally walked slowly around her apartment, touching things, smelling her cushions and taking in their musty scent, brushing her fingertips over the fudge stain on her couch. She went into her closet and ran her hands over plain cottons and rayons and blue jeans, all hanging on plastic and wire hangers. She went into her room and bounced lightly onto her bed, curling up in the tangled blankets. From the safety of her newly-made cocoon, she stared at her bedroom door, knowing the bathroom door was just beyond it.

A sadness overcame Ally then, and she didn't know why. She had her life back. She should be happy. And she was, happy not to be dead at any rate. But as she looked around her plain bedroom, and at the pile of clothes sitting on the garage-sale chair in the corner, she realized that the life she had gotten back hadn't really gotten better since almost losing it.

You still work at a dead-end job. You still don't have a boyfriend. You are still plus-sized.

Ally ran her hand over her stomach, squishing the soft rolls with her fingertips. She pulled her hand back and sat up, throwing blankets away from her.

There was one more place to check, to be sure.

Ally paused in front of the bathroom door, took a deep breath, and opened it.

Her own reflection stared back at her in the dim light. Ally turned on the light switch and walked toward the mirror, studying herself.

A pimple was forming on her forehead, and the pores around her nose seemed abnormally large to her. She scratched at a dry patch of skin on her jaw line, and pushed her tangled hair back behind her ears, which made them stick out funny. She tilted her head from side to side, trying to determine if she was pretty or not.

"Why do I hate myself?" she said out loud to her reflection.

"Because you're ugly, fat, and pathetic," her reflection responded. Ally watched in horror as her reflection shifted, the hair becoming bouncy, the skin smooth and tan, the teeth sparkling white, the figure fit and curvy.

Allison grinned evilly at Ally.

BATTLE OF THE BULGE

Ally stepped back, feeling the towel rack dig into her back.

"No!" she exclaimed, her hand out in front of her as though to ward Allison off.

"Yes," Allison said calmly. Then she stepped forward, out of the mirror, through the counter, and into Ally's face. Ally tried to dodge to the side, and got halfway out the bathroom door when she felt Allison grab her and throw her against the wall across from it. She slammed into Ally, pinning her shoulders against the wall, her face inches from Ally's face.

"You actually thought you could get rid of me? You, the fag, and that bitch witch friend of yours? Don't you know I'm part of you?"

"No," Ally said again, and helplessly struggled against Allison. Allison laughed.

"You made me super strong," she told Ally. "A super fighter. That's what you always wanted to be, right? Well that's what I am—all the things you always wanted to be. And that's how I'm going to stay. It's time for you to go Ally."

"No!" Ally cried out again, a whimper.

The air around her began to change, to take on a different quality, as though the light was coming from a filter. Allison grinned at Ally, then threw her down the hall and toward the bedroom. Ally landed face first on the carpet, felt it burn against her cheek as she slid across it. She scrambled around to face Allison, but a noise behind her caught her attention.

Ally looked over her shoulder into the bedroom. Where the

window should have been was a silver-blue surface, growing like a spill spreading across a wooden floor. The silver was swirling, like a whirlpool. And Ally felt herself being drawn toward it.

"No!" she screamed out again.

"Scream all you want but it's still going to be true," Allison exclaimed. Ally pushed up onto her feet and ran toward Allison and barreled into her. She should have knocked Allison down, but Allison stood strong, and flung Ally back away from her. Ally landed hard on the carpet, just inside the bedroom door, the vortex growing behind her.

"You can't fight your own creation," Allison told her, calmly smoothing her outfit. "You created me to be perfect, and perfection will always win."

Ally felt the pull of the vortex on her, and got to her hands and knees, tried to crawl away from it. It was strong enough now that it was pulling her backward, into the bedroom, closer to its center. Ally grabbed at the doorframe, tried to hold on against the pulling.

Allison laughed. "Oh just give it up. You don't want your life anyway. Might as well just let go."

"We defeated you," Ally cried out. "Sandra, Michael and I…"

"Kept yourselves from being sucked into my world last night," Allison said smugly. "Did you like the little light show? Did you think that meant you won?" She leaned casually against the wall. "I was taking you with me until you shattered my mirror and let me go again."

"You were killing her," Ally said, remembering the way Sandra's face had grown pale under the draining greenish light.

"Yes," Allison said with a shrug. "She pissed me off."

Ally glared up at Allison and opened her mouth to say something. Then her fingers slipped off the wood, and she felt her legs being sucked toward the vortex. She tried to grab the carpet, tried to find any handhold she could to prevent her from sliding into that silver-blue surface. She managed to grab onto the edge of the bed, and held on with everything inside her, wishing she had spent more time in the gym. For once in her life, Ally was glad she was heavy. The vortex was struggling to pull her weight in.

"Time to go now Ally," Allison said, walking forward. She kicked out her leg and it landed square in Ally's face. Ally let go of the bed involuntarily, felt her body sliding into the vortex. She couldn't see Allison past the pain, but could hear her musical, evil laughter, and Ally wished more than anything that she had something to hold onto, and reached her hands out desperately.

Her fingers found something that felt like a handle, and she closed her hand around it, her arm stretching out its full length as the vortex pulled her away from the handle.

Ally blinked away her pain and looked up at Allison.

Allison was frowning. "Quit fighting!" she said, and sounded annoyed.

At first Ally could only concentrate on holding onto the handle, and then, as she saw something flicker across Allison's face—fear maybe?—she looked down at the handle that was keeping her from sliding into the vortex and wondered how it had appeared. It was buried deep into the carpet, and presumably into the floor below, anchoring her. It was solid, and the same beige as the carpet, and looked as though it had always been there. Ally had wished for it, and it had appeared.

A wild idea was forming in Ally's head. But before she could act on it, another perfectly aimed kick connected with her face. Allison was attacking her again.

This time though, Ally managed to keep her hold. She put her free hand in front of her face in an effort to ward off any other kicks, and felt the coppery taste of blood in her mouth. Allison had given her a fat lip.

"You stupid fat cow!" Allison screamed. "Just let go already!"

Ally wished then, with all her might, that Allison would somehow be flung across the room and have to shut up, and definitely have to stop kicking Ally.

And suddenly Allison flew across the room as though she had been kicked in the stomach by a horse. Ally watched the apparition's body land hard against the wall and slump toward the floor, and she grinned. Because suddenly she knew what Allison was, and how to fight her.

"You're my fantasy," Ally said, feeling something new surge through her. It was an energy she never even knew she had, and it was coursing through her like electricity. Electric anger, and pride, and self-righteous fury. "You're my fantasy."

Ally wished for the sucking feeling to go away, and felt it slacken behind her. Allison was getting up from the wall, and glared at Ally.

"You can't win," she told Ally. "Don't even bother trying to fight."

"This is my fantasy," Ally said. "And I want the vortex to close now."

"It's my fantasy!" Allison screeched. "And I want it to suck you in!"

Ally felt the pulling at her feet again, and realized then that Allison was right. As her hand began to slip from her handle, she wished for another one, and it appeared. It was Allison's fantasy, but Allison was Ally's creation, and that meant it was her fantasy too. And that meant Ally could fight back.

Allison came forward to kick at Ally again, and Ally dodged out of the way, reaching for another handle that appeared as she wished it into existence. She reached for another, and another, and now she was to the side of the vortex, and away from its sucking power. She stood up warily.

"Stop that!" Allison screamed as she barreled into Ally. Ally was slammed against the wall. She snapped her head forward and felt it crack hard against Allison's nose, and the thinner woman released her, holding the nose that was starting to run bloody.

"You bitch!" Allison squealed.

"Yep," Ally said, and swung at Allison. Allison blocked it easily, expert fighter that she was, and returned with another punch that knocked Ally back against the wall. Ally kicked out her leg, and managed to hit Allison hard in the knee. As Allison cried out in pain, Ally looked over and saw that the vortex was shrinking. It didn't matter if she was winning or not, she realized, but she was fighting. And that meant that the vortex couldn't have her. She took another kick at Allison, but Allison grabbed her leg and used it to twist Ally to the ground. Ally rolled away just before the kick Allison dropped toward Ally's head could connect. Ally looked at the vortex as she rolled. It was a lot smaller now. She grinned, and charged at Allison's knees.

Her body made hard contact with Allison, and, because she was heavier, her weight managed to knock the thinner woman down. Ally scrambled to her feet then, and ran out of the bedroom, away from the remaining force of the vortex. She ran down the hall, feeling Allison right on her heels.

Allison reached out a hand and snagged Ally's shirt. She wrenched her to the side and into the wall of the hall, right before the kitchen. Ally swung her elbow back into Allison's face, and Allison let go.

Ally ran into the kitchen, opening the fridge door and slamming it into Allison, who was following close behind. Ally looked in the fridge and grabbed a bottle of ketchup, squirting it into Allison's face.

Allison screamed.

"I'm a better fighter than you!" Ally cried out, tossing the bottle at Allison and making her duck. Ally reached in the fridge and grabbed a carton of eggs.

"I'm better!" Allison squealed, then recoiled as an egg landed smack in her face.

"No, I am. You're from my imagination, your skill is from my imagination. You're just the copy—I'm the original."

"You're fat, and pathetic, and weak, and worthless!" Allison cried out. Smack. Smack. Two more eggs found their target.

"But I'm real!" Ally said. She threw more eggs at Allison, watched them explode onto that perfect hair, perfectly ruining it. Once the carton was empty, she threw it at Allison too, then reached in the fridge and found tomatoes, and tossed those Allison's way as well.

Allison was obviously beside herself. None of Ally's fantasies had featured a produce attack. More than that, Ally could see Allison weakening, becoming less solid, less real.

"You're nothing!" Allison screamed. "You hate yourself, your life, your fat. Your friends pity you, your sister barely tolerates you. You will never have a boyfriend, or be rich, or have any of the things you want. You can't even stop yourself from eating! Look."

And she pointed to the cake sitting spectacularly on the counter, its frosting thick and rich all around it.

"You were going to die and you made a cake! That's how weak you are. You couldn't even diet one day!"

Ally stared at the cake.

"It's just a cake," she said. "It's just food."

"It's everything that is wrong with you. Your weakness, your self-hatred, your inability to change."

"I'm pretty sure it's just a cake," Ally said.

She grinned then, looked over at Allison, whose face and hair was coated in egg yolk, whose outfit was smothered in ketchup, and whose formerly beautiful face was disfigured with rage.

"And the cake was for you," she said, and held it up so that Allison could see the writing on it.

"Eat me," Allison read, and sneered.

"Love, Ally," Ally finished. And then, with all the strength she could muster, she threw the cake.

It landed with a heavy plop on Allison's head, and slid down the front of her body to squish itself onto the floor. Allison had to wipe frosting from her eyes in order to see. Ally began to laugh.

"You're the pathetic one. You couldn't even have a life of your own, not even one as lame as mine. You had to steal it, take it from fantasies."

"You made me," Allison tried again, but there wasn't much energy behind it.

"No," Ally said, shaking her head. "You found me, and like a parasite you latched on. I don't know what you are, but it's time you went back to wherever it is you came from."

"I'm part of you," Allison said weakly. She was beginning to fade now, and Ally stepped forward, hands on her hips.

"Not anymore," she said with finality.

"Please," Allison begged. Ally wasn't sure what for. She

shook her head and made one final wish.

Allison disappeared.

There was a knock on her door, and Ally went to get it, her hand reaching up to touch her lip. It wasn't as swollen as it had been, but it wasn't normal sized either. Whatever Allison was, she sure had packed a kick.

Ally opened the door to an extremely worried-looking Misha.

"You didn't answer your phone," she said accusingly. "I had the strangest dream about you. You have no idea. And I called to tell you about it, but you haven't been answering your phone all morning." As startled as Ally was to see her little sister, Misha was even more startled by Ally's appearance. "Have you been in a fight?"

Misha reached out for her face, but Ally slid past her hand and pulled Misha into a hug. She held her close for a very long time.

"I missed you," she said into her sister's shoulder.

"Ally, what's been going on?"

Misha pushed Ally into the apartment, closing the door behind them. She made Ally sit on the couch.

"You were acting so oddly on Friday, just like, not yourself or something. And then I had this dream, and in it you were you, but you were someone else and you were mean. I get here, and you look like you've been fighting and..." her voice trailed off. "Your lip is getting really big," she said.

"I have had the weirdest week," Ally said.

"Yeah, I can tell."

"I'm okay," Ally said. "I really am."

"Okay. So then, I have something else to ask you."

"Shoot," Ally said.

"Did you maybe make out with Alex at my party?" Misha asked.

"I think I kinda did."

Misha stared at Ally and Ally wondered what she might say next. And then Misha broke out into a grin.

"How was it?" she asked.

Ally laughed.

THE SCARECROW AND CATTY MCWHISKERS

Monday morning found Ally in the filing room, flipping through musty charts. It seemed like such an ordinary thing to do after her extraordinary weekend that Ally actually enjoyed the reconciliation process for once. She flipped closed the chart in her hand, and grabbed the next in her pile. As she read the name, she froze: Robert Dominguez.

Bobby's chart.

She looked around quickly to make sure she was alone, and then opened it to the notes written in Dr. Barclay's loose scrawl.

She read the last entry.

Asked an interesting question today—was it bad to be happy if someone else was suffering, if that meant you didn't have to suffer? I asked him what he meant and he said....

Ally watched the clock carefully, made sure to be in the front office when Bobby came out of his session. She planned the moment out, and as the chubby boy walked by the front office she grabbed the bowl full of left-over Halloween candy Michael had brought in and thrust it toward him.

"Hey Bobby, want some candy?" she asked with a careful smile. He hesitated before coming over to her.

"Candy isn't really good for me," he said. He seemed nervous talking to her, like before. "Did you, uh, have a good Halloween?" he asked.

Ally studied his features—he knew, she decided. She wasn't sure what he knew, but he knew something.

"It's gone," she said quietly. He looked up suddenly, met her eyes.

"I didn't mean…" he began. "I never meant…."

Ally nodded.

"I know. But it's okay now. It's gone." She reached out a hand to him. He flinched slightly, but didn't pull away and took her hand. "For good."

He met her eyes and nodded.

"You're much stronger than me," he said.

His mother approached then, and Ally let go of Bobby's hand. He stepped away.

"Hello, Mrs. Dominguez," Ally said. The small woman smiled back and smoothed a hair off of Bobby's forehead. As Bobby was pulled away, he gave Ally a smile.

"Thank you," he mouthed to her, and then was dragged into the elevator and out of sight.

Ally stared at the closed doors.

He'd thanked her, thought she was strong. She shook her head and wrapped her arms around herself. She didn't feel strong. She didn't know what she felt, except relieved that it was all over. There were still questions to be answered, like why had Allison been able to take over Ally's life so much faster than Bobby's and what Allison was to begin with—but Ally didn't want to think about them.

She walked back into the filing room and began to sort charts. Losing herself in the routine kept her mind from drifting into another fantasy, and Ally spent the next several hours trying not to think about anything at all.

✴

The phone call came at lunch. Ally picked up her cell automatically, giving Michael a puzzled look as she did so. She didn't recognize the number.

"Hello?"

"Ally? Hi, it's Seth. The scarecrow from the Halloween party?"

Ally felt herself redden, even as her mouth turned up into a grin she couldn't stop if she wanted to.

"I remember," she said.

Across from her, Michael gave her a questioning look.

"Hi Seth," she said in response.

"Hi Ally." He had a nice laugh. "I'm betting Michael is near you, isn't he?"

"Yep," she said, and turned slightly away from Michael's enthusiastic smile.

"Yeah, Sandra gave me a pretty hard time when I asked her for your number. I hope you don't mind me getting it from her. You said I could call and…"

"No, I'm glad you did," she said. Michael was making mock swooning gestures and she turned even more away from him. "How was your Sunday?" she asked.

"Good," he said. "I went for a hike with my roommates. How about you? How is your sister's cat?"

Ally blinked in surprise before she remembered the lie she'd told him about leaving the party.

"Oh, Mort is good," she said. "Back with the sis. It was only a one-day thing."

"Your sister's cat's name is Mort? As in the Terry Pratchett character?" he asked.

"We both love his books."

"If you had a cat what would you name it?" he asked.

"I dunno," she said, thinking. "I once had a stuffed cat I named Catty McWhiskers. I'm not too imaginative with names."

"I dunno, you made your cat Irish. That's pretty imaginative."

Ally smiled. "Unfortunately, Catty McWhiskers had a tragic ending."

"Oh yeah?"

"Yep. He did the Monster Mash wrong and members of the Monster community retaliated by tying his tail to the bumper of a car."

Seth laughed, surprise making him snort.

"You gotta watch the Monsters," he said. "They're a mean lot…"

When Ally hung up the phone, having spent almost her entire lunch hour talking to Seth, she felt lighthearted and excited. She spent the rest of the afternoon recapping the highlights of the conversation with Michael. He made his own phone call, and by the end of the day had arranged a dinner party with Seth, Ally, him and his roommates Tuesday night. "So Sandra said Seth was kicking himself for not asking you on an actual date," Michael told her. Ally hadn't even considered that.

"But he had to get off the phone—we both did," she said. "He wanted to ask me out?"

"No silly, he just wanted to talk to you for an hour about nothing."

"It wasn't nothing!" Ally protested, trying not to blush or grin, and failing at both.

✳

After work on Tuesday, Ally went home and took her pre-planned outfit off its hanger and put it on, a nice button-down blue shirt over form-fitting black jeans and stylish black boots that didn't kill her feet. She pulled the frizz of her hair back into a half-pony-tail and secured it with a black butterfly clip. She brushed her teeth, refreshed her makeup. And then she stared at herself in the mirror.

It's amazing the power a piece of glass can have. She looked at the reverse image of herself. She played with her reflection, moving her hand slowly in a circle, crossing both her hands in front of her and then back out to her sides.

"Hello?" she whispered to the reflection, half expecting to hear Allison's voice answer her. Had she really won? Did she really get rid of Allison? She hadn't been able to look at her reflection without wondering about that.

She stared hard at herself, and tried to be objective, tried not compare her features to her memory of Allison's. Ally turned her head to the left, then to the right. She titled it from one side to the other. She moved her mouth into different kinds of smiles, some showing teeth, some not. She batted her eyelashes. She puckered her lips. And then she laughed at herself and her own foolishness.

Seth was already at Michael and Sandra's house when she arrived, and Ally was somewhat unprepared to see him before checking her outfit out with Michael. She smiled at him shyly, and shook his hand.

"Good to see you again," she said, wondering why it was so much easier to talk to him on the phone.

He looked different out of his Scarecrow costume, and she wondered how different she looked to him. She admired the specks of gold in his green eyes, the hints of red in his brown hair, all things she hadn't noticed the first time she met him. And he was cute, cuter than the costume made him look. His nose was long and narrow, his eyes framed by unbelievably long lashes, and his mouth full, wide, and smiling. He had a crooked bottom tooth that Ally decided was endearing.

"So then, the feathers are a once a year sort of thing?" he said, checking out her outfit.

"Unless you count feather boas," she said.

"And how often do you wear those?" he asked.

"I think it's way too early for that sort of talk," Michael said with a wicked gleam in his eye. "Sandra says dinner is ready." Ally followed him into the dining room. All evidence of the party had been removed. Ally sort of missed the decorations. The place looked plain without them.

She was seated between Seth and Michael and across from Tina. The fourth resident of the house was smiling, her dark hair down for once and her features calm. She explained that the movie she was working on just finished and she finally had some time off. By how different she looked from before, Ally guessed she needed the down time.

Tina's boyfriend, also in the industry, and Billy and his girlfriend finished off their dinner party.

Sandra had cooked, and the food was excellent. However, Ally found herself picking at her plate and had a hard time concentrating on the conversation around her.

"So we're like three hours past when we should have broken for lunch and then the boom mic goes out," Tina was saying. Everyone else seemed entertained by the story. Ally just couldn't follow along. Seth smiled at her, a concerned look in his eyes. She smiled back.

"Not a big movie fan?" he whispered to her.

"Just feeling a little tired," she whispered back. He reached over and took her hand. She felt chills run up her arm and her heart sped up.

"You okay?" he asked. Ally could only manage a nod. She felt really uncomfortable and couldn't say why. She discreetly took her hand out from under his.

"I'll be right back," she said and got up from the table. Michael gave her a concerned look, but she just smiled back and made her way to the bathroom.

She closed the door and turned to her reflection, glaring at it. She'd hiked into Vasquez Rocks at night, survived being flung like a rag doll, helped Sandra and Michael get back to the car, and defeated a parasitic spirit out to take over her life. So why did she still feel lethargic and numb? Why did a man showing interest in her make her feel uncomfortable? Why couldn't she just be a normal person and handle things normally?

Ally watched herself tug at the bottom of her shirt in a futile attempt to make it cover more of her stomach and wondered if she would ever get over feeling like she wanted to hide from the world. Her reflection just frowned back at her. As she turned to leave and flipped off the light, she thought she saw something else in the mirror, but when she turned the light back on to look, everything appeared normal.

She ran the water and then splashed some on her face, careful so as not to ruin her makeup. She just wanted to feel the coolness. She closed her eyes, kept her head hung over the sink for a moment.

I'm okay, she tried to tell herself. *I am normal. I'm okay.*

She didn't know why she didn't believe it.

She reached over for the towel and patted her face dry, and only then opened her eyes.

The reflection in the mirror had changed—Allison's smug smile sneered back at Ally. Ally stared.

"Not again," she said.

CHOCOLATE FROSTING

"What does it take to get rid of you?" Ally hissed at the mirror. Allison just laughed, and Ally covered her ears so that she could drown out the sound and think. "Do you know how crazy you look?" Allison said.

Ally ignored her. Why? Why had Allison appeared again? What was she missing?

The lake, Beauty, Tom-that-was.

"I found refuge in you, in your fantasies," Tom had told her. "Your dreams were so real. But, dangerous."

Ally had spent her entire life daydreaming. She was an expert at creating far away worlds, creating other people to be. Probably, she was better at fantasies than anyone she knew.

And that was what made her different.

Ally whirled to face the mirror. "It was my dreams you wanted, not me," she said. "You wanted the lives I created."

"Want, and will have," Allison corrected her.

"Want, and will never have," Ally said defiantly. "I know what you are."

"No, I really don't think you do," Allison said. "No one has ever figured it out, not fully. You certainly wouldn't be able to."

Ally took a deep breath. "Mirror," she said. "Shards of a mirror that gets into people's eyes and hearts, which makes things look ugly and horrible. I know what you are."

"You have no idea!"

It was said too adamantly, too forcefully. Ally was close.

"What I don't get is how you are able to make yourself

real. Or why. How did you get to Bobby?" she asked, and Allison flinched. "It was in Seattle, Michael said Bobby changed after Seattle. Was it one of his family members? And why go to him? Wasn't the person you were with before good enough?"

"Bobby was better," Allison said coldly. "He had a good imagination. You've seen the stuff he creates. Beautiful, really. Just not real enough."

"Not for you to be real," Ally said, nodding. "You needed something more..."

"And I found it. I found you." She grinned then, showing all her teeth.

"I gave you what you really wanted, what you needed—fantasies."

Allison nodded, rested her hands on her hips as though bored. Her eyes were sparking with emotion. Rage? Fear? Ally couldn't name it, but she knew she was getting to the spirit of the spirit.

"You spent more time in your fantasies than anyone I ever knew," Allison said. "Henry—the person you knew as Tom—he had some great fantasies too. Mostly they were pornographic though. He was really into T and A, you know? There's a version of me living the high life now, always surrounded by naked or nearly-naked beautiful women. Calls himself Hugh and has a freakin' huge house."

Ally shook her head.

"Fine, don't believe me," Allison said. "But Henry lasted longer than the others in the Realm. You wouldn't—sorry, won't— last a day."

"The place with the lake... That's where you're from."

"Close," Allison said, smiling.

Ally thought back, and heard Not-Tom's voice. *Ally, are you cold?* Every time. *Are you cold?* And she had been. For a long time, she had been.

"Mirror. Coldness. Shards. Ice. Snow Queen."

"A fancy name. Quite liked that one."

"You freeze hearts. You make everything look ugly, and hopeless."

Allison grinned. "I am older than you can ever imagine. More powerful. You won't ever be rid of me."

"And the lake?" Ally asked.

"Just one of the ways in and out."

And that's when Ally understood.

"You are the lake," Ally said. "Or you were."

"'First there was the word, and then the word became flesh.' Or, rather, first there was the lake and then the lake…well, you get the idea." Allison crossed her hands over her chest smugly. "Now how you going to defeat a whole lake?"

Ally stared hard at her, and her mind raced through the possibilities, through everything she knew.

Allison continued. "I'm everywhere, you know. Every time you turn on the television, read a magazine, look at a billboard, shop in the mall. You see what you're not and you feel bad about it. You can't help it. You know perfection exists and you know you will never have it. So you imagine it instead. And every time you do, you build me up, make me stronger. It's not just you feeding that lake. Everyone does to some degree. And everyone is fed by it. Everyone who compares and finds themselves lacking. Everyone who doubts. Everyone who has felt the chill, the numbness So I send tendrils out. I find weak spots and I wedge myself in. I don't want much, just to exist. Perfection wants to exist."

"There's no such thing as perfection," Ally said, shaking her head, still searching for the answer. "It doesn't exist."

"Sure," Allison agreed. "But the idea of it does. And all I need is the idea. Then I take over. There's more than one way to take over, you know."

"Oh?" Ally asked distractedly.

"Sometimes I just come in and let them destroy themselves. And sometimes, once in a very blue moon, I find a way out, into the world. I find a way to make all the people around me feel worse, all the time, by actually existing, actually walking among them. I become less perfect to do so, but I become more effective too. That's what I'm going to do when I take over your life. I'll make the people you knew feel horrible about theirs. Infect them. The way I infected you."

She seemed so pleased by the idea, so happy with her purpose.

"But where do you come from?" Ally asked. "What made the Lake?"

"People did," Allison said, and she shrugged. "It's always been there in one form or another. But in the last century, especially the last fifty years or so, it's grown, a lot. I'm more powerful than ever before." She flipped her hair triumphantly.

Ally's mind continued to search out the answer, the way she would beat Allison and the Lake of Perfection.

It came on like a reverse echo, and then it resounded in her head, tolling like a bell. In the Snow Queen, love melted the ice. Kindness. Purity. Compassion.

Ally blinked; it was so simple. To beat perfection, all she had to do was to give it up. Believe in herself, that's what Michael always told her. She was strong, and smart, and funny, and had a great imagination. She didn't need to be perfect. She just needed to remember the good things about herself, be grateful for what she had, and try to be happy.

She needed to love herself.

Ally smiled.

"I have an excellent imagination," she told Allison. Allison nodded.

"That's why I'm so happy to take you over," she said maliciously.

Ally nodded in turn, and kept grinning. Allison's gaze turned suspicious. "What? You think you can use it against me? Good luck, honey, because…"

She stopped. She had to stop because there was frosting covering her mouth, and her face, and the front of her body. There were eggshells in her hair tangled up in the yolk, and her arms were streaked with ketchup. Allison wiped the frosting from her eyes and looked down at herself in horror.

"What?" she asked.

"My fantasies," Ally said calmly. "They're why you exist, at least in this form. This one happens to be my new favorite fantasy. All the horrible voices in my head, the perfect image that haunts me, covered in a mess of food. Kind of poetic, don't you think?"

"This doesn't change anything. You think this changes something? You think that tomorrow you're not going to wake up, look at the rolls of your stomach and not want to kill yourself? You think you're going to be able to, what, write a gratitude journal and magically be better? You think you won't still have dark days and sad thoughts? You're a time bomb waiting to go off and when you do…"

Ally imagined a whipped-cream pie hitting Allison's face,

which cut the apparition off. Ally grinned and opened the bathroom door.

Michael was standing outside, looking concerned.

"I heard voices," he said.

Ally pulled him into a hug.

"This is going to be a long fight," she told him, stepping back to smile up at him. "But I'm very glad I have you on my side."

"We won," he said, worried. "You beat her…"

"I won the battle," she said back. "But this means war."

"So as long as you're still struggling with self-doubt, with how you feel about yourself, your life…." His voice trailed off. "Ally, dealing with those issues can take a long time for some people."

"But you'll help," Ally said. "And… and I think I'm going to talk to someone. Someone not you. Someone already licensed."

He took her hand.

"I'll help you find the right someone. You'll always have my support."

"Even if I hear voices?" she asked, smiling. He grinned back.

"Especially then."

She followed him back into the dining room. People were getting up, clearing their places. Ally spotted Seth and took a deep breath before approaching him.

"Hey Seth," she began, and then tried to will her voice to sound less nervous as she continued. "I was wondering if you were interested in seeing a movie this week. Maybe that new Melissa McCarthy comedy?"

His face lit up and he grinned.

"Actually," he said, "that's what I was going to ask you. So, yeah, sure. How 'bout Thursday?"

Ally nodded, relief spilling off of her.

"Thursday would be great."

✳

On Wednesday, Ally had her very first therapy appointment. Misha took her.

"What was it like when you first went to therapy?" she asked her sister.

"Weird. Scary. Like somehow the very act of going meant that there was something seriously wrong with me. Like, I could deny it before, but the moment I walked in to see the doc, that would be it. I wouldn't be able to pretend I didn't have a problem anymore."

"I get that," Ally said, staring up at the building in front of her.

"I'm surprised you asked me for help with this, instead of Michael."

"I actually think you understand what I'm going through better than he does. That whole struggle with perfection thing."

"So this therapist works with my group leader. She came highly recommended. I think this will be really good for you. And, I'm really glad you're going."

"Misha," Ally said, taking her sister's hand. "I should be the one being there for you. Not the other way around."

"You have been. You listen. I mean, I know I can be annoying or whatever, but you always answer my calls, and listen to whatever I have going on. You came to my party. You go shopping with me. I know it may not seem like a lot to you, but it really means a lot to me."

Ally pulled her sister closer and put her arm around her

shoulder.

"I can do better," she said. "I will do better."

"You need to get better, first." Misha turned and gave her sister a quick hug. "You have to stop being so hard on yourself. I mean, like, your therapist will help you with that. But like, that's one of the things you have to do. You have to stop trying to compare yourself to some other version of yourself who is like, perfect or whatever. Perfection doesn't exist. It's not really something anyone should try to be."

Ally shook her head.

"Sure, now you tell me." She smiled. "Okay, so, what, I just... talk?"

"Yeah. Pretty much. And be honest. That helps."

"Okay." Ally started walking toward the door of the office when it opened and a familiar figure with familiar perfect arms walked out, surprising her.

"Tom?"

"Hey Ally," he said. He smiled at her and Misha. "What are you doing here?"

"Starting therapy," Ally said without thinking. She almost instantly wished she could take it back. Tom just nodded.

"The doctors here are really great. Not that self-help books aren't also nice, but nothing beats professional help."

Ally felt her face redden, and then she smiled.

"Oh, this is my sister Misha," she said.

"Hey." Misha nodded at Tom, who nodded back.

"So, I know you probably have to head in, but I have a kind of strange question to ask you."

"Sure," Ally said. "I have a high tolerance for strange."

"Your friend Michael, from the gym? Is he, you know...single?"

Ally grinned.

"Let me give you his number."

✳

"How goes the war?" Michael asked as he flopped down onto Ally's couch, displacing a few kernels of popcorn from the bowl he was holding.

"It's been a few weeks, and she hasn't been in any of my mirrors," Ally said. "Still, I keep waiting for her to show up again. I am almost certain she will. I keep having nightmares. She's still in them."

"I'm not sure I understand any of this."

"Honestly, I'm not sure I do either. Sandra tried to explain it to me, but there was a lot of talk about life force and mystical energies, and when I told her about my Snow Queen theory, she went off about archetypes and ancient battles for the soul."

"Right," Michael said. "So, how do you kill the Snow Queen?"

"Well, I'm not sure you do." Ally took a handful of popcorn and popped a few pieces in her mouth, crunching down thoughtfully.

"So, you just have to live with this thing haunting you for the rest of your life?"

"Well, that's sort of how mental illness works," Ally said.

"I'm pretty sure it's not. I mean, Allison isn't something you can control with medication. I think this goes beyond the DSM. Fringe science doesn't even know what this is!"

"You and Sandra both have a habit of saying things no one else understands. Did you ever notice that?"

"I'm just saying—I haven't seen anything in the psychiatric and psychology journals even remotely like this. And I've been searching."

"I think the answer may be somewhere in the middle, between what you know and what Sandra knows. Only, I'm the one living with it."

"I refuse that as an answer. You have enough to deal with. Evil spirit-like things showing up in your mirror every time you're feeling insecure shouldn't have to be one of them."

"Actually," Ally said, brushing popcorn crumbs from her hands. "Sandra and I have a theory about that. And a plan."

"Does this mean we have to do another moonlight hike?"

"No." Ally grinned. "Actually, it's something I can do right here, right now. And, with you here, I think I'd like to try it."

"Okay." He put the bowl down and sat up. "How can I help?"

"Quick question: if you were going to show up in one of my fantasies, how would you want to look?"

"Like myself," he said. "Only with a feather boa."

Ally laughed.

"I can work with that."

She closed her eyes, took a deep breath, and let her mind drift away.

✳

Ally opened her eyes. She was in a large warehouse with metal sides and a small door off in the corner to her left. What little light there was came in from a large sky-light above her. Everything else was in shadow. She was sitting in a metal chair, a thick rope wrapped around her arms and pinning them to her side. She took in the details of herself quickly, and without the judgment she usually included. Thick thighs, protruding belly rolls, heavy arms. She was herself, and felt some small measure of relief for it.

She looked over to her right and saw Tom, also bound. His mouth was gagged, and his arm muscles strained against thick white ropes in a way that made them flex and ripple. This was Tom-Tom, she knew, and not Not-Tom, who was dead. She didn't know how she knew the difference, but she did. Tom appeared to be greased up for maximum muscle showing off. Ally had to admit it was a little distracting.

"Allison!" Ally called out. "This isn't going to work."

The apparition appeared in front of her wearing a sleek black latex suit with a deep V in the front that showed of a dangerous amount of cleavage. Any more, and the top of the suit would just be sleeves.

"This already has worked," Allison said. "This is where it all started—in your fantasies. And this is where it's all going to end."

She snapped her fingers and two more figures appeared: Scar Face and Turtleneck, the two men who showed up in Ally's fantasy of her life as a double-agent. They were wearing the same black shirts and pants they had on in the escape van, the last time Ally saw them.

"Those are my characters!"

"They're mine now." Allison grinned, showing off all her pearly whites.

Turtleneck had a knife out and was testing the edge against his thumb, cutting himself. Like any good melodrama villain, he raised his hand to his mouth and sucked on the wound. Ally was sure it was supposed to be threatening, but somehow it missed the mark.

Next to him, Scar Face pulled a gun out. He pointed it first at Ally, then at Tom. He did his best evil grin.

"I brought you company. Not the real thing, of course, or

the fake you had gotten used to. Last time we found ourselves here, Not-Tom, as you called him, pulled you away before we got to the good stuff. This time, there is no one here to save you."

She gestured slightly and Scar Face lunged forward in one quick rush and slammed the butt of his gun against Tom's temple, causing Tom to cry out in pain through his gag. Blood trickled down Tom's temple while Scar Face laughed.

"Allison, stop!"

"Why? I want you to suffer. First you'll watch. And then you'll be the target." She raised a gun and pointed it at Ally.

"I can't die in my fantasies," Ally said, though she was feeling less than sure about that after everything she'd been experiencing lately. She tugged experimentally at her ropes. They held tight.

"Maybe not. But you can feel pain. And you can watch other people feel pain. And you can watch them die."

Allison turned the gun toward Tom, who doubled his own efforts to escape. He seemed to be trying to say something, which Ally was sure was heroic and manly, but was coming out "gerkaha-hulleluwhahalahitch."

Ally took a deep breath. It was time to put her theory into action.

"Yeah, this didn't turn out quite how I had hoped," she said. "I mean, there are three of you, and only two of us. And we're both, you know, tied up."

"I can see that." Allison sneered.

"And you have proven, over and over again, that you are very powerful. And super mean."

"Do you have a point? Can I kill your imaginary lover now?"

"Super-duper mean."

Allison's perfect blue eyes had the perfect look of annoyance.

Ally smiled back at her.

"So, ask me why I'm smiling."

Scar Face exchanged an amused look with Turtleneck. Allison tilted her head.

"Fine, I'll play. Why are you smiling?"

"Because we're not here alone," Ally said. "Now!!"

Glass rained down from above, and a pink-clad form rappelled from the skylight in the ceiling, landing with a soft thud. The figure rolled forward and in one fluid motion got to her feet and pulled two short swords out from sheaths strapped to her back at the same time. As she stood in a perfect warrior pose, she tossed her blonde ponytail over her shoulders.

"Misha?" Allison stared, bewildered. "What the hell? This isn't how this is supposed to go."

"Why, because you control my fantasies?" Ally laughed. "Honey, that boat sailed a while ago. You're in my world now." She lifted her arms in one swift move, snapping her ropes, and stood up.

A small explosion blew the door to the warehouse open, sending a billow of smoke into the room. A shadowy figure dressed in a tight tailored black suit emerged from the smoke holding large semi-automatic guns in each hand. A long black feather boa draped across his neck and shoulders and billowed out behind him.

"Michael?" Allison asked. "What in the hell is he wearing?"

Ally shrugged.

"He said he wanted to wear a feather boa."

Just then, a motorcycle zoomed in from the darkness of the warehouse behind them, skidding to a sideways stop as Sandra flung her helmet off her head and shook out a wild mane of golden hair. She turned toward Allison and held out her hand. A glowing ball of greenish energy hovered just over it, tiny crackles of electricity shooting out, through, and around it, like the world's cutest lightning storm.

"This is a gun fight!" Allison protested.

"My world, my rules," Ally said. With a snap of her fingers, she made Scar Face and Turtleneck disappear. "You're completely surrounded. Outnumbered. Outclassed. You should probably just surrender."

Misha, Sandra, Michael, and Tom—magically and without explanation newly freed from his chair—created a circle around the two women.

"No!" Allison screamed. She fired her gun at Ally, but as the bullets shot out, they turned into little bursts of silver glitter that rained softly down on Ally and made her sparkle.

"How?" Allison asked. "You are not strong enough. This is not possible."

"I wasn't strong enough alone," Ally said. "But like I said before—I'm not alone anymore."

"This isn't over," Allison said. "It will never be over! I will..." But she couldn't talk anymore; her face was covered in chocolate frosting. She wiped it from her eyes and mouth and stared at Ally with a horrified look.

"I'm stronger!" It came out like a whimper.

"Sure," Ally said. "You keep telling yourself that."

"You can't kill me," Allison said. "You know that, right? I'm not something that can be killed."

"But you are something that can be contained," Ally said. She looked around the circle at each of her friends in turn before turning back to face Allison. "And I am strong enough to do that.

You will never be able to leave my fantasies, never be able to hurt another person again. And me? I have beautiful dreams. Beautiful, but dangerous." She lifted her hand. There was a gun in it, and she aimed it at Allison. "You might want to run."

"You don't want to do that," Allison said.

"Yeah, actually, I do." Ally squeezed her trigger.

✳

"Ally, you okay?"

Ally opened her eyes and looked into Michael's brown ones, a worried crease between his brows.

"You sort of drifted off there. Is everything okay? Is Allison...?"

"Completely impotent and currently staring down the barrel of a gun in a fantasy world of my own creation?" Ally finished for him. "She sure is!"

The crease did not leave Michael's eyebrows.

"Should I be worried about how sadistically gleeful you sounded just now?"

"Maybe a little," Ally conceded. "But it wasn't going to be a real bullet." She grabbed the bowl of popcorn from the table and shifted her position to get into a squishier spot in the cushions of the couch. "Do you want to hear about it?"

"Oh yeah," he said. "Every detail!"

"So, I open my eyes, and I'm in this warehouse, and Tom..."

"My Tom?"

"Yeah, your Tom, only Allison still hasn't figured that out yet. Also, how guilty should I feel about fantasizing about him?"

"Not at all. He was totally flattered when I told him."

"You told him!?!"

"You still blush every time you see him. I had to explain why."

Ally ducked her head down behind the bowl, hiding her face. Michael patted her gently on the shoulder in a move designed for maximum fake condescension.

"There there," he said. "Now get over it and get back to your story. What was Tom wearing?"

Ally sat up and stuck her tongue out at him, then smiled.

"Well, he was tied to this chair. But really, you should see how he was tied. I mean, it was like some sort of bondage porn ...."

Michael's eyes lit up.

"Oh! And I remembered your feather boa! Only wait, we're not there yet."

Michael laughed.

"Somehow, I am not that worried about Allison anymore."

"I dunno," Ally said, "Perfection is a hard thing to beat."

"True. So how do you keep defeating her?"

Ally thought for a moment.

"Chocolate frosting mostly," she said. "And one hell of an imagination."

ACKNOWLEDGEMENTS

As this is my first published novel, I am trying to fight the urge to use this space to thank everyone I ever knew, and particularly everyone who ever read a story of mine. Because if I were to start down that rabbit hole of gratitude, I know that names like Mrs. Smisko of Highland's Elementary School, and Rick Monroe of Woodinville High School would have to be included, even though the likelihood of either of my former teachers ever reading this paragraph are very slim. I would want to wander into the early days of this novel and list all the names of the first writing groups I subjected it to, people I no longer even talk to outside of social media now because we have all changed a lot in the past 10 years. I would want to start thanking people who never read any fiction I wrote but would have had I ever followed through and sent them something. I would list every family member, chosen family member, and friend, but I have been blessed enough that I would drown this space in names in the attempt.

I am left, instead, with those people who have had the biggest and most direct impact in bringing this book to life. Lance Yomtob, thank you for your endless support and for being the best dad a girl could ask for. Danielle Rago, thank you taking on a last-minute editing job because you were excited to read this book before everyone else. Laurie Temple, thank you for excellent feedback and copy-editing. Karen Harris Tully and Juel Lugo, thank you for believing in me enough to join forces on this crazy adventure we have embarked on. And finally, Bethany Maines, thank you for paving the way for the rest of us, being our biggest cheerleader, and the best publishing partner. You have helped me find faith in myself and in this book over and over again, and it literally would not be in the world without you.

ABOUT THE AUTHOR

 Jennae Phillippe spent the early part of her life in the deserts of Santa Clarita, California where she learned about fire season and idolized She-Ra; her adolescent/ young adult years in the ever-green Seattle suburbs where she gained an appreciation for walking in the rain and earned a degree in Journalism and Creative Writing; and her early twenties in Los Angeles where she tried to make a go of it as a freelance writer and thus learned a great deal about being an administrative assistant before ending up in public relations. Then she did the most LA thing she could think of — she moved across the country to go to graduate school in New York City. She has settled in Brooklyn, New York and became a licensed masters social worker and works as a family therapist. She spends her free-time decorating her tiny apartment to her cat Oscar Wilde's liking (which consists of having lots of interesting things to lay on), drinking cider at her favorite British-style pub, and training to be the next Karate Kid, one wax-on at a time.

Find out more at:

JennaePhillippe.com

BLUE ZEPHYR PRESS

Enjoy other fine books from Blue Zephyr Press!

THE FAARIAN CHRONICLES: EXILE

by Karen Harris Tully

Fifteen-year-old Sunny Price dreams of being an Olympic gymnast, but thanks to the worst custody agreement in the universe, she finds out she's half-alien and is exiled to her absentee-mother's home planet. She has to give up her friends and elite gymnastics career to live with a mother who only wants to give orders? This. Sucks.

AN UNSEEN CURRENT

by Bethany Maines

You never know what's beneath the surface. When Seattle native and ex-actress Tish Yearly finds herself fired and evicted all in one afternoon, she knows she's in deep water. And when she discovers the strangled corpse of grandfather's best friend, she knows she's in over her head. Now Tish must swim against the current, and depend on her nearly forgotten acting skills to stay alive.

blue zephyrpress.com